FORGOTTEN SINS

FORGOTTEN SINS

Anthony Mathis

Writer's Showcase
San Jose New York Lincoln Shanghai

Forgotten Sins

Writer's Showcase
an imprint of iUniverse, Inc.

For information address:
iUniverse, Inc.
5220 S. 16th St., Suite 200
Lincoln, NE 68512
www.iuniverse.com

Any resemblance to actual people and events is purely coincidental.
This is a work of fiction.

ISBN: 0-595-22285-4

Printed in the United States of America

To Mary Jean & Larry
For all your hours of support and constant reading.

CHAPTER 1

*T*he priest always hated hearing confessions. In his twenty-seven years of priesthood he had baptized, buried, married and consoled thousands of people. He didn't mind wakes and wedding rehearsals. He relished in seeing the school children receive sacraments for the first time and there was no greater joy than presiding at a wedding of a former grade school graduate.

But confessions were a different story. Every Saturday at 3:30 he went into the box. That dark cubicle of walnut and peg board that had its own smell. This Saturday was no exception. He opened the door and flipped on the switches. The light in his side came on and the little light on the bottom of the penitent's side flickered. "I'll have to look into fixing that." he thought, the same as he did every week. He took his purple stole off the hook and placed it over his shoulder. His grey hair rested gently over the stole, he was far overdue for a haircut. He sat in the chair and it creaked, the dry wood older than the priest himself. He settled back and opened the sliding wooden window so that he could hear the penitents clearly. And he waited.

Within five minutes the door on the other side of the confessional opened. He heard a body come in and kneel down, triggering the red light on the outside of the box, warning others that the box was occupied. He leaned a little closer to the mesh screen window so he could better hear the person on the other side.

The breathing was heavy, he could hear the person struggling to maneuver the hard kneeler on the other side. Then the unmistakable sound of rosary beads hitting the mesh screen could be heard. The priest knew at that point that it was an old woman on the other side. Actually she was the same old woman every week. She only occasionally missed, when she was sick, or when her knees hurt so bad that she could not get out of the house.

"Bless me Father, for I have sinned, it has been one week since my last confession." The beads hitting the screen as she made the sign of the cross.

"Go ahead, tell me your sins," he said, almost sighing.

She started as she always did, "Well, Father, I am an old woman and I do not have much to tell. I have missed my morning prayers two times and I had some impure thoughts. Of course I did not act on those thoughts, but I had them just the same. I also watched an R rated movie on the cable TV. You know my son Father, he lives with me, and he insists that we get those channels that get the R movies. I don't watch them all the time, but sometimes, late at night when there is nothing else on, I stop for a few minutes and watch."

The priest leaned back in his chair, nothing new from the cable lady, as he liked to think of her. "Go on, anything else this week?" His tone was not sarcastic but it could have been more compassionate and he knew this.

"No Father, only that I am short tempered with my son, many days I wish that he would get a job and get out of the house. He's 50 years old and I think it's time. Oh, yes and I would like to be forgiven for the sins of my past life."

There was silence in the box and all the priest could hear was the woman's breathing and the slow steady thump of the rosary beads occasionally hitting the mesh screen. He took a deep breath, knowing that what he was about to say was not any different from last week. "I suggest that you continue to try and live the good life that God has given to you and obey his commandments and feel his loving presence in your life. As for the movies, you know as well as I that you have control over that, so try to stay away from the things that you know will offend you and your relationship with God. For your penance I want you to say one rosary and to make the best effort to get along with your son. Make an act of contrition, and I will offer you absolution."

He ordinarily did not give an entire rosary for a penance, but in the past he had offered the woman to say only two Our Fathers and she baulked at the idea. She told him that it simply was not enough of a penance for her sins. He said the prayer of absolution and bid her peace. She opened the door of the box and held it for a moment while the next penitent came in. The priest sat back and thought that he heard a slight gasp from the familiar voice of the old woman. What was that she had said? "Oh my?". Well it could not worry him now. He sat up in the chair waiting for the next person to settle in and begin his confession.

The door closed and he heard the penitent kneel down. The person was obviously big for he needed to hold onto the ledge attached to the wall to kneel all the way down. The priest could hear the wood on the other side almost moan as the large body came down to its knees. The penitent leaned forward and placed his large hand on the screen. The priest could see the outline of the huge appendage covering most of the screen. In all his years he had rarely seen such a large hand lean against the confessional screen. The priest leaned back in his chair half in amazement, half still in boredom.

"Bless me Father for I have sinned, it has been a long time since my last confession." The voice was soft, so soft that the priest could hardly hear it.

"I am sorry," he said "I can barely hear you, can you speak up just a little?"

The soft voice came back, "No Father, I can't I was operated on last week, and my vocal chords were damaged, please lean in closer."

The priest could not place the voice, as soft as it was. Usually he knew if the person had been in his confessional before, he recognized most voices, but tried never to put a face with a voice. But this voice was so different. Not only was it soft, but there was a definite accent. Where was it from? It certainly was not Chicago. He knew all the Chicago accents, having served in three parishes and three different ends of the diocese. Was it Appalachian?

It was slow and almost a drawl, but not southern in nature. "Alright, I will come closer, but you need to talk a bit louder, or perhaps we can talk face to face, that is a part of the Rite now."

"No Father", the strange accented voice replied. "I never went face to face and I don't mean to start today. Come closer and you will hear me, but I won't be able to keep my voice loud for very long."

The priest leaned in, close to the screen. He had often had to ask the penitent to do this since so many of them were hard of hearing. "Okay, I'm listening".

"Father, I have committed a great sin, the sin of murder." The voice was stronger than before, but still hard to hear. "I don't even know where to begin or how to stop, because I am very afraid that I will kill again. Father you may have to stop me."

"My son, calm down." The voice of the priest was anything but convincing, murder was not one of the those things that happened in every confession. "Now if you want to be forgiven, you must be contrite, you must express your sorrow and promise that you will do your best not to commit the sin again."

"But Father, I don't know if I can do that. I mean I'm sorry, but what if I can't help doing it again? What if I kill and kill and cannot keep from doing it?"

The priest was nervous and sweat began to run down the back of his neck. "Listen to me, you can get help to stop this. Tell me that you are sorry and then the sacrament can be completed, then let me get you help, allow me to help you outside of the confessional."

"You are going to go to the police aren't you? You dirty priest, I knew I shouldn't have come here." The voice was stained, almost raw with anger. "Now my throat hurts so much, I can hardly speak again."

"I never said I was going to the police. I cannot go to the police even if I wanted to, I am bound by the seal of this confession, but I can get you help if you allow me to outside of the sacrament. Please my son, I know you are sorry, let me give you forgiveness and then get you help from a professional. You know that you do not want to kill again." The priest hoped that this would work. In the past he had been able to convince a child molester to get help and to stop his cycle of abuse.

"Okay, Okay, I'm sorry," said the scratchy voice. "I'm sorry so give me the absolution, give the forgiveness that you promised."

The priest took a breath and hoped his next words would not cause him to lose the man. "I also want you to show you are contrite, tell me that you are going to try and stop this madness, tell me that you are not going to kill again."

The voice was soft again, and the priest could hear the man crying gently on the other side. "I am sorry, I am sorry, Father I am so sorry. I don't want to kill." The voice was so soft it could hardly be heard even though the priest was only a few inches away. "Father, come close to me." The priest could see the huge hand pushed up against the screen again. "I will tell you what you want to hear."

"I am as close as I can get, unless you want me to open the door so that I…"

"No, no" interrupted the voice, "I want you to lean in so that I know you are close, this is so hard for me Father, dear Father."

The priest took a breath and leaned into the screen. He wanted to be compassionate, he wanted to help this man. His head pushed against the mesh, he could feel the heat of the man on the other side coming through the screen. The heat of a passionate man, he could smell the sweat in the box, was it his own, or was it the man's? He leaned in and heard the man put his hand to the screen. He felt the breath come through and the man sobbing again. "I am here," he said. "I am close."

"Yes, you are," the voice trembled. "I think you are a good man after all". The voice softened again. The priest put his head on the screen, confident that he had won the man over, sure that the man would seek help and that no one else would have to die. He turned to listen and could not quite make out the sound on the other side. Metal, yes metal hitting metal. What a strange sound to be heard in a confessional. Then silence, total silence.

Nothing moved in the confessional. There was no sound only the small drip of blood now coming from the ear of the priest, the blood mixed with small pieces of brain that the ice pick had attached to as it was pulled out of the priest's head.

CHAPTER 2

*D*an Gill was what was known as a veteran on the Chicago Police Force. He had been with the department for twenty-five years, working his way up through the often competitive rank and file. He was not a second or third generation cop like so many of his peers. His father was a quiet bookkeeper for a large Chicago department store. Dan grew up in a house that was filled with quiet. His parents rarely raised their voices to one another and the idea of breaking the law was unheard of in the small yet comfortable north side bungalow. Dan remembered his father as a man of high morals and personal values. He never heard him gossip and he never saw his father get involved in his neighbor's business. When Dan announced one day that he planned to become a cop, it was met with quiet reserve from his parents. His father had no plans for Dan's life, that would have been going against everything he believed. Joseph Gill was not about to pick the careers of his children.

In all his years on the force Dan had seen his share of unbelievable things. He had seen serial killers and domestic violence, he had witnessed child abuse and arson. After twenty-five years there were not many things that upset him or shocked him. As he pulled up to the front of St. Veronica's Catholic Church his own memory kicked into play. He had spent many a day as a youth in his own north side parish. He was baptized, made his first communion and confirmation and would probably be buried at his own home parish. Catholicism was ingrained in Gill and although so many of his contemporaries had fallen away from the church in the 1970's, he was still a faithful church goer, attending 6:30 AM mass each and every Sunday. Church remained important for him, although he could not always tell you why.

St. Veronica's, affectionately called St. Vero's was located on a residential street on Chicago's near south side. The neighborhood had been predominantly Bohemian at one time, but was now mainly Latino. The old people of the neighborhood still flocked to the Church, looking to hold on to some semblance of days gone by. The Latino community, which was mainly composed of Mexicans fresh over the border, were of course Catholics, but that sense of the parish and the neighborhood being connected was long gone. Neighbors didn't really know their neighbors anymore and youth organizations and sports clubs were quickly being replaced by gangs and violence. The parish, once a financial strong hold in the Archdiocese, had now become somewhat dilapidated and in severe debt. There was no danger of the parish closing, it served too many people to think of that, but there was always the constant worry about money and how the bills were going to be paid. The rich history of the parish was quickly being replaced with new stories of new people and the once almost incestuous neighborhood was rapidly becoming blocks of strangers.

Dan walked up to the crime scene, the yellow tape already in place and covering the entrance to the church. He stepped under the tape and walked into the darkened church. The only light was from the evening sun pouring in through the west stained glass windows and the flash of the crime scene photographer. The coroner's car was in front of the church and the medical examiner lackies were getting a gurney in place so they could remove the body. The body of the priest was still in the confessional, a small trail of blood dried on his ear . Dan walked up to a junior grade detective and shook his hand. "Hey Raferty, you got here pretty fast," Dan said.

"In all my years this is the first time I seen a priest killed," said the young detective. He shook the hand of Dan and stepped back out of the way.

"Yeah, I know it has happened in other places, but not here in Chicago." Dan moved closer to the confessional to take a look at the body. "What do you think caused the blood here?'

The young detective pointed to the mesh screen with a hole about 1/4 inch in circumference poked right through the middle. "Well, I would have to say that something came pushing through this screen with a pretty good force. The forensic guys have already determined that blood and brain particle can be found around the edges of this hole. Jesus, what kind of nut would stick something like that into the brain of a priest?"

Dan ignored the question, for it was a question that had no answer. "What do they think, some kind of surgical instrument, a wood worker's tool, what?"

"They say it was probably a sharpened ice pick, but they'll know more after an autopsy. They think they can actually get small flakes of the metal out of his brain and test it for all kinds of things. Man those guys are amazing."

"Yeah, well we'll see what they can find out." Dan was never overly impressed with forensics. They could make good guesses, but television shows and people's ignorance made them seem like gods. Dan looked at the mesh screen closer. The small prongs of the screen were pushed in toward the body of the dead priest. "Whatever he used had a handle bigger than a good portion of the rest of the instrument. Look how the prongs face in on the screen. He must have jammed this mother with some real force and pulled it back quick, not catching any of the broken screen."

The younger detective leaned in closer to Dan. "Good eye Dan. I guess that's why they sent you over and not Bartly, that fat piece of shit."

Bartly was John Bartleanowicz, a nemesis of Dan Gill and one of the most hated detectives in homicide. Bartly made enemies by grabbing the spot light, going for the big story and always managing to get his picture in the paper. He didn't care who he stepped on or how he solved his cases. Dan suspected that Bartly sometimes planted evidence although there was never anyway to prove this. He just knew in his gut that no detective could be that lucky that many times.

When they had entered the academy together almost twenty six years ago, Dan and Bartly seemed destined to become great friends. They were from neighboring parts of the city, both grew up as the sons of immigrants, both Catholics, both married their high school sweethearts. But it wasn't long before the two drifted apart. They were always in competition even in the early days. Gill would do a great job and few would notice his efforts. Bartly would do an adequate job and somehow always manage to get the attention of the Captain or even the Commissioner. Dan often had to stop and ask himself if he hated Bartly because of his tactics, or because he was jealous of all the attention that Bartly received.

Dan stepped back from the confessional and looked at the carpeting around the front. He looked over to the penitent's side and opened the door. He could see that the box and the door handles had already been dusted for prints. He also knew that they would not find anything because this killer was too smart to leave something as easy to detect as a finger print. He knelt down in the confessional and let go of the door. It was an amazingly dark place, as though the Church did not want you to see even yourself as you confessed your sins. He looked through the screen and saw that the priest's side was lit but he wasn't sure if that was because the door was open or because of a light in the confessional itself. "Hey, Raferty", he shouted to the young detective, "Turn on the lights on the priest's side of the confessional and close the door. In fact come into the priest's side and close the door."

The young detective walked over to the priest's side of the confessional and looked for the switches to turn on the lights. "Hey, Dan, this is kind of freaky, coming into the priest's side and with a stiff in here to boot."

"Don't give me any shit kid, just do as I ask." Dan was in no mood to play games.

Raferty moved into the box, closed the door and flicked three switches on the wall. One lit the box for the priest, one lit a very dim light on Gill's side and the other controlled the outside lights letting everyone know that the priest was available and that the confessional was occupied. Raferty felt strange being in the box. He too was Catholic as were most of the whites on the Chicago Police Force. He knew what confession was all about although he hadn't been to the sacrament for years.

"Why are you making me do this Dan?" he asked.

"I want to see if I can see you through the screen," answered Dan

"Well you didn't need me for that, there is another body in here you know."

"No shit Sherlock, but that body can't tell me if you can see me." Dan looked around and could see a bit of the priest and Raferty. Dan thought the picture was almost surrealistic, three men in a confessional, sounded like a Bergman film title. He grinned and then asked Raferty his question. "Now can you see me?"

Raferty looked but could not really see Dan very well. "Not really, it must be pretty dark on your side."

"Yeah it is, how about now?" Dan raised his hand to the screen and touched the mesh.

"Yeah, yeah, now I can see your hand, wow it looks huge from this side, it must be the back lighting." Raferty was pleased with his own sense of logic.

"You can't see me unless I move pretty close though right?" Dan leaned back away from the mesh. "How well can you hear me."

"I can hear you fine but you do sound a little more distant than before. Lean closer and I'll see if it makes a difference." Raferty was anticipating Dan's next command.

"Yes, Raferty, I was just about to suggest that." Dan moved closer to the screen and lowered his voice to a whisper. "How about now, he said ever so softly, "can you hear me well?"

"I can hear you," said Raferty "but you're not real clear. Why are you whispering so low?"

Dan leaned even closer to the screen and lowered his voice even more. "Come closer Raferty so you can hear me better." Raferty did what Gill told him to do.

"Man, I can barely hear you Dan." Raferty moved even closer to the screen placing his ear next to the mesh.

"Can you still see me Raferty?" Dan asked.

"Not with my ear so close to the screen," he answered with indignation.

"Good,." said Gill and with that he smacked the screen with the palm of his hand. Raferty's ear rung and he instinctively let out a few expletives even though he was in a church.

"Son of a bitch, that hurt Dan, what the hell's the matter with you?"

Dan opened the door of his side of the confessional and walked over to open Raferty's.

"Well," he said, "Its not too hard to see how the poor SOB was killed, now all we have to do is find out why.

CHAPTER 3

*T*he house of the Archbishop of Chicago had been a landmark in the city for over sixty years. Its eleven chimneys stood as a reminded to the people of the city of a more powerful time for the Church. The building sat on North Parkway like a guardian of the neighborhood, watching all that passed by in the nearby park and on the quiet tree lined streets. It was built at a time when the Archbishop of Chicago was considered by all, Catholics and non-Catholics alike, as a force with which to be reckoned. The people of Chicago, mostly European immigrants in the early part of the twentieth century, had given of their sweat and blood to build an Archdiocese that the world could look to as powerful. The Irish and the Germans were the first wave of Catholic Immigrants to Chicago. They brought with them their traditions and their religion. They worked hard to be accepted and made their names known throughout the city. A glance at the street names of Chicago reminded everyone of the power that once ruled the metropolis by the lake.

But times had changed and the house on North Parkway seemed in many ways to sit there as a anachronism. The Archbishop of Chicago was not nearly as powerful as he had been fifty or even twenty years before. The Church had a difficult time influencing her own people, let alone an entire city. Yet at the same time the office of the Archbishop still commanded respect in this diocese of more than two million Catholics. Catholics were by far the largest voting block in the county and in many ways among the richest people in the city and the surrounding areas. When the Archbishop of Chicago wanted something, he could, usually, still get it.

Detective Dan Gill wasn't really excited about going to visit the Archbishop on that Saturday evening. He had met the Archbishop several times before at police gatherings and other fund raisers. It wasn't that Dan didn't respect the Archbishop, he certainly did, but under the given circumstances Dan would rather had been home with a beer and the people he loved. He parked his car in the semi circular drive of the mansion and got out of the car. He extinguished his cigarette, figuring that it would be pretty rude to go to the front door of the Archbishop's house puffing away. He spied himself in the glass of the front door and shook his head, took out a small comb from his front breast pocket and combed down his hair. He straightened his coat and gave a quick spit into the side bushes so that he wouldn't cough later. He rang the bell and waited.

The door opened and a nun, maybe about seventy years old answered the door. "Can I help you?" she said, with a not too terribly friendly voice.

"Yes, Sister" he said nervously, always thinking of his grade school days anytime he saw a nun in habit, which these days was not too often. "I'm here to see Archbishop Tate, I'm Dan Gill, Chicago Police."

The nun opened the glass door and stretched her arm to hold it open for Dan. She eyed him from head to toe giving a little smirk as she came to his worn shoes. Dan hated to buy shoes and it was always that part of his suit that looked out of place. "Oh yes, Mr. Gill, the Archbishop is expecting you, please come in." She lead him through a short corridor to a sitting room filled with religious art. The paintings on the walls were of scenes of the life of Christ and the nick knacks were fine pieces of porcelain shaped like angels and saints. The room was tastefully decorated and not too pretentious.

Gill took a seat close to a lamp next to the fireplace. He was not surprised that the sitting room had a rather small fireplace at one end of the room. He had driven by the mansion many times counting the chimneys wondering just how many fireplaces the building held. He sat up straight so that he would look officious as the Archbishop entered the room.

After about ten minutes the Archbishop of Chicago entered the sitting room. Archbishop James Francis Xavier Tate was a sixty-four year old man who had seen his share of life. He had served as an army chaplain in the Vietnam War, taught in the seminary system, was made chancellor of his home diocese in Southern Illinois and quickly rose through the ranks of the Church. He was not a tall man, but his stature was still imposing. At five foot nine and two hundred pounds, his presence filled a room when he entered.

James Tate had been the Archbishop of Chicago for six years. He was by nature a southern boy in a Midwestern milieu and he often felt like a fish out of water. Everything in Chicago was different than it was in his home in Southern Illinois. The food was different, the people were different, the weather was surely different. Except for a six year stint as a professor in the Chicago seminary system, and his two years in Viet Nam, Tate rarely strayed from his Southern Illinois roots. In fact, Tate had been accused of being a bit too Southern when he had first arrived six years ago. His views on minorities came under close scrutiny and his own version of plantation politics were often seen as antiquated and out of place in a diocese like Chicago. His acceptance came slow, but eventually the people of Chicago accepted him as their spiritual leader. The priests though were a bit slower to accept him as the boss.

The clergy of Chicago had always had a reputation of being independent if not difficult. They claimed they wanted a strong leader but were always offended when they received one. James Tate was not an autocrat but he was outspoken and his ideas of how to save money, reduce the fat, and pull the clergy back in line were not met with open arms. His first five years were spent in constant negotiation with his priests, trying to get them on board with his programs and ideas. Now in his sixth year he had finally won most of them over and was pleased with the relationships he had formed. He had one advantage in that he knew some of the priests from his years of teaching in the seminary. At least when he first arrived he had some built in allies.

When the Archbishop entered the room Detective Dan Gill rose. He knew it was good manners and Church protocol to rise for the Archbishop. "Good evening your Grace," Dan extended his hand to the Archbishop.

The Archbishop extended his hand and warmly grasped Dan's. "Good evening Detective Gill, it is nice to see you again, although I wish it were under better circumstances."

Dan nodded his head as the Archbishop gestured for him to be seated. Dan explained the earlier happenings of the day giving details to the Archbishop that had not yet been released to the press. Dan was not too sure how much the Archbishop would want to know, but he decided that unless he was interrupted by the Archbishop that he would just continue on. He gave the Archbishop a detailed account of what they found. Dan thought that maybe the Archbishop would be shocked at what he heard, but the man listened intently taking it all in like a good mystery tale.

"You know Detective, I spent two years in Vietnam with our men in fox holes. I have seen a great deal of death and useless destruction. I hope that I don't seem cold, I rarely come across as an emotional man." The Archbishop stood and walked over to the fireplace and lit a match on the stone mantle piece. "Does it bother you if I smoke?" he asked.

Dan indicated that it not only did not bother him but would very much like to join him. Dan lit his cigarette and thought maybe he should stand too, so that the two men would be on an even keel, but he decided to remain seated.

"This is of course a very bothersome event Detective. I know that you see people in this city killed almost everyday, but it is rarely, if ever a member of the clergy." The Archbishop took a long drag of his cigarette. "I imagine this will make the national news tonight and tomorrow morning."

"Yes, I'm sure it will and I'm pretty sure that the television cameras will be outside your house looking for a statement before too long." Dan looked up at the troubled face of the Archbishop.

"Most likely before you leave here," he said.

Dan knew he was right, once the media got hold of a story like this they could be vultures looking for every angle. They would think that the most likely source of information would be the Archbishop, even though he didn't know anymore than anyone else. Dan explained that the department was ready to make a statement indicating only that the priest was murdered and that the case was under priority investigation. They would not reveal the type of murder or exactly where it took place, although the police tape around the confessional area might give that away. And given the natural gossip factor of any parish community, the details would most likely leak out. The police still wanted to prevent any copycat crimes at all costs. It was just too attractive for some nut to go around and start stabbing priests in the ears.

"Look Archbishop," Dan was a little nervous. "I don't want to tell you how to do your job, but I would suggest that somebody prepare a statement for the press. If not you then one of your assistants or somebody."

"Yes, Detective we have already done that, my chancellor Chris Rayday has prepared a statement that will be read tonight from the Chancery office. The office should be making calls right now to the media to meet there at 9:30. But I doubt that will keep the media off my doorstep."

"You know as well as I do sir that nothing keeps them away." Dan stood realizing that he had accomplished what he had set out to do.

He shook the hand of the Archbishop and headed for the door. It would be a long night of paper work. He knew he had to start looking for witnesses in the morning and get this damn thing off the front pages of the newspaper.

The Archbishop walked Dan to the door hoping that the media would not yet be gathered outside. "You know Detective I feel a very personal loss when one of my priests die. I don't even know how to feel now that one has been murdered."

"I am sorry Archbishop, I know this is going to be tough on you and the diocese. It's tough on us too, I mean quite honestly sir we have very little idea of who would want to do this."

"Don't be too naive Dan, you don't mind me calling you Dan I hope" said the Archbishop. "There are plenty of people who hate priests, some for good cause, some because they are just angry people. Of course we realize that the life of this dead priest will now be planted all over the front pages of the papers. We hope that there is nothing in his past that would give any cause to this horrible crime, but quite honestly you never know."

Dan turned to face the Archbishop "If there is something that you know Archbishop I hope that you will share it with us, we want to catch this guy."

"I wish there was something I could tell you Dan, but as far as I know, and I have consulted the files on this priest, there is nothing that indicates he was involved with someone who would do this. You know we keep a pretty extensive file on all of our priests, more extensive that even they themselves know." The Archbishop looked down at his own shoes, perhaps a little ashamed to admit this to an outsider.

"Well, sir if there is anything you can tell us please do so, in the meantime I'll drive by the Chancery and try to talk with the chancellor after the press conference. What was his name again?"

The Archbishop smiled, "Oh, not his name Detective, her name, Sister Chris Rayday. You see we are an enlightened archdiocese and raise both men and women to the highest offices allowed by the Church. I think you will find her very cooperative, she too is very anxious to solve your case."

Dan left the house and got in his car. The media had not yet arrived so he would have no trouble getting over to the chancery office before the show began. He lit another cigarette and thought to himself , "What could be in those files on the priests that even they themselves don't know?" He sped along North Parkway glancing at the clock on his dash. He had enough time to stop for a burger before hitting the chancery office.

CHAPTER 4

*T*he Chancery Office for the Archdiocese of Chicago had been renamed the Pastoral Center back in the late eighties as political correctness and change for the sake of change became vogue. If you told an older Catholic to meet you at the Pastoral Center, they would have very little idea of what you were talking about. If you told them to meet at the Chancery, they would be there.

The office was actually a building, a six story steel and glass monstrosity that stood in the heart of Chicago's Gold Coast, the city's most exclusive shopping district. The building was nothing to look at, having been built in the sixties when Mies Van der Rohe and the Bauhaus were the kings of Chicago architecture. Not that the master had anything to do with this building, it was, quite unfortunately, a bad mock of post modern design. While the buildings that surrounded the Chancery were considered world class pieces of architecture, the Chancery itself was little more than six stories of bad concrete, glass, and metal.

This was where the Chancellor was to hold her press conference, on the sixth floor. This was the floor that always entertained the media, although these days there was little cause for that. Church scandal was at a low and the Archdiocese was financially sound. No one important was sick and a press conference had not been held here for over a year. But now the sixth floor was buzzing. The city's various newspapers and television stations had all sent reporters because a priest being killed in an Archdiocese with over 2 million Catholics was still big news. The news trucks lined the front of the building with their satellite dishes up and their lights ready for on the street reporting. Dan was happy when he pulled up that he could park wherever he wanted with no fear of being towed.

Dan made his way through the crowd at the entrance to the building and flashed his badge to the guard behind the large marble desk on the ground floor. "Dan Gill, Chicago P.D., I'm here to see Chris Rayday."

The guard behind the desk quickly glanced at Dan's ID and waved him past, directing him to the sixth floor. As Dan rode the elevator up he marveled at the ease with which hired guards let people through. He thought how easy it would be for some nut to come through and kill the Archbishop himself if he showed the right badge to the idiot at the desk. When the doors opened Dan walked through the sixth floor lobby to a sea of reporters and cameras. He was still early and the only representative from the police department. He scanned the room and looked for someone dressed like a Chancellor, whatever that might be. He was pretty sure he could pick her out of the crowd of black suits and collars

"Detective Gill?" a confident voice asked.

Dan turned around, "Yes, I'm Dan Gill."

"Detective, I am Sister Christ Rayday, I thought you might be with the police, I can usually pick out a cop at twenty paces." The women speaking was well dressed. She stood about five foot six with perfectly styled hair and a suit that had to come from Marshall Fields or Bloomingdale's. Her posture was impeccable, she was a women who knew where she stood and was proud that she did so.

"I'm sorry Sister, you took me a little by surprise, I always thought that I could pick out a nun at twenty paces myself." Dan shook her hand and felt her strong grip.

"Yes, well there are some who feel the habit makes the woman Detective. I however feel that the women should speak for herself." She let go of his hand and gestured for him to follow her to a private place where they could talk in quiet. "There is very little I actually know about this case Detective. I am anxious to get your take on the details and on any question you might anticipate the press asking."

Dan followed the nun to a room set with a large conference table, one floor lamp and eight chairs. On the table were copies of the Archdiocesan newspaper and a commemorative book of the 150th Anniversary of the Archdiocese. Nothing radical, nothing even interesting. "I can give you some idea of the questions the vultures will ask Sister," Dan said as he sat in one of the chairs. I've dealt with this bunch for years, remember that with them, the best defense is often a good offense."

She took her seat at the head of the long table. "How do you mean Detective?"

"Well, they will all want some kind of an angle, you know, why did they want to do this to a priest, what's in his past, what are you doing to protect people from nuts like this in parishes."

She sat up straight in her chair. "Certainly they don't think they we could have prevented this, my God the man was killed hearing confessions, its not like you can lock the doors of the Church during sacraments. Perhaps they would like us to put metal detectors inside the church doors to keep the nuts out!"

"Easy Sister, I'm only the messenger remember?" Dan could tell she was a pistol waiting to go off. What was the Archbishop thinking having this woman speak for him. She'd surely put her size four in her mouth before the press conference was over. "Sister, you have to understand that this is big news for these guys. They haven't had a good church scoop in about 2 years. For us no news is good news, for them it's a kick in the pants."

"Yes, Detective, I understand. It's just so frustrating always trying to explain the inexplicable. This was a good priest. A man who gave of himself everyday. He was in a tough assignment but never gave up. I knew him personally and can tell you that there was no reason to target him as an individual."

Dan now sat up a little in his own chair. "What was in his file Sister? Not the general file but the special file?" He could see that the statement made her a bit uncomfortable.

"I see His Grace has been running at the mouth a bit,." she said.

"I've known him in social circles for a few years Sister, he has come to trust me, hope you can do the same."

"Yes, well, we'll see Detective. Right now my concern is for the Archdiocese and for the family of this priest. As for his file, including his special file, it is clean. Only three letters of complaint against him in his twenty-seven years of priesthood. Practically a record. There is nothing in there that would indicate a vendetta for death."

"Can I see those letters Sister? I mean I know I can see them, I can get a subpoena for them, but may I see them now?" Dan relished in using a bit of English grammar rhetoric on a nun.

"Yes, you may see them Detective. You may see the entire file, because I am as anxious to see this maniac caught as you are."

Dan looked over the file, surprisingly thin only about 10 pages of material. Not too much for twenty-seven years of priesthood he thought. Janitors at the police department probably had bigger files that this. He looked over the papers. The priest's name, Joseph Stanislaus Wysocki was in bold letters at the top of the page. Listed inside were verifications of degrees conferred. This priest was pretty smart. His B.A. from Loyola University, his Master in Divinity from the theologate in Chicago, and a J.D. from Georgetown.

Dan looked up at the nun. "He was a lawyer? Isn't that a bit strange for a priest?"

"Not in the least Detective." The nun crossed her legs a leaned back in the chair. "Many priests go on for continuing education. This priest was quite intelligent, and a favorite of the Cardinal Archbishop twenty years ago. He was given the opportunity to become a lawyer to help the Archdiocese in a time of need."

"What need?" he asked.

"It was a time when the Archdiocese was letting go of quite a bit of property. Convents were emptying, schools were closing. They needed someone personable and bright to negotiate deals and assure that the Church wasn't getting screwed."

Dan was a bit taken aback by her use of the vulgar. "Yes, well, it seems his services were no longer needed, since he spent the last 15 years in parishes."

The nun stood up and walked a bit closer to Dan. "Don't be naive Detective, the Church is not immune to politics. What one Archbishop likes in a person doesn't always translate to a new administration. Do you honestly think I would have this position under that last Archbishop of Chicago? He would have sooner seen Satan be the chancellor than a woman."

They stared at each other for just a moment, but Dan saw something in her that he did not like, or was it something that he admired? He never thought himself a sexist but that old adage that an aggressive man is admired while an aggressive woman is considered a bitch came to his mind. The nun straightened her suit and walked back to her end of the table.

"You know Detective, there is nothing in that file that is really going to help you. But just the same I think you should have a complete copy of it. Let me make one for you before you go." Dan handed her the worn folder and figured he would have time later to read the three letters of complaint and anything else that was in there.

"Sister, maybe I'm not being very helpful to you. You wanted to know what the media might ask. Let me help you on this tonight. Let me be up there with you incase they get a little out of control. There are bound to be questions that the diocese cannot answer and the vultures will be just as happy getting my blood as yours." He was genuine in his offer hoping this would allow them to have some kind of working relationship during this case.

"Yes, I think you're right Detective. I could use someone with me." She reached into her attache case and pulled out a single piece of beige bond paper. "I have a prepared statement that should at least look good for the cameras. Quite honestly I don't really have much to say. I know that details should come from your end."

They walked out of the room together, like a team of comic book super heroes, going out there to make the city safe. She had a real confidence in her walk. Dan was sure that no one could ever tell that she was a nun. He imagined her shopping a Marshall Field's fooling people behind the counters. She was a tough cookies alright, and maybe wouldn't be that bad to work with.

She stopped Dan halfway down the hall. "Let me copy this file for you Detective. It will only take a minute." She directed Dan to have a seat in the hallway. He sat down, longing for a cigarette, but knowing that to smoke here was for sure a big no no.

"Here you are Detective, his file for your perusal. All verification of degrees, his ordination papers, his letters from former supervisors, and the two letters of complaint from the faithful of his flock."

"I thought you said there were three letters Sister," Dan said firmly..

"Oh, no Detective just the two, you must be mistaken. As I said Joe almost set a record for lack of complaints, just two letters in twent-seven years."

Dan thanked the nun and slipped the dozier under his arm. "Shall we move forward Sister to face the wolves?" He smiled a reassuring smile.

"Let's Detective, we've nothing to hide." She was confident in her gait as she pushed open the doors to the reception room of the sixth floor.

CHAPTER 5

❀

*T*he phone rang at 1:30 AM in the rectory of the far north side church. The priest had the phone programmed to ring in his room after three rings so that he could deal with late night emergencies.

In the 1950's the phone rang at night all the time in church rectories. People needing the 'Last Rites' as they were known then. Today, very few people died at home and even fewer saw the need for the final sacrament of the Anointing of the Sick. The mystery had been taken out of the sacrament and only recent immigrants and old people saw the value in having the priest come to the house as a person lay dying. For these people the anointing was very important. The call would come through occasionally to anoint someone who had been dead for an hour or more, never a pleasant thing to do.

When the phone at St. Polycarp rang the priest answered it as though he were wide awake. "St. Polycarp, how can I help you?"

The voice on the other end was raspy and deep, with a heavy breath. "Father, we need you to come over right away, its my mother, she's dying."

The priest sat up in bed and cleared his throat because now it was important that he really was awake. He turned on the light by his bed and fumbled for his glasses and a pen and paper. "Alright, what is your mother's name?"

"Martha," the voice replied.

"Is she under a doctor's care, I mean is there hospice in the house or did she have a heart attack or what?" The priest did not mean to sound callous, it was just easier for him if he knew the full situation.

"No, uh, she's just really sick, I mean she needs a priest because she is dying, didn't I already say that?"

The priest moved a little farther up in his bed. "Alright, give me the address and I'll be right over."

The voice cleared his own throat and then hesitated as he answered. "Well, the number isn't on the building. It's the old Majestic Hotel on Irving Park just east of Clark street. We've been living there for a few months now even though it's closed."

The priest knew that there were many homeless in his parish. His boundaries included the rich yuppies along the lake front and the displaced people of what was known as Uptown. This was one of the few times that he had received a call from someone living on the streets, although it had happened before. "Yeah, I know the place. I can be there in about 10-15 minutes. She is still alive isn't she?"

"Yes Father", the voice answered. "She is alive. Come to the old hotel and park in the back, there's no electricity, but I have a flash light. Come in the back door and I'll meet you on the stairs. Don't worry though there isn't anyone else in here now, the city swept everyone else out last week. We managed to stay because there was a lock on our door."

"Okay", said the priest, "Stay there and I'll meet you in the back, and for God's sake call 911 and get an ambulance there."

"I'd rather not, I don't want anyone to know that we're here."

"Don't be a fool, either call 911 or I will, you have to get her medical attention."

The voice gave a large sigh, "Okay, I'll call them right now."

The priest got out of bed and turned on the overhead light in his bedroom. He dressed in his black pants which hung on his desk chair and threw on a clergy shirt. He headed quietly down the stairs and out to his garage. He did not want to wake the associate pastor, no need to, he would be back long before anyone else needed to be up.

The priest left the parish and headed west on Irving Park Road. Even at this time of the night roads in that part of the north side were crowded. People coming home from local bars, theater and late night dinners. The neighborhood was amazing, such a fantastic mixture of people. The same corner would have drug addicts and gay couples crossing at the light, each going different ways, living different lives.

As he drove west he could see the imposing building of the old Majestic Hotel. He knew that the building was slated to be torn down later in the year. He knew most things about the neighborhood because he served on his alderman's task force for urban renewal. He didn't think anyone could really be living in the building and he knew about the police sweeps of just a week before. In fact he remembered well the day it happened because the soup kitchen and food pantry were particularly crowded with displaced people.

His car pulled into the empty lot behind the hotel. This was not originally a parking lot, it was the site of the Majestic Ballroom and Theater which had been torn down almost ten years ago. The original hotel had no need of a parking lot. In its hey day people would come in taxis or on public transportation to the hotel and ballroom. People felt safe riding a bus at 2:00 AM. Those days were long gone.

The priest exited his car and hit his alarm button. The beep squeak of the alarm echoed off the building. It was a quiet night, only the sounds of a few people shouting and the rumble of the 'L' train going by disturbed the eerie silence. He reached the back door of the hotel and pulled on the door handle. It opened and he entered the building. "Anyone here?" he shouted.

No one answered.

"Martha? It's Father Phil from St. Polycarp. I've brought you the anointing of the sick, hello is anyone there?"

His heart beat a little faster and he stepped completely into the building. Why was there no answer? Perhaps the son wasn't back in the building yet. He could not have called from the hotel, there were no phones, no electricity. He must have gone down to one of the local bars, or the 'L' station to make the call. Now he was worried that something happened to the son. Even experienced street people could easily run into trouble this late a night in this neighborhood. He never thought about the paramedics and why they were not there yet.

He decided to climb the stairs and find the room with the woman in it. He thought of waiting at the bottom but his instincts told him that this woman was in pretty bad shape. He realized that the son probably spent all the change he had just to make the phone call.

"Martha? Can you hear me?" He wished he had asked the son his name so he could call that out too, or at least comfort the old woman by letting her know that her son had called. "Martha, this is Father Phil. Your son called and asked me to bring you the sacrament of the sick. I've come to pray with you dear if you can just let me know where you are."

The stairway was very dark, the only light coming in the windows at each landing. The city of Chicago had good street lights, but they weren't close enough to illuminate these stairs very well. He moved to the first floor and looked down the hall. No lights anywhere. He thought he would see at least a shimmer under one of the doors. It looked as though most of the rooms didn't even have doors on them anymore.

He reached the second floor and wondered to himself, why he did not bring a flashlight. He knew the building had no electricity and that it would be dark inside. He remembered the son saying that he had a flashlight, that's why he didn't think to bring his own from the car. At this point though his thoughts led him to believe that he should go to the car and get his flashlight and his cell phone.

He looked down the long hallway of the second floor and saw just a bit of light coming from the room at the far end. He breathed a sigh of relief and walked assuredly down the hall. "Finally", he thought. "There she is."

"Martha, this is Father Phil from St. Polycarp, I've brought you the sacrament of the sick. Your son called and asked me to come see you." He reached the door and knocked gently. The door creaked open slowly. He peered in, the light was extremely dim, and he could barely make out the figure that lied on the old broken down bed. He moved in a bit closer and bent toward the figure, but his nose, his sense of smell caused him to bolt upright. He had rarely if ever smelled anything like the odor of that room. It was pungent and grotesque. It made him want to vomit and literally made him dizzy. He staggered back against the door, sweat now pouring from his head. "What can that smell be?" he thought. "I know it, but can't place it." He wiped his forehead and again moved a little closer to the bed. He thought to himself, "That's the smell of death. But not recent death, death of a few days or weeks." He remembered the time the janitors had laid rat poison in the basement and how he had found the dead vermin from the smell when he went down there one afternoon.

He had hoped that the son wasn't insane, keeping the body of the mother in the bed for a few days after she died. He had read about that and seen it in movies, but this was real life. He approached the bed again, because although the smell was repulsive, he was not afraid of death or a dead body. He saw the candle that gave the only light to the room on the floor next to the bed. He bent down to pick it up and shine it on the old woman.

His entire body shook as he saw the deformed figure that lay in the bed. It wasn't a person, or was it? He looked closer, it was a dog, a huge dead dog, its eyes bulging and it swollen tongue hanging from its mouth. "What the hell is this?" he said. "What kind of sick joke is this?"

Suddenly the dog body moved, flung upward with the force of an erupting volcano. The priest shrieked with surprise and tried to jump back from the decaying animal. His face was covered with blood and the smell of death had permeated his nostrils. He reeled back and fell to the floor. Then he saw him. A massive individual with a huge pair of scissors in his hands. He tried to roll out of the way but it was too late, the hands had grabbed him and pulled him forward to the bed. His hands, the mad man was pulling so hard on his hands. He felt the sharp blade of scissors on his thumb and looked desperately at the man who tricked him into coming to this hell, this chamber of torture. He looked and saw only the foot of the man coming at his face the last thing he saw was that boot, steel toed, black and heavy as it crashed into his face, crushed his skull and took his life.

CHAPTER 6

✿

*I*t was 8:30 Tuesday morning when Dan got the call that another priest had been murdered. It was hard to believe that two priests could be murdered within three days. He knew in his gut that it was more than a coincidence. He knew that these two murders had to be connected.

He raced out of his house and drove to the Majestic Hotel on Irving Park Road. There were three squad cars in the empty lot behind the building. Dan parked between two of them and got out of his car. He saw Raferty waiting by the front door smoking a cigarette, with left foot propped up in the door jamb.

"Looks like another sick one Dan." Raferty said.

"What happened?" asked Dan.

"Looks like somehow the priest was lured here late last night. His car is there in the empty lot. Nothing touched on it, the alarm is still engaged." You can see where he pulled in off of Irving from his tire tracks. No other tracks near his car, no foot prints other than his own coming from his car." Raferty threw down the cigarette and exhaled a big puff of smoke.

Dan walked into the building, Raferty following in tow. "I thought they were going to tear this place down." Dan said.

"They are next week." Raferty leaned forward to look up the flight of stairs. "He's up here on the second floor. It's not a pretty sight Dan, much worse than the last priest."

Dan looked at Raferty with a knowing smile. "We don't know if these two murders are connected yet Rafts, let's wait and see huh?"

Raferty knew that Dan thought they were connected but let him have his say anyway. Dan never played his hand, and Raferty knew this too. "Well the M.O. is slightly different that's for sure, could be a copy cat or maybe a drug buy gone bad."

Dan started up the stairs taking two at a time, he looked back to Raferty. "We'll see. Let's get a look at things first. Have the forensics been here yet?"

"No not yet. Only the uniforms and the photographer. I guess downtown is going to send in the big guys on this one. I'm sure they'll be here any minute."

Dan walked down the short corridor to the room where the priest lay on the bed. It was truly a gruesome sight. Blood strewn across the old mattress, the priest's eyes closed but his face in agony as though he truly felt the pain of his death. Dan looked at the body and said, "This wasn't a drug buy gone bad. How many priests do you know that buy crack while they have their Roman collar on?"

Raferty looked again at the body. "Guess your right, would be kind of stupid huh?"

Dan walked around the bed to get a full look at the body. He could see that the priest had been cut several times on the left arm. Not only punctures but blade cuts, long cuts as though someone had slashed at him during a struggle. He looked at the priest's face and saw the horror in his expression. Then he saw the throat, pierced with a sharp object, a large gashing wound that proved to be fatal. The hole was large, much larger than the hole in the other priest's ear. This was no ice pick it was something much larger, a hunting knife perhaps or a pair of shears. It wasn't large enough to be a sword or a military weapon, but something definitely sharp.

Raferty stood in the corner and watched Dan as he observed the body. There was so much he could learn from this master detective, perhaps the most important thing being to remain cool and withhold judgement until all the facts came in. "Pretty gruesome huh?" Raferty said.

"Man it stinks in here." Dan said. "I can't believe this guy has only been dead since last night. What made you think it didn't happen earlier."

Raferty stood up straight. "The associate pastor at St. Polycarp, that's where this guy was pastor, he's the one who called us in the first place. Said he heard the guy leave the rectory at about 1:45 last night. He thought it was unusual, but he had heard the phone ring just prior to his leaving. He figured he was called out on a sick call or some kind of emergency. When he didn't show up for 6:00 AM mass he knew something was wrong. He drove around the neighborhood himself until he spotted the car then called it in."

"Still," Dan said, "It smells like something else died in here days ago. Is there a decaying rat or something in one of the corners?"

"I can look, but I didn't see anything. Maybe it's just the smell of a vacant building Dan, I mean a lot of homeless were in here until it was swept clean last week."

Down the hall Dan could hear the footsteps of others coming to the crime scene. He stepped out into the hall and saw the forensic team coming at him with equipment in hand. They wanted to get in and do a preliminary work up before the body was removed. At the head of the party was Dan's worst nightmare, Bartly.

"Gill, you piece of shit, what the hell are you doing here?" Bartly waddled down the hall closer to Dan.

Dan stood his ground and literally dug in his heals. "I might ask you the same thing Bartly." Dan said.

"Well, when I heard the call that the forensic boys were needed for a priest murder I jumped along for the ride. Looks like a big case and one that will need a competent detective to get it solved."

Dan looked Bartly square in the eye. "Like I said, then why are you here?"

There was no love loss between the two detectives. Bartly the climber had always managed to be at the right place at the right time. Dan Gill, the smartest detective in the Chicago P.D. always managed to be at the wrong place at the wrong time. But Dan believed this was his case. Bartly was trying to muscle in because now it would be high profile, but Dan was not letting go of this one.

"Why don't you blow it out your ass son. I have as much right to be here as you do." Bartly pushed past him and entered the room. He looked around saw the body and turned to the forensic guys who came in behind him. "Looks like Father here was looking to score a little smack or coke. You guys should check him for residue, bet he comes up reeking of the shit."

Dan leaned back against the wall and saw the look of astonishment on the faces of the forensic team. He walked closer to the body and said, "Bartly, you're nuts man. Always so quick to judge. Not a fucking clue about what happened here and disparaging the name of the dead. Shame on you." Dan made a tsk tsk sound and turned away from Bartly.

"Okay, big shot, what do you think happened?" Bartly stood taller so he wouldn't look as though Dan had just pulled the carpet out from under him.

"I don't know what happened yet. I'm waiting until I can do some investigating. But I'll tell you one thing for sure, the padre was not here to score drugs."

Dan knew that Bartly was stupid and that anything Bartly said was probably wrong. But in his heart he knew that the priest was not there for drugs. It didn't make any sense. Not that he didn't believe that Priests did drugs. He was sure some of them did. But no one would go to score dressed in his collar, and so close to his own neighborhood. Even a guy with a real addiction problem would go somewhere else to get the goods.

He needed to tune Bartly out and concentrate on what happened in that hotel room. He began to walk again around the body occasionally closing his eyes and imaging the scene. He could see the priest coming down the hall in his mind. Looking for the room, most likely coming here because he was called. He imagined that it was pretty dark since there had not been electricity in the building for quite some time. How did the priest see, there was no flashlight found in the room. Dan continued to walk around the body, he looked at the foot of the bed and saw an indentation in the old metal foot rail. Could it be a new dent or an old one? He looked closer, it seemed to be newer, there was no rust on the dent and metal that was bent was much more susceptible to rust because it had been weakened. He would have the forensic boys look at that to see if there was anything from the priest on it.

He looked again at the body. The priest's left arm was in front on the body as though it were grasping his chest. His right arm was under his body, almost hiding. Dan thought it odd that one arm would be up and one arm under if the priest were fighting for his life. Both arms should be in front if he were in a defensive position. Dan's train of thought was broken by the bright flash of the photographer as he again snapped pictures of the body.

"Make sure you get this exactly as it is now from every angle." Dan said. "There's something strange about the way the body is laid but I can't quite figure it out yet."

Bartly looked up, chewing a huge wad of gum. "The great detective can't figure something out? Well let me sit down before I faint!"

Dan glanced over at Bartly trying not to get into a confrontation this early in the morning.

He turned to Raferty and said, "This guy was placed like this on purpose. We were meant to find his body this way. Remember when we found the other guy. His head was against the screen of the confessional. It seemed natural at the time, but now that I think about it the thrust of the weapon should have driven him at least back a little.

He would have fallen back or sideways, not forward. We're supposed to find this guy like this, but I don't know what it means yet."

After the photographer finished shooting all his pictures the forensic men began to gather evidence in plastic bags and containers. They wore rubber gloves and masks. They did not want to contaminate the area. They used tweezers and long tongs to pick up items and move things around. One of the forensic guys worked feverishly picking up hair from the bed. He looked to the other workers and said, "Somebody was hairy in this bed, and I don't think it was the priest or the murderer."

Dan walked over to him to see what he was gathering. "What is it?" he asked.

"This hair is from a dog. Look at all the different colors, black, tan, white. Coarse too, like a German Sheperd or something. I'll have to analyze this, but it's not human."

Dan looked again around the room and took in a breath. He had been in the room long enough for his sense of smell to adjust to the odor that was present earlier. But now he purposefully smelled it again. It was the death smell. Not human death, but animal death. A dog had died in that room. But where was the body now?"

The forensic team began to move the body of the priest and pull his arms forward as much as possible. Rigor had already began to set in and moving the arm was difficult. Dan watched as they moved the body up and tried to give a little dignity to the priest's body. He noticed a pool of blood under the body, but it wasn't from the wound in the neck, it was too low. Dan walked closer to the body and looked at it again. The blood stain had been where his arm was.

"Is his right arm cut bad enough to leave this much blood?" Dan asked.

The forensic man looked at the arm and saw some wounds, none too deep, but still substantial. "Well, he bled that's for sure. But the shirt isn't really blood soaked from these wounds. Must be from somewhere else."

Dan looked at the arm and down to the priest's right hand. He saw the cause of the blood at the base of the hand. The thumb of the priest was missing, cut off clean like a butcher cuts the wings off of chickens. "It was scissors, or shears," he thought to himself. "The bastard took off his right thumb on purpose."

Dan stood up straight and said, "Look for his thumb dammit, it's missing. It must be on the floor or in the bed, look for the damn thing."

Bartly was shocked and bewildered. He stood up straight and turned a ghastly shade of white. "Excuse me boys," he said, as he walked into the hallway to puke.

The team looked for the thumb but to no avail. It wasn't in the bed or on the floor. It was gone, taken by the killer. Dan knew that serial killers often took trophies from their vicitms, pieces of their flesh or scraps of clothing. Dan thought to himself., "Now I have two things to find, that dead dog and that missing thumb."

CHAPTER 7

*B*y 10:00 AM Dan found himself back at the office. This case was about to make big headlines, it already was plastered all over the news stations on radio and television. He knew that he was going to be the top detective on the case, in spite of Bartly and his one upmanship. Dan sat at his desk and began to go over the events of the previous few days.

"72 HOURS–2 PRIESTS KILLED," he read aloud.

As he looked up from his desk he could see Sr. Chris Rayday enter the office area. She did not have a smile on her face and he was a bit surprised to see her coming to him. "Hello Sister." Dan stood to offer her a chair next to his desk.

"Hello Detective." Her face somber, her hair a bit out of place.

"I don't have to ask what brings you here this morning." Dan sat and leaned back a bit in his chair.

The nun took her seat and leaned into to Dan. "No, Detective you don't have to ask me. Quite frankly the Archbishop is quite disturbed about these events. He has never had to deal with something on this level and he's literally shaking in his proverbial boots." She leaned back a little opening the space between them. "Our two biggest fears are that this nut will keep killing priests, or that some other psycho will begin to copycat him, then where will we be?"

Dan leaned a bit forward himself, once again closing the gap, making the conversation more personal. "Obviously Sister, we are dealing with some kind of serial killer here. Now, the experts might not say that yet with only two deaths, but let's face it these two victims have an awful lot in common on the surface. What we need to do is search what else they have in common. That's where the diocese can be of great assistance."

The nun sat up straight in her chair, very professional, very business like. "I can assure you Detective that we will do everything that we can to see that the murderer is caught. You of course have our complete cooperation. The Archbishop has instructed me to give you anything that you ask for."

"Anything, Sister?" Dan asked.

"Yes, Detective, anything."

Dan again leaned closer, playing the psychological card of personal space. "Then how about giving me all the letters on our first victim. I know you left one out, I just don't know why."

The Nun made her own psychological play now and leaned even closer to Dan. "Yes, Detective you knew I left one letter out right away didn't you? I can only say that it was left out to protect Fr. Wysocki's reputation. It was a crack pot letter that should have been tossed in the trash. It was unsigned and in our view unsigned letters hold no merit whatsoever. "She leaned over into her attache case and pulled out the file on Wysocki. "Here is the letter Detective, I do hope that it will help you, but quite honestly I don't think that it will."

Dan took the copy of the letter from her hands and began to read it. It was typed, triple spaced, not done on a computer, but rather on a regular typewriter. He read the note aloud, "Dear Father, past memories do die hard, one cannot stand to hear the pain of our past deeds. What we do not hear, we put away. But you did and you must carry it now."

Dan looked up at the Sister in disbelief. "You didn't see this as important Sister? How in the world could you not see this as a threat?"

"Detective, I assure you that many of our priests get threats. It will surprise you to know that we have many letters similar to this on file. If we were to take each one seriously, we would spend thousands of hours looking for phantoms. My God, nobody gets more nut letters than the Archbishop himself!"

Dan leaned back again. "But Sister, why were you afraid this would tarnish the reputation of Fr. Wysocki? If there are truly hundreds of letters like this on file then it should have been routine."

"Not for Fr. Wysocki." She said. "He was a very good priest and something like this could only tarnish a very good image. We looked into it, the Archbishop himself looked into it shortly after he arrived in Chicago, which is when the letter arrived."

"That was what, about six years ago?" Dan asked.

"Yes, so you see I thought that an awful long time ago to take it as a serious threat."

"This is a copy Sister," Dan said. "I'll need the original."

"Yes, I anticipated that, unfortunately the original is no longer with us. Shortly after the letter arrived it disappeared from the file. It was only fortuitous that I happen to have a copy in my own files. When the Archbishop asked to see the original I was afraid that it might get lost, which of course it did. I am sorry that there is no original to give to you."

Dan gave out a big exhale, exasperated in nature, knowing that once again the amateurs had screwed up. "Well Sister, at least we have a copy, I guess that is better than nothing. Which by the way this almost was. Sister you must realize that you withheld evidence from the police. I hope that we can count on your full cooperation now."

"I assure you Detective that I did not withhold what I thought to be evidence. Had the court subpoenaed that file, it would have all been there." Her voice was filled with a bit of indignation.

"I am also hoping Sister, that your attache has another file for me and that all the information is in that one." Dan said.

She again leaned into her magic attache and withdrew and file on Father Phil Danner, the second priest to have been murdered. "I assure you that everything concerning Father Danner is in this file Detective." She handed him the file, a much more substantial one that Wysocki's had been.

"Well, this is a file! What had Father Danner done to merit so much attention from the Archdiocese?" Dan said a little too condescending.

"It wasn't that he did anything wrong Mr. Gill," She said. "It's just that this particular priest moved around quite a bit in his years. He had what he liked to call the wanderlust and asked to be moved every three to five years. Every time there is a move, there is an evaluation. Father Danner had 9 evaluations in his 25 years as a priest. Father Wysocki, far fewer."

"Are these all copies too, Sister?" Dan asked.

"Yes, they are. I have the original file at the Pastoral Center if you should need to see it, or if the court subpoenas it for evidence."

"Off the top of your head can you see anything that connected these two guys other than their priesthood?" He asked.

"Well, they were close in age, Father Wysocki being two years older than Father Danner. They did attend major seminary together, although I have no idea if they were friends or not. Other than that, I cannot think of anything that jumps off the page."

Dan stood so as to encourage the nun to stand. "Thank you Sister, I appreciate your cooperation and you bringing the file to me. Please assure the Archbishop that we are going to do everything that we can to solve these two crimes."

The nun stood and shook the hand of Dan Gill. "Yes, Detective, I'm sure that you will be doing all in your power. In the mean time, you have to know that there are quite a few clergy in Chicago who are scared to death of being murdered. I want the Archbishop to reassure them that they are going to be safe."

"We have already anticipated that Sister," he said. "The Mayor wants the Church to know that we have beefed up patrol at all the parishes in the city. No small task, I'm sure you would agree."

"Thank you Detective, that will make the Archbishop sleep a little better tonight, though I'm afraid not too much better." The nun turned and walked out of the office, her attache swinging loosely from her side.

Dan sat back down at his desk and prepared to look through the file of Father Philip Danner. It was considerably fuller than that of Father Wysocki. Perhaps the nun had been right, it was filled with evaluations and more letters from parishioners. Having moved so much in his twenty-five years, that seemed to make sense. What amazed Dan was the number of letters from each parish. There were a total of forty copied notes, some typed, some hand written. It painted a vivid picture of the priest and how he related to his parishioners. It also gave Dan a view of the faithful and what made them tick and what was important to them.

Dan was looking for something specific. Something that could link the two priests together. The nun had already told him that they went to school together so he could wait to look at the academic records of the two priests. He was looking for something more up to date, something like the letter that Wysocki had received six years earlier.

As he went through the letters Dan separated them into piles. Letters of complaint from parishioners, that were signed went into the first pile. Letters of praise from parishioners that were signed went into the second pile. Letters that were unsigned went into the third pile. Unfortunately Dan knew that he was most likely going to find his clues in the unsigned pile.

There were all kinds of letters. Of the forty that he perused, twenty-six were letters of complaint that were signed. Ten, were letters of compliment that were signed and four were unsigned, not very complimentary at all. But that seemed to make sense. People rarely write letters of praise. Generally the pen only comes out when someone has something negative to say. "A sad commentary on our modern society," he thought.

The bitch letters seemed normal enough. Common complaints were that Danner had been snippy or rude, that he would not do a certain baptism or circumvent church procedure for a 'special' parishioner. The letters of praise seemed to directly contradict the others. Danner was commended for being present at the illness of a child, or very understanding during the death of a parent. The only conclusion that Dan could draw from these letters was that you can't please everyone all the time.

When he got to the pile of unsigned letters, the tone changed a bit. Sr. Rayday had said that the archdiocese did not put stock in unsigned notes. Dan thought that to be a smart idea. If the person doesn't have the balls to sign a note, why bother to take it seriously. But threats were another matter. Dan was surprised that notes that were threatening in nature were not looked into more deeply. He looked at the four unsigned notes. Two were hand written, one was typed on a typewriter and one was done on a computer, the type face at about 15 point, much too big for a typewriter.

The typed note was unfortunately nothing like the one that Fr. Wysocki had received. It was not threatening and was actually rather coherent. It was a complaint about Danner's tardiness to a wedding rehearsal. "Big deal," thought Gill. The hand written notes were also harmless in nature. One parishioner had seen Danner drink alcohol at a local restaurant and the other note was reporting that Danner left a copy of "Valley of the Dolls" in the confessional one Saturday afternoon. Dan looked over the notes and shook his head, "These asinine ' people need to get lives."

The computer generated note though was a standout from the rest. It was hand dated five years earlier in red ink, apparently by someone at the Chancery Office. It was similar to the letter that Wysocki had received in its innocuous tone. Like the first note he saw earlier in the day, Dan read this one aloud, "Dearest Father, What you touch may not always turn to gold. Your fingers loosen and it slips away. When we hold something so dear, so valuable it is a shame to keep it to ourselves."

Dan saw the connection immediately. The same sappy syntax, the same strange reference to knowing something but holding it in. There was no doubt in Dan's mind that the same person had written both letters. Proof would not be easy. The first letter, typewritten was not even an original, so forget finding anything on it. The second letter should have an original in the file at the Chancery, but how many people had handled it over the five years? The chances of getting anything off that page was minuscule. Dan wondered if the nun still had the original envelope, but he knew that was surely an impossibility.

Dan swung in closer to his desk and reached for his Rolodex. He looked up the number he desired and dialed the phone. "I would like to speak to Archbishop Tate please, this is Detective Dan Gill."

Dan waited for a few moments and then heard the voice of the Archbishop on the other end of the phone. "Dan, thank you for calling, I understand that you met with Sr. Rayday again this morning."

Dan was surprised that the nun had reported back so fast, it had only been an hour since she left. He cleared his throat and said, "Yes Archbishop, she was here and she gave me the file on Fr. Danner and a letter that was previously misplaced on Father Wysocki. Archbishop, we need to meet about these files. There is something you need to see and give me your advice about. I think it should be soon, because not only do I want to catch this psycho, I want to stop him from killing again."

CHAPTER 8

By 2:00 PM Dan was again at the residence of the Archbishop. Dan held the files under his arm as he rang the doorbell of the mansion. The same nun answered the door and gave a half smile to the detective. This was his second visit and she did seem a bit friendlier. Dan figured that by his tenth or eleventh visit she might even give him a cordial greeting.

"I'm here to see the Archbishop Sister," he said.

She opened the iron and glass outer door, "Yes, Detective he is expecting you. I can't remember the last time that the Archbishop has spent so many daytime hours here at the mansion."

Dan held the door and followed the old nun to the sitting room where the Archbishop was seated next to the massive fireplace. He walked toward the Archbishop who seemed to be lost in thought. He noticed the Archbishop had a cigarette going and a glass with what looked like scotch in his hand, straight up, no water, no ice.

"I am so sorry to have to interrupt you Archbishop," said Dan.

The Archbishop looked up, very slowly and intent. He was not surprised to see Dan. "Oh, Dan, please come in, have a seat. Can I get you something to drink?"

Dan shook his head. "On duty still, not really allowed."

"Yes, well it's not really allowed when I am on duty either, but if I followed that train of thought I would have to drink between brushing my teeth and taking my shower."

Dan smiled. It was true he thought to himself, the guy is in everyone's eye all the time. "Archbishop, I brought the files on the two priests with me. They are of course copies, so I am sure you have seen the originals already. I thought that we could go through a couple of things that might help us to narrow down possible motives and then possible suspects."

The Archbishop took a drink of the scotch and nodded his head. "Yes, Dan, I have the files here with me. I asked Sister Rayday to drop them off right after her meeting with you this morning. I don't usually have cause to look through these files. I have to say, it is amazing how different these two files are."

Dan opened the file on the first priest killed, Father Wysocki. He looked through the small manilla file folder and specifically pulled out the letter that was unsigned. "Do you by any chance remember this note Archbishop?" He handed the note in front of the Archbishop who then pulled the other copy out of his own file.

The Archbishop read the brief typewritten note to himself. He looked up at Dan, visibly shaken. "Yes, Dan, I do remember this note. I found it more disturbing than the usual run of the mill nut letter. I tried to look into it deeper, but it was unsigned. The note came to us rather than to the priest himself which was quite unusual. I had Sister Rayday try to do some investigating but nothing ever turned up. I am not even sure we told Fr. Wysocki about the letter."

Dan looked up at the Archbishop. "You can't remember if you told the priest? Excuse me for saying this Archbishop, but you went to the trouble of looking into the letter and you can't remember if you told him? That just seems a bit odd. Plus, the letter was addressed to Fr. Wysocki, I would have assumed that it was mailed directly to him."

The Archbishop glared at Dan. "I run the third largest archdiocese in the country Detective, I have control of over three hundred parishes and seven hundred priests. Sister Rayday handles the everyday things like this. Maybe she knows if Wysocki was informed or if he received a letter himself. People often send copies of letters that they address to priests to the Archdiocese."

Dan was taken aback by the Archbishop's tone. Perhaps he had been a little too accusatorial or sarcastic in his own tone. "Archbishop, I am sorry if I offended you, but I thought that it was important enough to bring this up. I mean if Father Wysocki knew about the letter, he could have perhaps let you know who would write such a thing. Doesn't it make sense that he should be informed?"

"You're right Dan, I am sorry if I was curt, its just so much to handle some days. My guess is that Sister Rayday discussed this letter with Father Wysocki. But quite honestly, nothing ever came of it. At least nothing that was ever brought to my attention." The Archbishop had set down his drink and put out his cigarette and was wringing his hands.

"This letter seems quite disturbing to me Archbishop. I know that you get many letters every year, Sister Rayday told me than no one gets as many as you yourself. But I have to say that there is something quite out of the ordinary here. It's cryptic, there is some kind of message here don't you agree?"

The Archbishop looked over the letter again. He looked up at Dan, "I guess you're right Detective, I guess I thought that six years ago too. But what could it mean? Now, because of my carelessness we cannot ask Fr. Wysocki can we?"

Dan was shocked. Was the Archbishop somehow blaming himself for the death of the priest? "Sir, this priest didn't die because of you. You can't think like that."

"I realize that Dan. But if I weren't so busy or if I paid more attention to things like this I could have some better answers for you. I should have taken the time to call him in and ask him about this. You know, I knew both these priests when they were seminarians. Maybe that is why I am so terribly disturbed by this. I mean of course I would be shaken by these events in any case, but I knew both of these men for decades."

"No, I didn't know that. When I go to the seminary for their records we may have to go over those together. I guess you would know then if they were friends. I mean did they hang around together?"

The Archbishop picked up his drink again. He looked at the bronze liquid and finished what was in the glass. "Let me explain something to you Dan. The seminary system thirty years ago was quite different than it is today. In those days, the seminarians were kept away from one another. They each had their own room and their own bathrooms. The idea of preventing 'particular friendships' was actually pioneered in Chicago. There was silence in the halls and free time was always closely supervised. Meals were generally quiet because scripture was read at the front of the dining hall. That's not to say that friendships didn't develop, obviously they did. But it would be anachronistic to say that anyone 'hung around' together."

"Pardon me for saying this Archbishop, but it sounds more like it was a prison than a school," Dan said.

"Dan, it was a different time. We wanted to avoid any kind of inappropriate liaison between students. In hind sight, it was probably overdone, we had whole generations of priests that were not quite socially ready for parish life. Of course we tried to bring community life to those guys. They had gym time together, drama plays in the auditorium. There was even a golf course at the seminary. But all of that was done with a priest present. The bonding was always done on a group level, rarely on an interpersonal basis."

"If you don't mind me asking," said Dan. "What was your role at the seminary?"

"I was the Dean of Formation," said the Archbishop.

Dan gave an unknowing look at Church leader.

"You wouldn't really know what that is, would you Dan?" said the Archbishop. "The Dean of Formations was responsible for the formative life of the seminarians. Everyday, in addition to their studies they had a program of priestly formation. It involved talks from priests, psychologists, bible scholars, etcetera. It lasted one hour in the evening. I had to put the program together each year. I also had the responsibility of discipline. Not that there was too much of a need for that. Mostly school boy pranks that got a little out of hand."

"So you were the bad guy huh?" Dan asked.

"Sometimes, I had to yell a little, take away a privilege like smoking after choir or a movie on Friday nights. But for the most part they didn't get into much trouble."

"So with all that responsibility I don't suppose you would ever remember Wysocki or Danner getting in to any real trouble?"

The Archbishop took in a deep breath and then paused. "No, Dan. I don't remember them getting into any serious trouble. They were good guys. They were even a part of my bridge club that met after formations. Such a great game, but I could never get more than six or seven of them to learn it every year or so. I guess in that respect, those two did 'hang around' as you say."

Dan sat back in the chair he had taken. "Archbishop, again pardon me if this seems rude, but, yes, I would call that hanging around. I mean they played bridge together I would guess that they had the chance to exchange ideas, and share common interests. "

"I am sorry Dan, I guess I wasn't thinking like that. I thought that you were perhaps thinking of other kinds of relationships. I mean, oh my this is embarrassing, but I thought perhaps that you were asking if they had a 'particular' friendship." The Archbishop leaned back in his chair, looking exasperated and ready to throw in the towel.

Dan felt the embarrassment of the Archbishop and even felt a little flushed himself. "No, Archbishop, I wasn't trying to insinuate anything. I guess I should have been clearer. You see, the only connection that I have so far is their two years in school together. I haven't had a chance to do any real searching yet, beyond their files. I thought that if I could show some kind of friendship in seminary that it could lead to something."

The Archbishop nodded his head and took another cigarette. "Of course you're right Dan. But as I told you, beyond choir time, play rehearsal, and activities like the bridge club, these men could not really form strong social groups."

Dan leaned in a little closer to the Archbishop. "Your information is very helpful Archbishop. I really didn't know that the men had such lack of freedom or social time. But they certainly did know one another. They were two years apart but still seemed to share at least one interest. Now I know that this is not earth shattering information, but it is a start. Can you remember other men that were in this group?"

"Well, that was a long time ago Dan. Not all the men in the club were ordained and I added at least four a year while I was there. But, yes I suppose if I saw the records from that time that I could remember at least some of the men. You know, not all of them played with the group all four years. Bridge is not the easiest game to master and some men stayed only a few months, or even weeks. But, yes I suppose I could search my memory a bit."

Dan now picked up the other manila folder with the information about Fr. Danner. He watched as the Archbishop did the same and pulled out his own copy. "This file is considerably larger. Sister Rayday told me it was due to his moving so often. I read through the file and beyond this one letter, I can't see anything out of the ordinary." Dan held up the computer generated note with the red date written on it by someone at the chancery office. "I would really like the original of this if at all possible."

The Archbishop looked over the note and shook his head. "Dan, I can't honestly remember ever seeing this note. I don't know where I was when it came in, I may have been in Rome, or on vacation, but this doesn't ring a bell for me."

Dan looked incredulously at the cleric. "Is it possible that someone in the office just didn't think this was important enough?"

"Dan, I'm just not sure. I'm not even sure if the letter was mailed to us or to Fr. Danner. He may have given us a copy himself, thus going through other channels. The Vicar for Priests may have dealt with this rather than the chancery and then it may have just ended up in our files."

Dan smiled and shook his head. "You're throwing things at me again that I don't understand. Who is the Vicar for Priests?"

"He is a priest elected by the other priests to oversee situations unique to the priesthood. For a long time he only dealt with things like health problems, nervous breakdowns, financial problems and other things. But in the late 80's, when the accusations started to come forward against the priests dealing with inappropriate behavior the job took on new meaning. The Vicar had to deal with the press, with the legal office, and unfortunately with law enforcement, no offense, Dan."

Dan nodded. "Tough job, who would ever want to have to deal with that stuff?"

"That's always been the problem," said the Archbishop. "There have been five vicars in the last six years. Many men have turned the job down even after they were elected by the presbyterate."

Dan knew the answer to his next question before he even asked it. "So the man who was Vicar for Priests when this note came in is not the man who is Vicar now?"

"No, he certainly is not. Let me look at that date again." The Archbishop looked over the hand written date from the chancery. "Not only is the man who was vicar when this came in no longer Vicar. This man is dead."

Dan was shocked as he looked into the face of the Archbishop. "Dead?" he asked. "What happened?"

"The Vicar for priests when this letter was sent was Monsignor Robert Carmichael. He was a very popular priest among the clergy.

He was appointed by my predecessor and served longer in that job than any other priest. The late 80's really took their toll on him though and he turned to alcohol. The saddest thing was that he was the one who was supposed to deal with alcoholic priests. There was no one to challenge him and he hid his problem very well. Shortly after I came back to Chicago, he was killed in a car accident. I am sure that alcohol had something to do with it because an empty bottle of Jack Daniels was found at the scene of the accident. The coroner found that his blood alcohol level was three times the legal limit. I honestly did not even know until that point that he was such a heavy drinker."

Again Dan was shocked. He was learning more about the Church in this one visit than he had in twelve years of Catholic school. Dan told the Archbishop that he planned to look deeper into the files, particularly at the letters that seemed so similar. He offered his thanks to the Archbishop and returned to his car.

❦   ❦   ❦

The Archbishop picked up his files and told the nun that he was going to his room on the third floor. He walked up the grand wooden staircase and set the files on the desk in his suite. He walked over to his closet and opened the door. In the floor of the closet was a loose piece of carpet. He took the piece of carpet up and revealed the door of a floor safe. He carefully spun the numbers on the dial in the safe and opened the steel door. He reached in and took out a file folder wrapped in plastic.

The Archbishop went to his bed with the file in his hand and sat at the edge. Slowly he removed the plastic wrap and opened the folder. Inside was the original letter written to Fr. Wysocki. He looked at the slightly yellowed page, placed it down on the bed and began to sob uncontrollably.

CHAPTER 9

*I*t was time for Dan to do some 'at the scene' investigating. He got in his car and drove to St. Veronica, the church where Fr. Wysocki had been killed in the confessional. He parked on the street where it said No Parking, knowing that he would not get a ticket. He walked to the top of the church stairs and tried to open the large steel door. It was locked. Dan remembered the days when every church in the city was open all day long. In his head he knew it was necessary to keep the doors locked, but his heart still fell.

Dan walked over to the rectory where the priest had lived. It was a beautiful Georgian house. Two floors, all brick with framed windows. Considering that the neighborhood had changed several years ago and the income level of the parish dropped dramatically, the rectory was in pretty good shape. Dan walked up to the door and rang the intercom. He waited at the entranceway looking down the block at the many children playing in the street.

The intercom buzzed back "Yes, can I help you?"

"This is Detective Dan Gill from the Chicago Police Department, I would like to get into the Church please."

The faceless voice answered back. "Just one minute please, I'll be right there."

Dan waited for the door to open. A middle aged woman answered the door with a key in her hand. "I'll be glad to open the door Detective. Do you mind if I ask you for some identification?"

Dan reached to his side and removed his badge from his belt buckle. He held it up for the woman and she glanced at it rather quickly, probably embarrassed that she asked to see it in the first place.

She smiled at Dan. "You can never be too careful," she said. "One of my friends knew a lady who let a guy in the house who said he was a cop, and she was raped."

Dan nodded. "I'm sorry to bother you, but I need to get in and take a look around the church. If you don't mind I'd also like to talk to you after I'm done. Is there anyone else in the rectory that I could also talk to, I mean other staff?"

"Sure," she said. "That's no problem. There's only two of us here today, me and Mrs. McGovern, she's the housekeeper. I'm Marge Gonzalez, I'm the secretary here at the parish."

Dan extended his hand to the woman. "Nice to meet you Mrs. Gonzalez."

The secretary shook Dan's hand and walked down the street to the church entrance. She unlocked the door and entered the building. She walked to the side of the entrance and flicked a few switches to illuminate the church.

"Do you want me to stay with you Detective?" Mrs. Gonzalez asked.

"No, that won't be necessary" he said.

Dan watched as the secretary walked out of the church. He went over to the confessional area and began to look around. The church was beautiful. Dan knew that no suburban parish could match the grandeur of this building. The amazing thing was, it was built over one hundred years ago by European immigrants with little more in their pockets than dimes and nickels. Dan thought that the churches being built today were little more than lifeless bricks and mortar, no character and certainly nothing explicitly Catholic about them.

Dan bent down to look at the handle of the confessional. The forensic lab had determined that there were no latent fingerprints on the knob. That meant that it had been wiped clean. With the traffic in and out of the place, there should have been lots of prints to pick up. Dan grabbed that handle and pulled the door open. He went into the confessional and looked around. It was dark, the only light coming from the church itself. It was plain inside, nothing special. The police had told the diocese not to allow anyone to use the confessional after the murder. Since it was now the middle of the week, that wasn't a very difficult task.

There was nothing in the confessional that Dan had not seen before. He knelt down on the kneeler and felt it give a little, triggering the light on the front to indicate that a penitent was present. He looked at the wire mesh screen. The forensic lab had determined that the weapon was some kind of tool. Almost certainly it was an ice pick because the mesh screen was still bent in toward the priest's side. This indicated that the tool was larger at the back than at the front. Not too many tools fit that description. A screwdriver would have been too blunt and the metal would have been too soft in the long run to go through the priest's head.

Dan tried to look at the angle of the entry. It was significantly bent down. To Dan, this meant that the murderer must have been rather tall. Dan was about six one and he could see that he could have easily put the tool directly into the priest's ear from where he knelt. Given the angle, this guy must have been about six three or larger. And he must have been pretty strong. The mesh was old, but sturdy. Dan walked out of the penitent's side and into the priest's side. He looked at the screws on the screen and realized that they were loose, and a bit rusty. They must have been as old as the screen and over the years loosened up. For the murderer to have put the weapon through the screen without making the whole screen fall off his force must have been swift and mighty.

So Dan had some sense of the size and strength of the murderer. He was tall and strong. This narrowed his search down to only a couple of hundred thousand guys in the greater Chicagoland area. Dan sighed and went back into the church. He walked down the center aisle and went into the sacristy where the priests got ready for mass. He flicked another switch and the sacristy lit up. There was a faint smell of incense, probably left over from yesterday's funeral of Fr. Wysocki. Dan poked around and found a drawer marked FR JOE. Dan opened the drawer and peered inside. There wasn't much there. A small thin purple stole, used for sick calls, a bronze pyx used for bringing communion to the homes of the sick, some prayer cards with various saints on them. Dan dug down a little deeper, removing all the objects on top. He saw something small on bottom of the drawer. He reached into his pocket and put on a rubber glove. Then he reached in a pulled out a pair of small tweezers. He held the tweezers gingerly and grabbed the object. It was a small medal, like ones that many Catholics wore. Dan held it the grasp of the tweezers and looked at it closely. It was not a Catholic medal though, it was something more secular it nature. It was silver, about one inch in diameter. Dan held it up to the light. There was an inscription on one side that read, "Never Trump". Dan turned the medal over and saw a heart engraved on the medal. He reached into his pocket again and pulled out a small plastic bag where he deposited the medal. He put the bag in his pocket and flicked off the light. He walked down center aisle and out the front door of the church.

Dan went back to the rectory and rang the buzzer again. The secretary answered and after identifying himself, he waited to be buzzed in. The secretary greeted him at the top of a small staircase and brought him into the front office.

"I know that this is a difficult time for you Mrs. Gonzalez, but I would like to ask you a few questions," Dan said.

"I understand Detective, I want to help you in anyway that I can. Please take a seat." The secretary gestured for Dan to sit in the chair next to her desk.

Dan took out a small note pad and a pen from his coat pocket. He never understood why women felt the need to carry purses when so many things could fit in a jacket. "Mrs. Gonzalez, how long have you been the secretary here?"

She brushed a lock of dishwater blonde hair from her eyes. "Five years. I was hired when the former secretary died. I'm bilingual and Father Joe thought that I could be of help. My husband is Mexican, and I learned Spanish when we got married. I'm Polish myself, so I guess Fr. Joe figured he was getting the best of both worlds."

Dan scribbled on his note pad. "So you knew Fr. Joe before he hired you?"

"Yeah, he married me and my husband ten years ago. We have been pretty active in the parish ever since. I still can't believe he's gone, he was really a good man." She took a tissue from the desk and blew her nose.

"This may sound like a strange question, but do you know anyone who would have wanted to do this to him?"

She sniffled a little. "No," she paused and put the tissue up to her eyes. "I mean he was well liked here in the parish. Of course there were always people who complained you know? People are never completely satisfied, but I can't think of a single person from this parish that would have wanted to do that to him."

Dan sat up a bit. "I really doubt that it was a parishioner Mrs. Gonzalez. But you would have taken calls for him right? Can you think of anything in the last week or even few months that would have seemed strange?"

"No, not really, well wait let me think a minute. We take so many calls here, I always try to screen the crazies before I pass them on to Fr. Joe. Let me think, unusual nutty calls." She looked up at the ceiling as though searching her memory. "You know about three weeks ago a guy called and asked for Fr. Joseph. I figured it wasn't a parishioner because every one here called him Fr. Joe. Usually that meant it was a candle salesman or magazine salesman. But this call was different. The voice was deeper than any I have ever heard before. Yeah know it reminded me of that guy from that singing group, uh, Sha Na Na, what his name, Bowler, Bow Wow, Bowser, yeah that's it Bowser."

Well anyway this guy asked for Fr. Joseph and when I asked who was calling he said an old friend, he wanted to surprise Fr. Joe since they hadn't talked for a long time. So I figured what the heck I'll put it through. I called Fr. Joe on the intercom and he took the call. Usually if I put the call through he didn't bother to ask who it was, cause he knew I screened out the crazies."

"So he took the call. Did you see him after that?" Dan asked.

She thought for a moment. "Yeah, as a matter of fact I did. About two minutes after the call he came flying down the front stairs from his room and went out the front door without saying a word. I think he went over to Church because he didn't have his coat on and he was only gone for about five minutes. I remember asking him when he came back if everything was all right. He said yeah, he just needed to check something in the sacristy."

"Do you remember if Father Joseph was prone to wearing jewelry? I mean like rings or medals?"

She grinned. "Father Joe, no he definitely didn't wear jewelry. It was always a big joke with us that knew him well. He didn't even wear a watch because he had some kind of metal allergy. Deep down I always thought he made it up so that he could be just a few minutes late for things." She smiled and then tears welled up in her eyes.

Dan pulled the medal out of his jacket. "So he would have never wore something like this?"

She looked at the medal in the plastic bag. "No, never. He supposedly would have broke out from it. Come to think of it one time when he was over at the house for dinner, he had his arm resting on one of my mom's good silver forks. When he got up to leave you could see where the fork was, I mean he had a nasty rash from it."

Dan put the medal back in his pocket. "I see. So it wouldn't be unusual for me to find this in his drawer in the sacristy, if say someone gave it to him."

"I suppose not. I know he wouldn't wear it."

Dan stood up. "There are two more things I'd like to do before I go. One is to visit Fr. Wysocki's room and the other is to talk to the housekeeper, what was her name?"

She stood too. "Mrs. McGovern. You take care of both at the same time. She's up in his room now getting boxes ready to pack up Fr. Joe's things." She hasn't touched anything, because the police and the archdiocese told us not to disturb anything. We only got the call today that it was okay to start packing things up"

She walked around the desk and led Dan up the large wooden staircase outside the office. He followed closely behind as she led him into the priest's room.

She knocked lightly on the open door. "Mrs McGovern? Katherine are you in here?"

The housekeeper came from the priest's bedroom into the sitting room where the secretary and the detective were standing. She was an elderly woman, maybe sixty-five. She was plump but not fat, her red hair just beginning to turn white at the front. She wiped her hand across her forehead and then wiped her hands on her apron. Dan couldn't remember the last time he saw someone wearing an apron.

She answered the call in a slight yet present Irish brogue. "I'm here Margie, what do you need?" She was a bit startled when she saw Dan with the secretary.

The secretary walked further into the sitting room. "Mrs. McGovern this is a Detective from the police department. He wanted to see Fr. Joe's room and possibly talk to you if that's okay."

Dan could see that the secretary paid great deference to the older housekeeper. Even rectories seemed to have their pecking order. "Mrs. McGovern, I'm Detective Dan Gill from the Chicago Police. I hope you don't mind me asking you just a few questions. Maybe we could have a seat."

The housekeeper looked around and offered Dan a chair in the sitting room. She took a chair next to him. The secretary excused herself and went back to the office. Dan looked around the room and couldn't help but notice all the clutter. Books on the floor and papers all over the end tables. File folders were strewn across the coffee table that sat in front of a small fireplace.

"Mrs. McGovern. I know that this is a difficult time for all of you and I won't keep you but a few moments. But I do have some questions I need to ask."

The housekeeper nodded, never really looking right at Dan. "I understand Detective, you have to do your job and believe me, I want you to catch the monster that did this to Fr. Joe."

Dan again pulled out his notebook. "How long have you worked here Mrs. McGovern?"

"This April will be forty-five years. This was my first and only job after coming here from Ireland."

"So it's safe to say that you know all the things that go on here in the rectory and in the parish," Dan said.

"Well, I don't know about that Mr. Detective man, but I have been here a long time."

Dan smiled, an Irish brogue could bring out the best in anyone. "What I meant Mrs. McGovern is that you have a sort of inside tract to the goings on here. You have seen a few priests come and go in your day I suppose."

She sat up a little straighter. She loved to get respect and this guy apparently knew how important she was in the scheme of things. "Yes, I have seen my share of priests here and I've seen this neighborhood and parish change too. Fr. Joe was a wonderful man, he was always very good to me and to my boy Patrick. He's a retarded boy you know, he goes to a special school run by the church and Fr. Joe got him in there. I waited fifteen years for him to get on that list to get in, and Fr. Joe was able to do it for me in one month. He has some good connections in the diocese." She brushed the wisp of white hair that had fallen into her eyes.

"That was very nice of him Mrs. McGovern. Can I ask you something about visitors that Fr. Joe might have had, especially over that past few weeks or months?"

"Fr. Joe didn't have visitors," she answered quickly. "Not any that I seen. He was a very friendly man, but he did his socializin' on his day off, not here at the rectory. Where would they have sat for goodness sake, the man was a pack rat, God rest his soul." She made an impromptu sign of the cross.

Dan grinned again. "I can see that, must have been hard to clean up after him with all this stuff in here."

"Not so bad, I just lift a pile of papers and dust around the other things. He wasn't a pig yeah know, just liked to save things. He probably has his grammar school report cards in here somewhere."

Dan looked around again. "Yep, it was going to take a while to go through this room," he thought.

Dan reached into his pocket one more time and took out the plastic bag. He held it up to Mrs. McGovern. "Do you recognize this medal?" he asked.

She looked closely at the bag. "I don't recall seein' it, he didn't wear jewelry you know, didn't even wear a watch. Always a little late for everything, that one was."

"I was just wondering if you ever saw anything like it around the room, anything that might ring a bell."

She looked at it again and put the glasses that were hanging around her neck on the bridge of her nose. "Never Trump," she said aloud.

"Yes," he said. "Never Trump, seems like a strange medallion, to me."

She sat back and gave a little huff, letting the glasses fall back onto her hefty bosom. "Doesn't seem strange to me," she said. "The man lived to play bridge, never missed a game in the twelve years that I knew 'im."

CHAPTER 10

*D*an knew that he had his work cut out for him. He had already gotten permission from the archdiocese to go through the priest's room and take into evidence anything that he needed. Dan had learned that the Archdiocese of Chicago was one of the few dioceses left in the country that was known as a Corporation Sole. That meant that everything, from the funds in the banks to the pencils on the desks were the property of the Archbishop.

Illinois was one of the last states to still recognize Corporation Sole status for certain dioceses. It was something that was devised in the mid nineteenth century and because of the power of the Church in Chicago had managed to stay on the books. What this meant was that anything in the priest's room, unless otherwise specifically noted in his will, was the property of the Archbishop. Dan had gone directly to the Archbishop and received permission to go through anything in the priest's room. In his busy life, Fr. Wysocki had failed to leave a will, so technically everything there was property of the Church.

Dan looked around and heaved a large sigh. "Man, this guy was a saver," he thought. Dan walked toward the desk that was at the far side of the large room. It was loaded with papers. They were in piles and Dan was sure that the priest had some kind of filing system that only he understood. Dan knew what he was looking for, the priest's calendar. Surely the calendar would give him some insight into the life of the priest. He rummaged on the desk and then he saw it under a pile of old newspapers.

Dan picked up the book and flipped it open. The priest had terrible handwriting, again Dan was sure that the priest himself could decipher what the book said, but to anyone else it might remain a difficult task. Dan looked at the entries for the previous Saturday. From what he could tell it was probably an ordinary day. 7:30 AM–Mass, 10:30 AM–Baptisms, 12:00 PM–lunch w/Bill, 3:00 PM–Confessions, 5:00 PM–Mass, 7:00 PM–visit Patrick, call Katherine. That was the end of the entries. It was not easy to interpret, but it was certainly possible. Most of the entries seemed like ordinary priestly things. The only out of the ordinary thing was the lunch date with someone named Bill. He would ask Mrs. Gonzalez if she knew who that was.

Dan then flipped through the book to look for other entries that might be of help. He didn't see anything out of the ordinary. Most of the entries were for parish appointments, sacramental preparations, and other meetings dealing with parish life. He noticed that there was never anything on Thursdays, he assumed that was the priest's day off. He thought it unusual that he didn't indicate where he was going on those days, but maybe it was the same place each week. He set the book down and looked again on the desk. He began to look through the papers, but there were so many that he didn't know how he would possibly find anything helpful. Maybe he kept a file of letters, Dan knew that as a professional it would be to his benefit to save letters from parishioners or the diocese.

Dan looked around for a file cabinet, thinking that he would not see one because there seemed to be very few things organized in this room. There was no file cabinet but there was an accordion style file folder on the floor next to the desk. He picked it up and opened the elastic band that kept it closed. It was mostly canceled checks and old bills. It was surprisingly organized. The checks were filed by number and they dated back about five years. Dan sat down at the desk and began to look through them.

The checks were mostly for ordinary things, car payments, charge cards, an IRA, some personal checks apparently to relatives with the notation of 'Happy Birthday!' filled in. As he went through the checks he noticed that there was one check every month made out to "Cash" for $250.00. The notation line was marked on each one with a small hand made heart, like the one you would find on a valentine, like the one on the back of the medal Dan had found in the sacristy.

"Finally, a connection." Dan thought. He leaned back in the chair and tried to put everything together. Fr. Joe was a player of bridge even back in his seminary days. He owned a medal that had an obvious connection to bridge. Every month he wrote a check to cash, which in itself might not be too unusual, except for the heart on the bottom of the check. But why? What could this mean and did it have anything to do with his murder? Dan sat up and leaned on the desk, it was then that he saw it out of the corner of his eye. How could he have missed it before? There on the calendar, on the Thursday before the murder in the lower left corner of the day was a little hand drawn heart, just like the one on the bottom of the check.

Dan picked up the book and began to flip through it, every Thursday in the same spot was the little heart. It went back all the way to the beginning of the year and as Dan flipped forward it went everyday until the end of the year! Dan set the book aside and began to pull out the checks from the file folder that had hearts on them.

"What else, what else?" Dan said aloud.

"Maybe you should look in that top left hand drawer."

Dan looked up and saw Mrs. McGovern standing by the door. "I'm sorry?" he said.

"Look in that top left drawer, it was where he kept more personal things. And I want you to know that I never snooped in there, he just happen to have told me that he kept things in there that were personal. I'm only tellin' you 'cause it might be helpful."

Dan nodded his head. "Thanks Mrs. McGovern, it just might be helpful."

Dan pulled at the top left hand drawer, it was locked. He looked over the desk for a key but didn't see one in plain sight.

Mrs. McGovern came a little closer pretending to dust a little on the chair next to the desk. "Try lookin' under the desk, a little hook hangin' near the back. I think I've bumped into it a coupla times while I was runnin' the sweeper."

Dan smiled at her. "Thanks Mrs. McGovern." Dan pulled the chair back a reached his hand under the desk. He felt around toward the back a found the key hanging from a hook just like the housekeeper said it would be. He lifted the key off the hook and held it in his hand. He sat up and pulled the chair back to the desk and slipped the key into the lock. A perfect fit. "Thank God for nosey housekeepers", he thought to himself.

Dan opened the drawer and looked through its contents. There were a few letters, out of their envelopes, about two dozen old photos, a deck of cards, some holy cards that Dan recognized as funeral remembrances that people picked up at wakes, and a receipt for a money order from a currency exchange downtown.

"Well, Mrs. McGovern, I think this just might be helpful after all."

"Well I wouldn't know, I just thought that if it was locked it might have somethin' of interest in there." She moved a little closer and peered over Dan's shoulder hoping to get a glimpse of the drawer's newest contents. Dan thought he heard a definite "hmph" over his shoulder.

Dan wasn't really sure what he was looking for. He couldn't quite put all the pieces together, he wasn't sure that any of this even could have a connection to the murder, but his instincts told him otherwise. Dan pulled out all the contents of the drawer and began to look through each of them. First he went through the letters hoping to find something that would connect to the letter in the possession of the Archbishop.

He unfolded the first note and looked it over. It was hand written, a bit yellowed from age and only written on one side of the page. It was short and to the point…

"Joe,

Since we've been cooperating there have been no problems, but it seems that things are changing. I don't want to meet this week at the usual spot, let's go to the old watering hole instead, less people that might know us. See you then at 12:00. TB."

"Great", thought Dan. "What the hell does this mean?" He folded the note again and opened the other one, this one was newer than the other, the paper stiffer and white all around.

Dan glanced over the note and saw that this one was type written, perhaps computer generated…

"Father,

Saw you back up north a few months back, meeting just like the old days huh? Well I was glad to see both of you there because it helps me to know that things are being kept in order and that we can go on with business as usual. Funny that you changed places though, you're not planning any changes in the near future are you? ME"

Dan shook his head, it was obviously a connection to the first letter but who the hell wrote it, for that matter who wrote the first letter? Who did Fr. Joe meet on his day off? Who would know this and who was following him and this TB guy?

Dan next looked at the receipt from the currency exchange. It was for a money order for $250.00. It had the address and the phone number of the store on the receipt. Dan put it on the pile of things that he was going to take with him.

Dan next began to look through the funeral cards. They were small and Dan had many of them himself from various funerals he had attended over the years. There were about twenty cards from various dates going back as far as thirty years. There were cards from what seemed to be the priest's grandparents and parents. There was one from a young boy aged six years old with the name Stanley

Wysocki, perhaps the brother or cousin of Father Joe? Most of the names were Polish in origin. Only one card stood out. It was not an ordinary holy card because it didn't have typical holy pictures on it. Most of the cards had pictures of Jesus, Mary, St. Joseph or St. Jude. This card had a purple border around it and a picture of a girl. The back of the card indicated that her name was Mary Kate Riley. Born in 1952 , Died in 1972. Under the dates was the Our Father prayer. Dan didn't think much of the card but set it aside anyway in his pile of things to take.

Next he went through the photos. There were about two dozen of them, mostly black and whites with the old crimped edges, some with dates on them like they used to do until the mid seventies. Some of the photos were marked on the back indicating those in the picture.

He saw pictures of the priest's family. The mother and father in front of their wooden frame house. The same couple with a new baby. The same mom and dad with a young man in a collar and a younger boy next to them. Dan turned over the picture and saw in perfect handwriting, "Joe's first day in major seminary, September 1969. Joe, Stan, Papa, Mama."

"So", thought Dan. "That was his brother that died in 1970."

There were other family photos and some photos from what looked like the seminary. As he flipped though the photos one caught his eye. It was unusual because it was a rather large group and Dan recognized three of the subjects. There were eight men and three women in the photo. Fr. Joe Wysocki, Fr. Phil Danner who was also murdered, and the Archbishop before his current position was granted him. Dan glanced at the photo. The men were all in cassocks and roman collars. Dan knew that in those days that was normal garb for the men in the seminary, it wasn't until about 1975 that the students were allowed to wear lay clothing around campus. As Dan scanned the picture he felt as though he knew one of the girls. Yes, he knew her but from where? The funeral cards, yes that was it, the girl was the same as in the funeral card he saw. Mary Kate Riley who died in 1972.

He went back and pulled out the funeral card. It was definitely her. He then went back to the photo and flipped it over. As he hoped the back was marked. The handwriting was terrible, it was the same as the writing that Dan had seen in the priest's calendar. "Seminary, 1972—The Gang" No indication of who the gang was, why they were together or why there would be women present at the seminary. But Dan knew someone who would know everyone in the picture. He just hoped that the Archbishop wasn't getting too tired of seeing him for the fourth time in three days.

CHAPTER 11

Dan knew that the Archbishop would be presiding over the funeral of Father Phil Danner the next morning. He figured that he could talk to the Archbishop after the mass or at least see him to make an appointment later in the day. Why bother the old guy tonight, he's had enough for one week and he wasn't going anywhere that Dan couldn't find him.

Dan decided to head back to the precinct, no sense in trying to go through Father Danner's things today, surely his family would be around the church since he had read that the wake for the priest would be the next day at St. Polycarp. Priest's were always laid out in the center aisle of the last Church in which they served. Tomorrow Dan could kill two birds with one stone and talk with Archbishop and check out things in the rectory.

As he came into the precinct and began to walk toward his office Dan heard his name being called down the hall. "Hey Gill, come in here a minute will you?"

Dan recognized the voice of the Captain and turned on heel to answer to his superior. "Sure thing boss," he said.

Dan came into the office of the Captain and took a seat in front of the desk. "Just going into the office to figure out some of this priest killing stuff."

Captain John Kelsh was about fifty years old and looked every day of it. He was a tall man with grey balding hair and a pot belly that came from too many beers after work. He sat behind his desk with his feet propped up and his hands entwined behind his head. "That's just what I want to talk to you about," he said.

"It's pretty perplexing Captain, I really think it's safe to say that we have a serial killer here, but I know that department frowns on us saying things like that when only two people are dead."

"Well, Dan, not only the department, but the Mayor's office too. His Honor called me this morning and was very explicit that we are in no way to give the impression that there is some kind of priest killer roaming the streets of Chicago."

Dan smiled at the Captain. "Even though we know that there is."

"Like I said, Dan, we don't know that and your investigation needs to treat these two killings as separate entities until we can absolutely prove a connection." The Captain took his feet off of the desk, stood and walked behind Dan to close the door. "We don't want to incite panic among the Catholics of the city."

"I agree Captain, but I do hope that the priests and their faithful flocks are being a little more cautious in light of what has happened. I mean if two lawyers were killed, or two butchers were killed within three days of one another no one would think twice about it, but there are less than 500 priests living in the city, they are a pretty rare commodity these days."

"Of course," said Kelsh. "I am sure that all the good church people are watching a little more closely over their clergy. But I am fearful that we will encourage copycats and nuts to go on priest killing binges if we play this up with too much publicity. The Mayor has every precinct in the city on extra alert and every church has a cop car in front of it. That's a pretty big commitment considering there are over 150 parishes within the city limits, shit, not even the 'L' has that kind of protection."

"You don't have to worry about any leaks from me boss. I am doing all my dealings with the Archdiocese, not with the press."

The Captain sat down behind his desk again. "Speaking of the Archdiocese, a Sister Chris Rayday called this morning. Seems you and she have had a few discussions concerning the murders. She is quite impressed with you and I don't think that she is a woman who impresses too easily."

Dan gave a little smile to the Captain. "She has been helpful for the most part. She wasn't too willing to hand over all the evidence at first, I think she was trying to protect one of the dead priests from bad P.R., but she eventually came around to seeing things from our point of view."

"That's good, she will be a very valuable to you Dan. She knows her stuff and she knows the workings of the Archdiocese. Hopefully we won't have to deal with her on any other cases, but in terms of these two she may know more than the Archbishop himself."

"I doubt that Captain. The Archbishop knew both of these priests personally, not only as their boss, but from their seminary days. There's something there in the past that I can't quite unlock, but I'll get to it, hopefully tomorrow."

"Now Dan, I don't want you badgering the Archbishop, he has had enough to deal with without you making him feel worse."

Dan was incredulous. "Feel worse? How could he feel worse? He has lost two priests to murder in three days, that hasn't ever happened here before. He knew them both very well and when I talked to him yesterday afternoon he wanted to tell me something. I don't know what, but I could feel it."

"Okay, Okay. But I want you to remain respectful to that man and give him the leeway that he needs to sort things out."

"I will," Dan said. "Is there anything else you needed to tell me?"

"No. Oh yeah, I want you to take Raferty with you on the rest of your investigations. He needs that practice and this case seems to be a good one for him to cut his teeth on."

Dan stood up and walked out of the Captain's office and toward his own cubicle at the end of the hallway. He reached his desk and sat down taking out all the things he had found in Fr. Joe's room. He looked again at the funeral card of Mary Kate Riley, the name of the funeral home was printed at the bottom of the card. O'Connor and Son's Funeral Home, 105th and Western Ave. Chicago. There was no phone number but it certainly would not be too difficult to find out if they were still in business.

Dan picked up the phone and dialed 411 information. He got the number of the funeral home and dialed it up. The phone rang four times and a pleasant sounding woman answered the phone. "O'Connor and Sons Funeral Home, how can I be of assistance?"

Dan cleared his throat a little. "Well, I hope that you can help me, I have a rather strange request."

"Yes, go on." she said.

"I am looking for Mr. O'Connor or perhaps one of his sons, I have some business to discuss with them that dates back to 1972."

"1972? May I ask who this is calling?"

Dan wasn't too sure he wanted to play his hand yet, he didn't want to send her into panic or cause her to start gossiping around the office. But he didn't really know how to make this work to his advantage. "Well, it's rather personal, my name is Dan Gill and it would be most helpful if I could talk to one of them."

"Well, that's not going to be too easy. You see, Mr. O'Connor died in 1990 and he had no sons, that was just a way to get people to feel a bit more comfortable with business. The company is now owned by a corporation, Eastern Crematoriums Incorporated."

"I see," said Dan. "Well, maybe there is someone there who was working at the funeral home back in the early 70's who could help me. This is a police matter." He hated to do it but he had to use a bit of authority to get what he wanted.

"Oh, I'm sorry I didn't know this was police business. Isn't it more customary for you fellas to come in person and not do investigating over the phone?"

He was a little embarrassed "Yes, it is and I will most likely be coming down to the parlor, but I was hoping to talk to someone who might remember a few details for me to see if a trip was really necessary. I hope I don't sound lazy."

"No no, not at all officer. I am sorry that you can't talk to Mr. O'Connor, but perhaps you could talk to Shannon Wallace, she's his daughter."

"I see," he said. "I guess O'Connor and Daughters wouldn't attract too much business eh?"

"Unfortunately, yes. I would like to blame it on the notion that it was a different time back then, but you still don't see too many women in this business and the one's that are don't advertise their femininity on their sign boards. Most people don't associate women with the funeral industry, which is a shame, because in my experience women make the best and certainly the most compassionate funeral directors."

"Yes, well I am sure that is true, after all you would know better than I." Dan felt himself blush a little.

"Would you like to talk with Ms. Wallace?"

"Yes very, much, thank you."

"Hold please." The next sound that came over the phone was Muzak.

After a few moments the Muzak stopped. "This is Shannon Wallace how can I help you?" The voice was quite pleasant.

"Ms. Wallace, this is Detective Dan Gill from the Chicago police department. I don't know if you can help me, but I am hoping that you can. I am trying to investigate a death that your father's funeral home took care of back in 1972. Is there a chance you would know anything about the funerals done back then?"

"Well, Detective I was all of 18 years old in 1972, just out of high school and just starting my first year of mortuary school. I was working here as a receptionist at night so I saw all the funerals that went through this place. But that was a long time ago and I doubt that I will have much recollection of a specific one."

"I understand. I was hoping though that this one may have stayed in your mind because it was a young person. Mary Kate Riley, she was only twenty years old, I thought that might be a bit rare." His statement was greeted with cold silence. "Hello, Ms. Wallace, are you still there?"

"I'm here. What do you want to investigate about that death Detective, it happened over 28 years ago and you people seemed to have done quite a bit of investigating at the time."

"I'm sorry," he said, I was unaware that the police had investigated the death, I had no idea that there was foul play indicated."

"There was no foul play Detective. At least none that could be found. She died of a drug overdose. Heroin is what the coroner told us and that is what they put on the death certificate. I remember it like it was yesterday."

"Why's that?" he said.

"Because I knew her. She was a year ahead of me in school. We both went to the Divine Mercy Academy for Girls on 103rd street. It was a big school but kids from the same neighborhood all knew each other. I don't believe for a minute that she took drugs. I mean I know that it was the 70's and there was a lot of drugs all over the place, but this girl did not do drugs. She worked at the parish office five nights a week for God's sake, her family was very religious."

Dan interrupted. "I'm sorry did you say that she worked at the parish office? Which parish would that be?"

"St. Edmund Campion on 101st and Oakley. I can see the steeple if I look out my back window."

"And she worked there even after high school?" he asked.

"Yes, lots of the girls from Divine Mercy worked at their parish rectory offices. It was good part time work and the parent's saw it as a safe way for the girls to get a little extra money. I think a handful of them even became nuns at one time. But the Riley family was very religious, attended mass together every Sunday, never missed a novena to the Sorrowful Mother, volunteered all over the place. There is just no way that girl did drugs."

"I don't want to sound rude or callous Ms. Wallace, but even the best of girls could have gotten into trouble if the right people offered her drugs. It was really a wild time in our country."

"I know Detective. If it had been any other girl I could have bought it. But Mary Kate was straight laced. Hell, she didn't even drink. I remember one night when I was a junior and she was a senior in high school and we had a sleep over at another girl's house. Well things got a little wild, I mean at least wild for high school girls. Someone had brought a bottle of cheap wine, Annie Green Apple or something like that. Well there wasn't enough alcohol in those bottles to get a gerbil drunk but we all took swigs and started to act a little silly. But not Mary Kate she just wouldn't do it. She was adamant that she was not going to drink and she was adamant that she was not going to smoke when someone broke out the Virginia Slims. She just couldn't bring herself to do it. I guess of all the girls I knew she was loaded with the most Catholic guilt. Besides she always said she couldn't do those things because it would disappoint her brother."

"Her brother?" he asked.

"Yeah, her brother Jerry. He as a seminarian, the pride of the parish, was going to be the next Pope, you know? What a shame that he never saw that dream come true."

"Why's that?" he asked.

"Because he left the seminary two months after her death."

CHAPTER 12

$\mathcal{D}$ an knew that he had some serious investigative work ahead of him. Tracking down this Jerry Riley would not be too easy, the name was common and there was bound to be more than one listed in the Chicago phone book. He knew that he had three options, first he could call information which he knew would not be much help, he could also put the name through the main computer with hopes that the guy had some kind of criminal record and trace him that way. He also knew that he could call the seminary and try to find out some information that way.

He picked up his phone and began his task of searching for Jerry Riley. The first call he made was to the central information office of the Chicago Police Department. He had friends in the central information office and he knew they would help him get through the red tape. It was not legal even for a cop to run a report on someone unless they were being charged with a crime, but in cases of investigations those rules were often bent.

"Central Information, this is Officer Carlisle," the familiar voice answered.

"Ginny, this is Dan Gill, how are you?"

"Dan you old son of a dog! I'm great, how about you?"

"I'm good, in the middle of an investigation and I need to track down a possible lead, can you help me?" Dan knew Ginny Carlisle for years and he had a good rapport with her.

"Is he being charged with anything Dan?" she asked.

"Uh, no he's not, but I think he could really be of help in tying down some loose ends for me. I would consider it a personal favor."

"Of course you would sweety. How come I only hear from you when you need personal favors? I would love to have you call and ask me out for a drink some night."

Dan cleared his throat. "Ginny, I would love to go out some night, you and me and Maggie."

She gave a little laugh. "Are you still seeing her? My God Dan either make an honest women out of her or let her find someone who will."

Dan had been dating Maggie Cleveland since his wife died three years ago. At their ages neither one talked about marriage too often, but it was something that occasionally crossed Dan's mind. "Don't you worry about that, she's honest enough. So what do you say, a little spin through the database for me?" he asked.

"Sure, what's the name?"

"Riley, Jerry. Might be under Gerald or Gerard. My guess is that he would be about fifty two or fifty three years old. I'm taking a bet that he has a record."

"Hold on, let me enter it." There was a pause on the other end and Dan could hear Ginny entering the information on her keyboard. "Okay, here we go, there are three Riley's with the first names of either Gerald or Gerard. The first is Gerald Riley, date of birth December 21, 1925, that's makes him a little too old for you. The second is a Gerald Q. Riley, date of birth July 28, 1950, that's a little closer. The third is a Gerard A. Riley, date of birth January 19, 1975, that makes him a bit too young. You want the info on the middle guy?"

"Yeah," he said. "It's pretty close to the date I might be looking for and I can cross match it to other information that I can get. Hey, how about the DMV, can you access those records for me?"

She laughed. "Sorry Charlie, no can do. I only have access to plates and numbers, no reverse search by names. You would think they would expand the database for that. But you might try calling there yourself and asking, I hear they're very cooperative, and I also hear they're now passing out ice water in hell."

"Yeah, very funny. I don't know how they expect us to fight crime with all these confidentiality laws. Liberals! Maybe if the president of the ACLU's daughter gets in trouble they'll loosen the laws up a bit."

She laughed again. "Don't hold your breath. But here's the info. Gerald Q. Riley, DOB, July 28, 1950. Arrested July 18 1973 for a DUI. Spent two days in county and was released when he made bail." He could hear the keys on her computer click a few more times. "Oh, Jerry, you were a bad boy. Seems he never showed up for the court date, skipped the bail and hasn't been seen or heard from since. So, the last address is pretty old, but here it is, 10261 S. Oakley. Ah, a good south side Irish boy, what's the world comin' to?"

He wrote down all the information that she gave. "Who posted the bail for him?"

"I work in central information Dan, not 'Prophets Are Us' You'll have to call county for that and I doubt that those records are even kept after more than twenty five years."

Thank's Ginny, you're still the best. Hey let's go out for that drink real soon, Maggie would love to see you."

"Thanks Gill, but no thanks, you give me a call when you're about to propose to the poor girl, then I can go out and drown my sorrows with some of my other friends." She hung up the phone. Dan knew she was a good soul, and thought she would be a great date if he didn't already have such a good thing going with Maggie.

Dan next called 411 information and learned that there were over one hundred Riley's in Chicago, 15 with the initial G or J. None of them were anywhere near 103rd street and the operator on the other end wasn't too happy to give him thirteen phone numbers and addresses. If he didn't inform her that he was a cop he wouldn't have gotten anywhere. She ended their call by informing him that phone books were readily available even to civil servants.

Dan then decided to call the seminary. He didn't know how far he would get, but he figured that if all else failed that maybe Sister Rayday or the Archbishop would be of help. The phone rang six times before an elderly voice answered.

"St. John Vianney Seminary." The voice said.

"Yes, this is Detective Dan Gill from the Chicago Police department, with whom would I speak if I wanted to find information concerning a former student?"

"A priest?" she asked.

"No, someone who dropped out."

"Registrar's office, hold." The phone went quiet.

"Not too up on their manners," Dan thought.

"This is the office of the registrar." Another female voice, about the same age and attitude as the receptionist.

"Yes, this is Detective Dan Gill from the Chicago Police Department. I am doing an investigation and I need some information concerning a former student." He waited for a response.

"Priest or drop out?" She asked.

Drop out sounded so cold to Dan. "Um, he was never ordained."

"I see, well we don't give out information Detective even to the police unless they have a warrant. Now if you have a warrant and you want to drive up here, I am sure that the Rector would be glad to open the files for you. Our files are sealed unless the student himself requests his transcripts and even then it must be done in writing with a valid signature and a check for five dollars."

"No, you don't understand I'm not asking to see his files or his grades, I'm just…"

She interrupted, "Oh, but I do understand, you want information on a former student and I don't give that out. Perhaps you would like to speak to the Rector, I apparently can be of no help to you." The phone again went silent as Dan was put on hold. It was easier to get information from the FBI than it was from this place.

"This is Father Sheahan, how can I help you?"

"Father, my name is Detective Dan Gill from the Chicago Police Department, your name was given to me by the Archbishop and I was told that you would be very cooperative in our ongoing investigation into the deaths of two priests." Dan figured what the hell, the Archbishop did say he would help in anyway possible. Right now this was the best way that he could help.

"Yes, Detective, what can I do for you?"

"I am looking for some information about a former student named Jerry Riley. I know that he was never ordained and that your records are sealed and that I can only get them with a warrant, but...."

The priest interrupted him. "Detective, I can see you went to the registrar's office before being patched through to me. I am sorry, they are the watchdogs of the seminary in that office. I would be glad to help you. Let me put you on hold and pull Jerry's file."

Dan waited again in silence. Finally someone who would help him.

The priest came back on the phone. "Here we go Detective, Gerald Q. Riley. Jerry was a student here about four years after me. I never knew him personally but stories have a way of staying on here at the seminary and I certainly knew of him. Let's see yes, he was a student here from 1970-1972. It appears that he was a good student his first two years but then something happened in his last quarter because he received all incomplete's. I'm not sure you know this but his sister died that quarter. He apparently took it pretty hard because he never really went to class after that. His final evaluation recommended that he take some time off from the seminary, get his head together maybe get into a program for grieving relatives."

"Was that the scuttlebutt about him in your days?" Dan asked.

"Yeah, more or less. Not so much about the sister dying, many of the men had relatives, even siblings that died while they were in seminary. But more about his demeanor those last few months he was still here. The story went that his sister had died of a drug overdose. He became quite scrupulous about drugs in general, especially about alcohol for some reason. He would walk around campus like Smokey Bear putting our forest fires every time he saw someone with a drink in their hand. It supposedly got so bad that one day at mass he walked up to the altar and tossed the Precious Blood on the floor insisting that Jesus would have never approved of alcohol in his services. Something like that tends to leave a lasting impression at the seminary."

"I take it that after that he was asked to leave," Dan said.

"Definitely," the priest said. "But I don't want to make it sound like he was thrown out into the streets. I heard that he was very close to the Dean of Formation at the time, you know him as Archbishop Tate, the man we affectionately call The Boss. He supposedly arranged for him to get into some kind of program and kept up with him after that. I'm surprised he didn't tell you that himself."

"Yes, uh, the Archbishop did indicate he knew him rather well," Dan lied.

"I would be glad to give you a copy of these files, but as our friendly registrar said, they are sealed. I mean we can't give them out by law. But you can look at them, there is no law against that."

"Well, I may just do that Father Sheahan. I will also want to see the records on Fathers Wysocki and Danner if that's alright."

"Not a problem," said the priest. Of course if you want to take them into evidence you'll have to subpoena them. Sorry about that."

Dan smiled to himself. "That may not be necessary, but thanks for the information. By the way, were there any stories floating around about Wysocki or Danner?"

"Those two? The only stories about them dealt with their notorious bridge games with the boss, I mean with Archbishop Tate. When he was Dean of Formation he had a group that played all the time, the group lasted for years, as long as Tate was Dean. But the stories were harmless, motivated by jealously. Other guys who didn't play didn't like Tate because they weren't part of the group. You know how it is."

"Yes, I do," Dan said. "How about you Father, were you a part of the group?"

"No Detective I was not. I don't think I was quite intelligent enough for that group. They were really the cream of the crop. Smart guys, most of them were very good a math in their college days. Some people said that the first thing Tate did when a new batch of students arrived was to check their math grades from college. I don't think he would have invited me to play a game of go fish."

Dan laughed along with the priest. "Well, thank you Father Sheahan, you have been of immense help. Again before you go. Did you ever hear of Jerry being arrested for anything after he left the seminary?"

There was a brief pause on the other end. "Detective, there were a lot of seminarians in my days here. The one's who left rarely if ever made contact with those who stayed. They were unfortunately known as the 'dropouts'. Not a very nice nomenclature I'm sorry to say. I can't recall hearing anything about Riley in his post seminary days. Seems like the stories about him ended with his being shipped off to that program by Tate."

"Thanks again Father, I may be in touch." Dan hung up the phone and sat back in his chair.

Dan was really given a lot more information that he thought he would get over the phone. But this he knew, Gerald Q. Riley, the south side Irish boy had been a seminarian the same time that Wysocki and Danner had been. He was a member of the elite group of bridge players, and odds were pretty good that his image was on that picture that he found in Wysocki's room. He had to be a member of 'the gang' in 1972. If his sister was there then he couldn't be far away.

But for as much information as Dan had, he still had no where to go with it. Okay so a girl in a picture with Wysocki and Danner died tragically. She had a brother in seminary, the boys all liked to play cards with the Dean of Formation. At least three people in the picture were dead. With leads like this Dan could arrest any Catholic with a propensity for playing cards.

"There is a connection here," he said aloud. "I know it."

Dan stood up and decided to head home. He hadn't seen Maggie in two days and her dander was getting a little ruffled. He would call it a day, have a nice dinner with the woman he loved and get more answers tomorrow at the funeral of Father Phil Danner.

CHAPTER 13

*D*an parked his car in front of his northwest side home. He bought the modest bungalow five years after joining the force. He and his wife were so proud of the yellow brick house in the middle of the block. Over the years Dan had fixed up the place, adding a family room in the basement and finishing a dormer in the attic just a year before his wife died. She always wanted a large master bedroom that they could call their own, some place off limits to all the kids. After the kids were all away at college or married, Dan finally had time to make her dream come true. After she died, he stopped going up to the room, the memories were just too painful.

Maggie came into Dan's life shortly after the death of his wife from ovarian cancer. She was a wonderful woman who had lost her husband in a traffic accident five years earlier. She was from a good Irish family and a her dad and brothers were all cops. Dan went through the academy with one of her brothers and had spent many a Sunday afternoon at the house of her parents during his rookie year. Had he not met his wife just before entering the academy he would have thought about dating Maggie then.

Dan lived alone in the bungalow. He didn't want to have Maggie move in just yet. Two of his kids were still in college and the other two lived just a few blocks away. It's not that Dan was ashamed of Maggie or of his relationship with her, he just didn't believe that people who were not married should live together. Although they rarely if ever discussed marriage, in the back of his mind Dan could see himself spending the rest of his life with Maggie. Once the last two kids were out of school they would most likely get married.

Even though they did not live together, Maggie did have her own key to the house and her own spot in the garage. Many nights Dan would come home and find her sitting in the family room watching television or reading the latest bestseller. She was a fantastic cook and occasionally Dan could talk her into doing up a big meal just for the two of them. It was a comfortable relationship and neither one of them was in a hurry to make any changes.

Dan came into the house and could hear the television in the basement. "Wheel of Fortune" was on, he could hear the familiar spin of the big wheel and the dings as Vanna turned the letters around for the contestants who bought vowels. He walked into the kitchen and grabbed a beer out of the refrigerator. He threw his keys on the kitchen table and walked down the stairs to see Maggie.

"Johnny Cash and Carry," he said.

"Dammit Gill, you know I hate when you walk in here and solve the puzzles like that!" She turned around and saw him at the foot of the stairs.

"Can't help it sweety, I'm a Detective, always looking for clues."

She got up from the couch and walked over to him and put her arms around him. She gave him a kiss on the lips and little pat on the behind. "Yeah, yeah, you just like to show me how smart you are. How was your day today? Any better?" She knew that he was really having a difficult time with the murders of the two priests.

"Actually it was a better day. I think I have some leads. Not evidential leads, but circumstantial. I mean, I think I can make a connection between some things that I uncovered. It's a little frustrating, has a lot to do with deaths from over twenty-five years ago. I don't know babe, I think maybe I'm getting a little to old for all this thinking."

She took his hand and led him back up the stairs to the kitchen. "Nonsense, you're the best damn detective they've got and don't you forget it. You wanna tell me about it? Bounce your ideas off of me a while?" This was a common practice for the two of them. Dan liked to talk out loud about his ideas and Maggie was the best person to bounce them off of. She had helped him to see the light and make connections in more than one case.

"Yeah, maybe that's a good idea," he said. "Okay, we have the murders of two priests, the department is saying that as of now they are unrelated except that they are both priests. You know how they frown on the serial killer stuff. Anyway, I haven't had too much time to dig into the second priest, but the first one, that Father Wysocki, remember I told you yesterday I was going to his rectory today, he had some stuff in his room that really got me thinking.

"I found about five things that may somehow lead me to a motive for his murder, but they're so damn shadowy. Like a medal with a heart on one side and an inscription on the other that says NEVER TRUMP. What the hell is that, shouldn't priests have religious medals?"

Maggie shook her head in agreement. "Well did he wear it like a religious medal?"

"No, I found it in a drawer of the sacristy of the church. Apparently he was allergic to metal so he would never have worn it. But it seems so strange to me. I know it's only one little thing and lots of people have medals and coins and other crap that they keep, but I'm telling you Maggie this medal was talking to me."

Again she nodded. "So tell me what you think it is."

"It's a token of some kind. The housekeeper and the Archbishop both told me that the guy loved to play bridge. Trump is word that you use in bridge. But it's more than that. The medal was," he hesitated, "ritualistic or something. It was as though it was a sign of membership or something."

"Like a bridge club?" she asked.

"Yeah, exactly like a bridge club. And that in itself is no big deal. So I guess it really leads me nowhere. Then there was this picture that I found." He opened his brief case a took out copies of the photos and the mass cards he had taken from the desk. "It is a picture of Fr. Wysocki when he was in the seminary, that's him there in the middle."

"Nice looking young man," she said.

"Yeah, well you were always a sucker for a guy in a uniform. Anyway his picture is not the only one I recognized. See the man standing to the left of everyone, the slightly older looking guy? Do you recognize him?"

She shook her head. "No, not really, why should I?"

"Well, maybe. That's Archbishop Tate before he was a bishop, while he was still a Dean at the seminary."

"So they knew each other, lots of priests know each other."

Dan nodded in agreement. "I know, but look over here to the right of the photo, that young man there is Father Danner, the other priest that was murdered."

Maggie held her arm around herself as though she was cold. "Okay, now that is weird. I mean there are only eight men in this photo and you know three of them?"

"Not only that," he said. "See this girl here next to Wysocki? I know her too."

"How?" she asked.

"Look at this funeral card, recognize the girl?"

"Well, sure she's the same girl as in the picture."

"Exactly, and she died shortly after this photo was taken. The writing on the back of the photo said 1972, the year she drug overdosed."

"Drug overdosed? She looks so sweet and young, not the type to do drugs."

"Yeah, well you're not the only one to think that," he said. "I did a little investigating on her and it seems that she was a very good girl.

Straight laced all the way. Her brother was in the seminary at the same time as these guys but he was never ordained. He left shortly after her death. I am sure that he is one of the guys in this photo, I intend to ask the Archbishop tomorrow which one he is."

"I know you're playing hunches here Dan, and that always works for you. But why does this make you think there's a connection to the murder?"

"I know, it is far fetched, after all its not a crime to have a medal, belong to a club, to have known people who have died under strange circumstances. But Maggie there is something there. Look at it with me and help me put the puzzle together."

Dan and Maggie looked over all the copies again. They went through the funeral cards and the photos. Dan had shown her copies of the canceled checks and the two letters that were found in the desk. Maggie and Dan poured over them for an hour bouncing questions off one another and looking for any clue they could find.

"You know Dan, I was thinking about this letter signed T.B. It doesn't seem worthy of keeping in your desk drawer along with other memorabilia. Why do you suppose he kept it?"

Dan looked at the letter again. "It is odd, I mean its not really a big deal, a schedule change for a meeting. The envelope didn't even come through the mail, see no postmark."

Maggie held up the copy of the letter and the envelope together. "Not even a name on the envelope, why did you bother to copy this?"

"I don't know, it was evidence, I assume that was the envelope that it came in, that was the envelope it was found in."

"Okay, so he saved it in a locked drawer so that no one would know he was having a schedule change. Who the hell would care? Who would see his calendar?"

Dan thought about it. "Maybe the secretary, she was a good friend of his and probably knew where he was most of the time. But also the nosey housekeep. She had access to his room and would have seen his calendar on his desk, maybe he didn't want her prying eyes to know he was having regular meetings with anyone."

"Or maybe," she said, "he didn't want anyone to recognize the handwriting on the note. Some people can look at a letter and know immediately who it's from. Maybe he wasn't so worried about people knowing that he was going out as much as he was concerned about them knowing WHO he was going out with."

"Of course, Maggie you are soooo smart. Nosey housekeeper, friendly secretary, visiting friend, maybe one of them would have been able to identify the writing. I'll be sure to take this copy back to them and ask. I'll lay ten bucks that the housekeeper not only knows who wrote it but that she knows what kind of pen he used."

"Did you think abut this T.B. thing Dan?" she asked. "Did you look through his telephone book or see anything else with those initials?"

"Yeah, I went through his personal calendar and it had a telephone directory in the back. No T.B. in there. I also asked the secretary on the way out to look in the diocesan directory and to let me know if any of the other priests had those initials and that came up negative. Maybe the housekeeper will know that too."

"Well, maybe. Could be just about anyone. When I worked at Ashton Middle School a few years back the principal used to sign all her notes T.B. It was supposed to be a big inside joke, she always like to be called "The Boss.""

"Yeah, some people are big into the power thing, I had one Captain who...," he stopped in mid sentence. "The boss. Oh my God Maggie that's it, T.B. is the boss and I know exactly who the boss is and I just happen to have a date with him tomorrow morning right after a funeral.

CHAPTER 14

*D*an woke up at his customary 6:30 AM. He never minded the morning, it gave him some chance to think and clear his head from life's problems. He rolled out of bed and headed into the kitchen to put on a pot of coffee. He never got used to making only two or three cups for himself, old habits die hard. He went to the front door to pick up the daily paper, sometimes there were good clues in there as to how his day was going to be. The mood of the city was often reflected in the headlines of the daily newspaper.

Dan glanced down at the paper. The headline read "Second Priest Murder Victim Buried Today." The story was about the upcoming funeral of Father Danner. The paper had indicated that it was going to be large, even bigger than that of Father Wysocki. The Archdiocese had time to let all this sink in and people from all over Chicago were expected to attend. The article noted that for the second time in three days the Archbishop would be the Presider of the mass. There were also side stories on the two murders and detailed obituaries of Father Danner. So far there was not flack from the press about the inept job that the Chicago police were doing in solving the murders, but Dan knew that it wouldn't be long before the press would start pushing hard for answers.

Dan left the paper on the kitchen table and went into the bathroom to take a shower. There was nothing better for him than a very hot shower in the morning to get going. It was even better than that first cup of coffee that would be waiting for him when he got out. He turned on the shower and let the hot water rise. As he got ready to enter the shower when he heard the phone ring. He let the water run and went back to the kitchen to enter the phone. It was pretty rare for someone to call him at this time of the day.

"Gill here," he said.

"Dan, it's Maggie. I was thinking all night about the case. I know there was something that I was seeing but couldn't quite put it together. It was in the picture of the eight men and three women."

Dan pushed aside the newspaper and looked again at the photo he had copied at the office. "Yeah, Maggie I'm looking at it, what did you see?"

"Look at the girl, what was her name, Mary the one who overdosed. Look at her neck Dan there is something shinny there."

Dan glanced down at the photo. "I'll be damned," he said. "There is something there."

"I knew I saw it, but it just didn't register with me. Doesn't that look a lot like a medal on a chain?" she said.

"It sure does, I wonder if I can get this blown up downtown and get a better look at it."

"Dan," she said. "Look at the other girls, any of them have charms on their necks?"

Dan looked over the photo again. "I don't think so, let's see, the one girl here on the left has what look like pearls, the other girl has on a loose neck blouse and there is definitely nothing there."

"I didn't think there would be. Dan, I know this sounds crazy, and there may never be anyway for you to know this or not, but I think she is wearing that medal like a steady pin."

Dan sounded a little confused. "A steady pin, what do you mean?"

"You know," she said. "When a boy and girl go steady, the boy gives something to the girl. When you're in college you pin a girl. I know kids don't do that now, but they were still doing it in the seventies. But maybe a pin was a little to obvious for this girl, maybe she needed to wear something that wouldn't draw a lot of attention, something her parents wouldn't ask questions about."

"You are a smart one, Maggie my dear. That female perspective always comes through for me. I'm going to go back to the original photo this afternoon and take a good look at that little charm around the neck of Mary Riley. Something tells me that you are right on the money with this one."

"Well," she said. Chalk it up to experience, I was a twenty year old girl once myself."

"And as I recall a pretty darn cute one. Did you hide things from your parents?"

"Me? Only all the time. And wearing a charm rather than a ring or bracelet or a pin was something that they would never have noticed. You be careful out there today Gill."

"I will," he said. "You be careful too, and have a good day. I'll call you later in the afternoon. And Maggie, thanks again."

Dan hung up the phone and rummaged through what he affectionately called the junk drawer for a magnifying glass. When he found it under the duct tape, the half pair of scissors and the three pens that didn't work, he went over to the table and looked more closely at the picture.

He could see the medal around the neck of Mary Riley. It wasn't necessarily meant to be seen. It was on a long chain and it was hanging a little to the side like it had accidentally fallen out of her blouse. If Maggie was right, then she probably kept it hidden under her blouse so that only she knew it was there. Of course there were lots of explanations for the presence of the medal. Maybe she was a great bridge player too, or maybe it wasn't a NEVER TRUMP medal at all, maybe it was a locket or something else all together. He would know a little more when he had the photo lab blow up the picture.

He glanced at the clock in the kitchen, it was 7:00 AM and he was running behind schedule. He wanted to get in the shower and head down to his office before he went to the funeral at St. Polycarp. He put down the magnifying glass and headed to his respite in the bathroom. The water was hot and the room was steamy. As Dan walked into the shower all the dirt and grime of this case rinsed off his body, at least he would feel clean for the next fifteen minutes.

Dan went to his office and picked up the original photo that he had put in his desk. He didn't enter anything into evidence yet because he had permission from the Archbishop to take anything that he needed and he knew that there would not be any fingerprints on the old photo that would offer him any help. He grabbed the photo and started down the hall when he heard his name called again from the Captain's office.

"Gill, come in here for a minute," the Captain shouted.

Dan walked toward the office and saw the Captain and Detective John Bartly sitting at the desk having a cup of coffee. Dan's face flushed red with anger. He couldn't stand Bartly and he knew that if Bartly were in the office the news could not be good. He hadn't spoken to or seen Bartly since the night of the second murder in the hotel.

"What's up Captain?" Dan asked.

"Dan, I was talking over this case with Bartly and I was thinking that it might be too much for you to be handling both cases."

Bartly turned his massive body in the chair and flashed a fake smile at Dan. "Yeah, I been tellin' the Captain here how you should let me take over the second case, since you seem pretty wrapped up in the first one," Bartly said.

"Captain that makes no sense what so ever. You know these two cases are related and the investigation will go better if I can trace down the leads on both of them. The only reason Bartly wants this one is because of the publicity. The second murder made pretty good headlines."

"What are you sayin' asshole, that I only take high profile cases?" Bartly asked.

"No, not at all Bartly, you only take cases that make you look good, if you thought it wouldn't benefit you, high profile or not, you'd be running from it like a cow from a prod."

Bartly struggled to stand up, his huge belly coming in direct contact with Dan. "You shit, I oughtta punch you right in the fricken head."

"Enough!" shouted the Captain. "You two are like little kids fighting over the last piece of candy. Dan, I just thought that it would make sense to allow you to spend more time on the Wysocki murder, I mean we can't show the two murders are related yet, so it's not that unusual to assign two of you, wouldn't you agree?"

"With all due respect, Captain, no I don't agree. These two murders are related and I am very close to figuring out how. I know the Mayor and the boys downtown don't want to make this look like a serial killer, you know I agree with that. But I also know that there are many things that connect these two guys beyond the priesthood. They were friends, they had common friends and I can't put that puzzle together without all the information in place. My esteemed colleague here has been know to withhold evidence in the past, and quite frankly I just can't afford that right now."

Bartly snorted again. "Withhold evidence? When did I ever withhold evidence Gill? Huh? You give me just one example."

"I can give you ten examples shit head and you know it. Remember the Luis case, the Mexican who was tried and convicted for the killing of three prostitutes on 26th street? You knew that he was innocent, you knew that there were witnesses that placed him at other places at the probable times of the murders. You not only ignored them, you paid the witnesses to stay quiet. The press was getting on your ass and you sent an innocent man to jail."

"That's not true! Captain, don't listen to this shit head, he doesn't know what he's talking about."

"The Captain knows damn well what I'm talking about, he just can't prove it," Dan said.

"Alright, enough of this, I can't take it," said the Captain. "Dan, you're out of line here. Bartly has never been brought up on any charges regardless of what the criminals he arrested have charged him with. But I do see your point Dan. I guess I would really like to deny that these cases are related to the same killer. But if you have evidence that links them, stay on both cases."

"Captain, that's not fair!" shouted Bartly.

"Yeah, well, life's not fair Bartly." said the Captain.

Dan smiled at Bartly. "Tell you what Bartly, the next time a movie star or a television guys gets knocked off in the city, you can have the case. I'm sure the press will be there too." Dan turned and walked away from the office. He could see Bartly giving him the finger in the reflection of the office glass.

Dan got in his car and went downtown to the central police headquarters. It was an impressive building with state of the art technology. It was relatively new and was being constantly updated. The Mayor had made fighting crime a priority and money was pretty free flowing for everything except salaries. He went to the photo lab and talked to the technician about blowing up the photo. She told him that it would be no problem but that there were nine cases ahead of his. He would have to come back later in the day or early tomorrow for the results. Dan explained that he was particularly interested in the neck area of the girl next to the priest in middle. He also wanted her to try and blow up each of the neck areas of the other girls to see if they had chains around their necks.

Leaving the photo in the hands of the tech, Dan left the building and got in his car. It was already 9:00 AM and the funeral for Father Danner was starting at 10:00 AM. He didn't have to worry too much about traffic because he was going the opposite way of rush hour, but he was concerned about parking. He wouldn't be the only official car there and it might be difficult to park just anywhere he wanted.

Dan got onto the expressway and tuned into the news station on the radio. There was the usual stories for the morning rush, traffic, weather, sports, fires, corruption, robberies and murders. The news anchor then told the story of Father Danner's Funeral. Dan listened to the pleasant voiced woman read her copy.

"The funeral of Father Phil Danner will take place today at St. Polycarp parish on the North side. Father Danner's body was found at the old Majestic Hotel on West Irving Park Road earlier in the week, in what appears to have been a violent Murder. Police Superintendent Wang has said that there is no conclusive connection between the murder of Father Danner and that of Father Joseph Wysocki last Saturday. When asked if these murders could be the work of a serial killer, the Superintendent said that given current investigation that it was highly unlikely

"The funeral is expected to draw large crowds, reports have indicated that the Mayor himself will be in attendance at the funeral. People traveling the Uptown neighborhood are advised to stay off of Broadway between Irving Park Road and Hollywood as that is the route the funeral will be taking at approximately noon."

Dan switched off the radio. How the hell could the Superintendent say that there was no connection between the murders given current investigation. He didn't even know what current investigation was. In all his years on the force, Dan had only met any superintendent twice, both times were for press pictures after big cases. "These big shots are all the same," Dan thought.

Dan exited the expressway and headed east on Irving Park Road to the Uptown neighborhood, it wasn't the fastest way to get to the parish, but he thought it would be his best bet for finding parking if he came from the west rather than from the east with everyone else. He could see the bell tower of the parish in the distance and turned down a side street to get a better chance for parking. About a block away from the parish he found a spot between two television vans. It wasn't ideal because they might recognize him as the detective on the job, after all he was at the press conference with Sister Rayday after the first murder, but he couldn't find anywhere else to park.

Dan walked briskly over to St. Polycarp. He was always amazed at the disparity of this neighborhood. High rises along the lake front held very wealthy tenants, while halfway houses could be found up down Broadway for blocks. He got to the church and walked up the steps. At the door he was stopped by a uniformed officer.

""Do you have a pass for the funeral?" the officer said.

"A pass, you have to have an invitation to come to this?" Dan asked.

"Actually yes, you do. Parishioners and friends were able to pick them up yesterday at the rectory. Do you have one?"

"No, the only pass I have is this one." Dan showed his badge and his identification.

"Oh, sorry," said the officer. "Go right in Detective."

Dan pushed past the officer and thought he heard the guy mumble something about big shots under his breath. Dan smiled to himself, it all trickles down doesn't it? His dislike of the higher ups was not different than the officer's dislike of him. As he entered the church Dan looked to see where the priests were vesting for mass. He didn't want to bother the Archbishop now, but he did want to try and let him know he wanted to talk to him after the funeral.

Dan walked to the front of the church behind two priests who held white vestments in their arms. He walked with them into the sacristy and looked around. He couldn't see the Archbishop and the room was a beehive of activity. There were about 50 priests in the sacristy and at least another fifty already sitting in the pews of the church. Dan saw an older man trying to get the attention of the priests so that they could get the show started.

"Please, Fathers, please take a program from the table and take a seat in the church along the front with the other priests," the old man said.

The priests slowly started to obey the old man and one by one filed out of the sacristy. Dan walked up to the old man hoping to find out where the Archbishop was. "Excuse me," Dan said. "Do you by chance know where the Archbishop is?"

The old man looked up, the funeral had not even started and he already looked exhausted. "Listen sir, you have to get out of here, this is for clergy only."

"I realize that," said Dan. "I'm a Detective from the police department. The Archbishop knows me quite well and I am sure he would talk to me if he knew I were here."

"Yes, I'm sure." The old man gave Dan the one over with his eyes. "Well he is in the rectory at the moment. He wasn't feeling too good this morning. He has a cold or the flu or something. He needed a place to sit down and get a little air. He should be coming in here any minute. I am sorry if I was a bit curt with you. But you can't believe the people who have tried to come back here this morning. The press alone have taken ten years off my life!"

"I can understand that. Can I sit here and wait.?" Dan asked.

"No need, here he comes now," the man said.

"Dan, I didn't expect to see you back here," said the Archbishop.

"I hope you don't mind Archbishop, I know how hectic this is for you, but I needed to ask you some very important questions after the funeral. Will you have any time?"

The Archbishop gave a little cough and then a sneeze. "Excuse me, I have a cold or something. But yes Dan, actually that would be fine. They are having a luncheon right after the funeral before we go to the cemetery. I have no appetite so we can meet in the rectory after the mass. That way I can avoid the press too."

The little man came up to the Archbishop. Your excellency, I set aside a separate chalice for you just as you asked. I told the altar servers to direct the priests to the other four chalices on the altar."

"Thank you," said the Archbishop. "I don't want to give my cold to anyone else, this is just safer."

Dan shook the Archbishop's hand. "Thank you so much Archbishop, I will come to the rectory after the mass is over. I really think you of all people can tie up some very important loose ends for me."

"Glad to do anything I can Dan. I just hope we can get to the bottom of this. Personally it's scaring me to death and I don't scare too easily." The Archbishop turned and glanced in the mirror to be sure that his vestments were in order. He wore the vestments that he had been given from a group of friends when he was consecrated a bishop. It had embroidery of his coat of arms on the back of the chasuble. A beautiful design with a cross, two doves, a large M for the Virgin Mary and a blood red heart.

CHAPTER 15

❀

*D*an walked out of the sacristy and back into the body of the Church. The funeral was about to begin. Dan saw the funeral directors placing the lid on the casket of Father Danner. Dan saw that the casket was a full couch.. The dead priest was laid out in mass vestments and the lid was one piece rather than the customary split lid. Next to the priest was has chalice and patten and a Book of Gospels. Dan scanned the assembly of mourners trying to decide where he would sit. The church was filled to capacity, not unusual for a priest's funeral. Dan saw Raferty sitting toward the back of the church and walked down the side aisle so that he could join him.

"Hey, Raferty, save me a seat?" Dan asked.

"Sure Dan, there's a little room here," Raferty said. Raferty was wearing a long black over coat over his suit. He had been on the force for ten years and was just made a detective four months earlier. He was young, smart, and liked to dress the part of the detective. He always wore a suit to work, not just the usual shirt and tie like many of the older detectives. Dan figured that Raferty spent more on his wardrobe than on his rent.

Dan took a seat next to Raferty and waited for the mass to begin. He glanced around the church to see who else he knew. He saw what appeared to be the family of the priest being ushered into the first pew across from the more than fifty priests who came for the funeral. He also saw Sister Chris Rayday sitting in the pew behind the family looking very proper but not very nun like.

Dan watched as the lid was completely closed on the casket. The chalice and the patten were removed from the table next to the casket. As though on command the priests all stood and filed into the aisle as the Archbishop approached the casket from the front of the church. It was quite an impressive sight. The aisle of priests wearing white vestments made a kind of honor guard for the beginning of the mass. The Archbishop approached the casket with five altar servers, one carrying a large white cloth, one carrying a cross, one carrying a holy water bucket, and two carrying candles. There was also a master of ceremonies dressed in black cassock and white surplice.

The Archbishop took the sprinkler from the holy water bucket and blessed the body of the dead priest. The undertakers then took the large white cloth from the server and covered the casket with it. The Archbishop turned and the priests dutifully filed back to their pews. The Archbishop then proceeded into the sanctuary of the church flanked by the servers and two of the auxiliary bishops of the Archdiocese. They went to their respective chairs and began the with a prayer.

After the readings from scripture, the Archbishop prepared to give a homily for his friend Father Danner. He moved from his seat to the podium at the left side of the altar. He glanced down at the podium and then back up at the assembly. He seemed to be nervous or shaken. He reached under his vestments and pulled out a handkerchief to wipe the beads of perspiration that had formed on his forehead.

"Let me begin this morning by saying how terribly sorry I am for the loss of Father Danner," the Archbishop said. "I have had the pleasure of knowing Father Danner for many years and not only was he one of our finest priests, but he was truly a great friend and a confidant."

Raferty leaned over to Dan. "Could you imagine a funeral for a priest where the Archbishop wouldn't say he was one of our finest?" he asked.

Dan looked back a Raferty and told him to be quiet. The Archbishop again wiped his head. He has his homily written out but he seemed to be having a difficult time focusing on the text. He looked back to the assembly with sad eyes as though to say release me from this task. Dan thought how difficult it must be for the Archbishop, to bury two priests within three days, both of them murdered.

The Archbishop continued his homily. "We have come here today with a sense of hope in our Christian hearts. We pray for Father Danner's salvation and his entrance into the heavenly kingdom of God. We pray for the souls of all those who have died and especially those who have died by violent means."

Dan could see that the Archbishop was no longer looking down at his text. The old man had apparently decided to wing it and speak from the top of his head or from his heart."

"We have all suffered a great loss here today," he continued. We have all lost someone who is very dear to us. Jesus tells us in the Gospel today that there are many dwelling places in his Father's house. I know in my heart that Father Danner is being welcomed to the kingdom of God. He was such a good man, a man of duty and responsibility.

"I recall when he was a seminarian. His love of theology and his love of mathematics. It was an unusual combination but one that helped him to serve the Archdiocese well for these many years. His dedication was without equal and we should always remember him for the many good things that he did in his life. I know that when my own time comes, that I too will be remembered for the good things that I have done and not for the sins that I have committed."

Again the Archbishop stopped and wiped the beads of sweat that were forming on his forehead. Dan could not figure out what he was doing. He had obviously strayed from his text, why was he talking about his own sins?

The Archbishop looked again at the assembly. He glanced over at the priests who were sitting in the pews. His look was forlorn, like he was a lost soul who did not know what to say. "I have always appreciated the priests of this Archdiocese," he said. "They have been pillars of faith to the larger community of Chicago. Father Danner was one of those pillars. He gave and gave of himself, it does not surprise me that he gave even his life in the line of duty. When a police officer or a fire fighter dies in the line of duty he is a hero. Cannot the same be said for Father Danner? He answered a call, just who called or why they called we cannot know. Neither could he have known what awaited him. But he went nonetheless. He answered a call, just as he had answered a call earlier in his life.

"No matter what he encountered as a seminarian or priest, he continued on with his mission. You see, nothing could stop his dream of becoming a priest. Even when times were difficult he persevered. It was not always an easy road for him, he faced many obstacles even while in seminary. But in the end, it was God who made the call and it was a call he answered. The events that happened along the way were just detours you see! He took the right path, and I know that he was convinced of that in his life." The Archbishop was getting very emotional, and tears were visibly forming in his eyes.

"When we are faced with decisions of our own mortality, we must make decisions that will impact the greater good. This is something that this priest knew in his life. Yes, there were times when those decisions were difficult and times when they were easy. But he did not falter. I told him many times that his decisions were good ones, that they were good for the entire Church and not just for himself. That, my friends is what a servant does. He thinks of the larger picture and makes sacrifices for the good of the whole."

Dan looked over at Raferty and then glanced around the church. People had no clue what the Archbishop was talking about. What was all this discussion of decisions and mortality? People began to whisper and wondered to themselves what was wrong with their spiritual leader. Dan strained to look to the front pew of the church, he could see the family of the priest talking among themselves, as though they too were confused by what was happening.

Dan was at a loss for words. He could see that the Archbishop was losing his audience. He was struggling to stay on track and his words were not making much sense to anyone. It was as though he had allowed a stream of consciousness to overtake his voice. It was as though he was talking to himself rather than to a congregation of worshipers.

"Oh, yes," he went on. "This man gave of himself and he could be trusted. With such a fine mind he could be trusted. Trusted to keep God's commandments and trusted be a true friend. He was the model of discretion, you could trust him with your life if you needed to. That was something on which many people counted. It is a complex day for all of us. We are called to rejoice in the resurrection of the Lord Jesus Christ, and yet we mourn. Let us mourn this priest, this man, this friend, but also let us rejoice in his share in the resurrection of Christ. Pray to God that all of us, yes all of us, will one day be reunited in His sight."

The Archbishop again wiped his brow and put out his hand to the master of ceremonies who guided him back to his chair. He sat down and put his head in his hands, it was obvious to everyone that he was weeping. For many who were gathered there this did not seem unusual. He had lost one of his priests, he was known to have treated many members of the clergy as though they were his sons. But to others it seemed strange. Dan was one of those others. He could understand the outpouring of emotion, he had wept many times at funerals himself. But he could not understand the apparent sporadic nature of the homily. He was all over the place talking about sins and choices. Dan just could not figure out what all that was about.

The mass processed as usual with beautiful music, incense and dignity. It was like a high mass of old. People were extremely moved and there were many tears that flowed from their eyes. At the sign of peace the Archbishop went to the family of Father Danner and embraced each one of them. It was a very moving scene, one that did not go unnoticed by many of the people in the assembly.

Dan watched as the Archbishop prepared for the Communion Rite. He held the host high over the chalice and proclaimed that the bread and wine he held were the body and blood of Christ. He then consumed the host and drank from the chalice in the center of the altar. After he drank the other priests went up to receive the chalices in two lines, one at each end of the altar. The master of ceremonies came and removed the chalice of the Archbishop. After the priests had all received from their chalices they too were removed and taken to the sacristy where they were immediately rinsed and dried.

The Archbishop went down the center aisle and began to give communion on one side of the casket. One of the other auxiliaries took his spot on the other side of the casket. As the people came to receive the body of Christ, it was obvious that there was something wrong with the Archbishop. He began to slur his words saying "bofy of rist", rather than body of Christ. He even dropped the host on the floor several times either missing the tongue or the hand of the intended recipient.

When communion was over the Archbishop sat back in his chair. His color was gone and he looked like a ghost. He leaned over to one of the auxiliaries and told them to finish the prayers, that he intended to stay seated until it was time to walk out. The auxiliary bishop did as he was told and the funeral ended with a song of fare-well for the priest. The people were invited to attend a memorial luncheon being provided in the school cafeteria before going to the cemetery. The Archbishop slipped into sacristy and quickly removed his vestments. He was sweating profusely and could not get his balance.

Dan made his way through the crowd, going against the flow of body traffic with Raferty directly behind him. He reached the sacristy and could see that the Archbishop was in no condition to talk. "Your excellency, I know this is not a good time," Dan said.

"Dan, I'm glad you're here. I guess this is not going to be a good time after all. That really took a lot more out of me than I had hoped."

"Archbishop you look terrible, are you in pain?" Dan asked.

There were many people standing around the Archbishop it was difficult to get air and even Dan was feeling warm. "I'm feeling rather weak Dan," the Archbishop said. "I think I might need a drink of water and some air."

The old sacristan came into the room and looked around. There were far too many people in there for his liking. "Alright, you priests," he said. "Get moving, the Archbishop needs some air and you're making a mess back here. Grab your things and go."

The priests were a little miffed at what was said to them but they did as they were told, some of them mumbling under their breaths about the attitude of the sacristan. Dan leaned in close to the Archbishop and gave him the glass of water he had gotten from the sink in the sacristy.

"That's better," said the Archbishop. "Dan, there is something that I want you to know about these murders." The Archbishop took a deep breath, it was obvious he was having trouble breathing.

"Hold on Archbishop, you really don't look good. We're going to take care of you." Dan turned to Raferty and told him to radio for an ambulance. Raferty left the sacristy and ran to his car to get the radio. "Go on Archbishop, is there something you want to tell me?"

The Archbishop looked up at Dan with tears in his eyes. He was shaking on one side and his other side a completely limp as though he were paralyzed. Dan's first thought was that the Archbishop was having a stroke. The Archbishop tried to lean a little closer to Dan, his voice was soft and his words were beginning to get jumbled again. "Lifen to me Dan, there is somefin' that you need to know. These murders, they're not goin' to be the onfy two. There's gonna be more, I just know it. But I need you to figure it out Dan. You can't let him do this to my boys, they're good boys." His words were becoming more and more slurred.

Dan was so close to the Archbishop that he could smell the wine from the mass on his breath. "Who Archbishop, who is doing this?" Dan asked.

The old man was fading fast and Dan wondered where in the hell the ambulance was. "Liften to me Danny. There's too muff to tell you now. I'll tell you later. Now I have to reft, I'm fery tired. But Danny, if somefing happen to me remember that my heart was always in it, I was always true to my heart."

Dan tried to hold up the body of the Archbishop but it was just too heavy. The breathing was slow and very shallow. His limbs were limp and he was going fast. Dan could feel that his left side was completely cold and his lips were beginning to turn a pale shade of blue.

Dan saw Raferty come back into the sacristy with the paramedics behind him. "Where the hell have you guys been?" he shouted.

"Take it easy sir," said the young paramedic. "There's about five hundred cars in front of this place, it wasn't easy to get here." The paramedic came in close to the Archbishop and took his vital signs. He could see that he was still alive and moved quickly to get his oxygen and onto a gurney to be placed in the ambulance.

Dan and Raferty moved out of the way as the Archbishop of Chicago was placed on the collapsible gurney and loaded onto the waiting ambulance. Dan looked at Raferty and waved him toward his car. "Let's go Raferty," he said.

"Are we going to the hospital?" Raferty asked.

"You bet you're sweet ass we are, now let's go."

All the commotion of the ambulance and the scene with the Archbishop caused a stir among the people. There were already some reporters there, reporting live back to their television and radio stations. Dan knew that with his siren and lights he could tail the ambulance, something the reporters could not do.

He turned on the radio to see if the news station was reporting the events that had just occurred. He was not surprised that they were all over it like white on rice.

"This is Laura Morales live at St. Polycarp Church where Archbishop Tate was just taken away by ambulance. The reason for this is not yet known. We hope to have a spokesman from the Archdiocese give us information at any moment. Again, the Archbishop has been taken from St. Polycarp Church on the North Side by ambulance. He was presiding at the Funeral of Father Phil Danner, pastor of St. Polycarp, who was murdered earlier this week. We will break into our regular news when we have more details. Back to you Charlie."

Dan sped behind the ambulance hoping beyond hope that they would get to the emergency room before too many reporters could clog the streets. His siren was blaring as he tailed the ambulance into the emergency entrance of St. Hedwig Hospital on Lake Shore Drive. There were nurses and doctors waiting at the entrance as the ambulance pulled up.

"Holy shit Dan," said Raferty. "This is unbelievable. I mean I could see he was distraught but what happened?"

"I'm not a Doctor Raferty," said Dan. "But that looked like a stroke to me. He really wanted to tell me something, he knows something about these murders."

"What do you think it is?"

"That's what we need to find out Raferty. That's the sixty four thousand dollar question."

CHAPTER 16

The two detectives got to the emergency entrance of the hospital at the same time as the ambulance. Dan pulled the car right behind the large red and white wagon with his portable Mars light still flashing. They both jumped out of the car and followed the paramedics into the emergency exit. There were already about three reporters there looking for an edge on the breaking story.

Dan followed the gurney carrying the Archbishop and flashed his badge to the waiting hospital security. "Gill, CPD, I'm going in there with them." Dan pushed his badge back in his coat pocket and told Raferty to wait for him outside and watch for Sister Rayday. "Let her know that I am in there with him and that I want to talk to her when she gets here."

Dan pushed his way into the emergency room and found the curtain draped cubicle where they were working on the Archbishop. He knew enough to stay out of the way, but still get a good view of what was going on. He could see the emergency room doctors and nurses working on the Archbishop, checking his vitals and applying various IV's to his arms. He didn't understand all the medical jargon, but he could occasionally catch a phrase that made sense.

One of the doctors, a young man of about thirty looked over at Dan standing at the corner of the cubicle. "What the hell is he doing here?" he asked to no one in particular.

Dan looked over at the doctor. "Official business, Doc, I won't get in the way."

The doctor worked on the Archbishop some more and spouted out some orders for treatment. He turned back to Dan and said, "See that you don't".

The doctor looked intently at the all the diagnostic equipment and seemed dismayed. Something wasn't right. He looked up at blood pressure machine, it didn't look good, the blood pressure was dropping fast and the Archbishop's breathing was so shallow that his chest was no longer moving up and down.

"Dammit intubate him nurse, he's barely breathing." The doctor was looking all around at the various machines. Shaking his head. "He has some of the symptoms of Cerebral Vascular Accident, but it just isn't adding up on the machines," he said.. "If we can get him stable then we'll run a CT Scan and see what has happened in his brain. If it shows a stroke, I want him started on Heparin right away."

Dan wasn't sure if he should interrupt and tell the doctor what happened right before the Archbishop went limp. The doctor turned to him, "You were with him when this happened?'

Dan shook his head. "Yes, I was in the church when he started acting funny and I was talking to him when he collapsed."

"What was happening to him in the church, was there anything peculiar?"

Dan moved in closer to the doctor. "Yeah, he started to slur his speech, at the end of the mass."

"Slur it how?" the doctor asked.

"You know, slurred, like he was drunk or something," Dan said. "But he was also sweating a lot. And after mass we talked briefly just before he collapsed. He was sweating like crazy and not making much sense."

"It sounds, like a stroke, that's for sure," said the doctor. But if it is, it's a whopper of a stroke. He's more than hemi-pelagic, he is in full paralysis. I just ordered them to put him on a breathing machine, he'd never survive without it. I mean I've seen some pretty bad strokes and certainly this is not unheard of, but I believe there is very little hope of ever stabilizing him or any hope at all for a recovery."

As the doctor was speaking the curtain to the cubicle was pulled open. Raferty and Sister Rayday entered. "What's happening to him?" she asked.

"I'm sorry, who are you?" asked the doctor.

"I am the chancellor of the Archdiocese of Chicago, Sister Rayday. I need to know what is going on and I need to know now!"

"Yes, Sister, it honestly doesn't look good. He seems to have had a massive stroke, I'm quite surprised that with what has happened that he didn't die on the spot. There really may be nothing that we can do. He is not even breathing on his own anymore."

Sister Rayday moved closer to the gurney where the Archbishop was laying. She put her hand on his and she could feel that it was already cold. She bent down and whispered something in the ear of the dying man. She stood up and turned to the doctor and saw Dan standing in the corner. "He would not want to live like this," she said. "He has a do not resuscitate order in his living will. He would not want to be kept alive on machines."

The doctor looked at her somewhat in dismay. "That generally comes from the family Sister, are you family?"

"The Church is his family, doctor. He has no other family, has been an orphan for most of his adult life. I am the one who worked this living will out with him, I assure you I am authorized to make this decision."

"Yes, well that may be the case, but we will have to have a copy of the order in hand before we pull him off the breathing machine. I want to add, that there is still some chance that he may recover and I don't feel that taking him off the respirator after only thirty minutes is the best plan of action."

Rayday looked at the doctor. "I'm not an idiot, doctor. I realize that we cannot take him off support at this moment, I just wanted you to know that this is what he wanted. I will produce his living will, it is at the Pastoral Center and another copy is kept with his attending physician at University Hospital. It will of course take some time to get those papers in order. In the meantime I suggest you make him as comfortable as possible. I need to address the media and get some things in order. How long do you think before we can say one way or the other if he is beyond hope?"

Dan could not believe how cold and callous this woman seemed to be. She seemed more concerned with the media than with the state of the Archbishop. He walked over to her and put his hand on her shoulder to comfort her, but also to test her reaction. "Im sorry Sister," he said. "I know this must be difficult."

She looked at Dan, her eyes were moist, she wasn't so cold hearted after all. "Thank you Dan, this is so much more difficult than you can know. But I won't see him suffer. He never wanted to suffer. This is for the best, believe me."

The doctor interrupted. "I think that it would be safe to say that he cannot be taken off the respirator until we run a CT scan. I need to know his brain wave activity before just abandoning him."

"Fair enough," said Rayday. "You run your tests and I'll be back with the documentation. In the meantime I do not want anyone, including your media representative talking to the press. The Archdiocese will handle that, your people will be needed after he dies to explain what happened."

As she turned to leave the alarms on the machines in the cubicle began to go off. The flat line beep was the loudest as the doctor and his assistants rushed to assist the Archbishop. "Dammit, he's going, we're losing him!" yelled the doctor.

Dan and Sister Rayday moved back to the corner of the cubicle, out of the way of the medical team. They worked feverishly to revive the dying man, they seemed to be yelling out all sorts of strange names of medicines and procedures to save him. The doctor could be seen pounding on the Archbishop's chest pulling tubes and opening sterile packages.

Suddenly all the furor died down. The medical team, as if on cue, stepped back from the Archbishop. A nurse walked over to the heart monitor and pushed a button to make the noise cease. The doctor looked up at the clock on the wall. "Time of death 12:48 P.M., presumed cause of death Cerebral Vascular Accident."

Dan looked on in disbelief. This couldn't be happening. Three priests in just a week. Something wasn't right. He looked over at Sister Rayday, tears welled up in her eyes. She put her hand on the hand of the dead man and stroked it gently. "You won't have to suffer, you're where you should be now, we all know that." She brushed the tears from her eyes and walked past Dan to the outer area, just outside of the general waiting room.

Dan followed her out as the medical team began to remove the machines from the Archbishop's body. "Sister, I am very sorry for your loss," he said.

She looked at Dan put her hand on his. "Thank you Dan," she said. "He was a good man, he's where he should be now. I need to talk to some of the other members of the cabinet before we go out to the media. There are probably some of them here in the waiting room already. I need to go out there and get them."

"Sister, I know this isn't the best time to talk about the other events that have happened, but I will need to talk to you soon about something that the Archbishop said to me before the stroke."

She looked intently at Dan. "What did he say, was it something about the murders?"

"Not exactly, but he seemed to know something and if he knew something then we have to investigate it deeper. Something was gnawing at him, something was weighing heavy on his mind."

She took Dan by the shoulder and squared up to him. "Of course there was something on his mind Detective. He just buried two of his friends, two of his priests. He was distraught, I doubt that he was even very coherent at the end, with all that slurring. He wasn't even rational. Exactly what did he say to you?"

"It wasn't what he said, it was what he didn't say. He wanted to unburden himself of something. If he had another priest there I think he would have gone to confession."

"He was dying, of course he wanted to unburden himself. He could barely breath," she said. "This will have to wait until later. I cannot deal with this right now."

"Of course, I understand. But we will need to talk and not before too long either. Perhaps we should plan to meet later tonight."

She gave Dan a look that went right through him. "Fine, meet me at the mansion, no you better make that my office, tonight at 7. I'll be in the lobby so I can escort you upstairs."

"That's fine Sister, I don't want to add to your own stress, but this simply has to stop."

"What has to stop?" she asked.

"These killings, we have two priests who have been brutally murdered, and if I'm not mistaken a third that has been added to the killer's list."

She removed her hand from his shoulder. "What are you saying Detective?"

"I want to know what killed the Archbishop."

"You heard the doctor, it was a stroke."

"I'm not so sure, we'll know more though after an autopsy."

"You can't be serious," she said. "You're not thinking that I will allow him to be cut up do you?'

"It's not going to be up to you Sister," he said. "It's the law, he was brought here under suspicious circumstance in an ambulance and not under a doctor's care. You have no choice."

"This was the Archbishop of Chicago, I am not going to allow him to be dissected!"

"Sister, I'm not going to rest on this until I know what happened. I'll get a court order if I have to, but he is going to be autopsied."

"Well, Detective, we will see about that!" She turned and walked into the general waiting room, flash bulbs and television lights hitting her as she entered the room.

"Yes, we will see about that, won't we?" Dan said as she disappeared into the lights.

CHAPTER 17

For three days the city of Chicago was buzzing with the news of the death of the Archbishop. Headlines everyday discussed some aspect of the death. First there was the shock of the news, then the pending arrangements, then the questions that were bound to be asked when a celebrity dies. The archdiocese of course made an official statement concerning the death of the Archbishop. In their own diocesan paper they wrote a small story on the death itself and dedicated page after page to the impending funeral arrangements.

The body was to lie in state at the cathedral for two days with an open casket and public viewing from 10:00 AM to 9:00 PM. The funeral mass itself was to be held on the morning of the third day at 11:00 AM. The media anticipated that there would be over 1000 people at the mass. Admission by ticket only. They also speculated that there would be a host of celebrities at the mass from both the political and entertainment world. The Archbishop was well known and this was still a Catholic town. The papers reported that the Governor, the Mayor, both Senators from Illinois, and maybe even the Vice President would be there. Among the whose who list there were local actors, newspaper columnists and television hosts that would be at the church.

Dan decided to forego the wake services. He drove by the Cathedral both days that the body was on display and the lines were wrapped around the block. He thought that it was ironic how many people vocally disliked the Archbishop in life, but how these faithful came out to view the dead body and offer prayers. Death tended to bring out the best of people, he thought as he drove by. He knew that he would go to the funeral and would not need a ticket other than his badge to get in.

On the morning of the funeral Dan woke up at his usual 6:30 and made his pot of coffee. He showered and sat at the kitchen table going over the headlines for the day. The details of the funeral service were laid out on the front page of the paper. There would be final viewing of the body at the cathedral from 8:00 AM until 10:30 AM. The funeral would take place at 11:00 AM and then the body would be taken in a police escorted motorcade down Ogden avenue to one of the far western suburbs where most of the bishops of Chicago were buried.

Dan read the article and noticed that the funeral services were being directed by O'Connor and Sons on the south side. It stood out immediately in Dan's mind and he remembered the connection between the funeral home and the dead girl in the photo he had found. He reached for his notebook and looked for the name of the woman he had spoken to on the phone last week. He found it scribbled in his own bad handwriting about a third of the way down one of the pages; Shannon Wallace. Dan wrote the name down on a blank piece of paper at the end of the book and tore the page out placing it in his pocket.

Dan finished his coffee, dutifully rinsed the cup and walked over to the phone. He dialed

Maggie and waited patiently for the phone to be picked up.

"Hello," she said.

"Hi darling," Dan said.

"Danny, how are you holding up?"

"Okay Maggie, hangin' in there. Gonna head down to the funeral this morning."

"You feeling up to it?"

"No choice babe, gotta go. I need to pay my respects and I'm hoping there is going to be someone there that I need to talk to."

"Who's that?" she asked.

"The Funeral director, a woman who used to be acquainted with the dead girl in the photo. She was somewhat helpful on the phone, but I think I can get more out of her in person."

"Oh, sure Danny, use those sexy eyes to get what you want," she laughed.

"These are eyes are only used for you, Miss Maggie, don't you forget it. I'm gonna head out in a few, wanna get in before the crowds. I'll call you when I get home tonight."

"Okay, Dan, be careful today. Don't tread into any dangerous waters. Love you."

"Me too babe, bye." Dan hung up the phone and headed upstairs to finalize his morning ritual. He grabbed his gun and his badge, slipped on his sport coat and headed for the front door.

Dan started the car and drove down the expressway to the Cathedral. The traffic was already terrible at 7:30 AM and had been backed up for about an hour. The gridlock was getting on his nerves because he rarely took the expressway at this time of the day. The station was closer to the house than the Cathedral and he could take side streets all the way. At one point he contemplated turning on the Mars light and riding the shoulder all the way in. He'd seen it done a million times before. But true to his nature Dan obeyed the law and sat in the impossible traffic for forty-five minutes.

When he arrived at the Cathedral he was able to find parking in the lot across the street. He parked the car and quickly crossed the street to the enter the limestone building. The Cathedral stood as a monument to Catholicism in Chicago. It was not as majestic as the European cathedrals that he had seen years before, but for the relatively young city of Chicago it was an impressive sight.

Dan bolted up the stairs and was greeted at the door by a guard hired by the diocese from a local ushering service. He anticipated the need to flash his badge but was surprised when the usher simply opened the door for him. He was informed that public viewing was being held until 10:30 and at that time everyone would be asked to leave the Cathedral unless they had tickets.

Dan walked down the long aisle and saw the casket of the Archbishop placed at the front of the church. On either side of the casket were men from the Knights of Columbus, dressed very formally with sashes over their black suits and their plumed hats under their arms. There was a short line waiting to go past the casket. Local mourners who came to pay their last respects to their shepherd. Dan got in the line and waited to do the same.

As he moved to the front of the line he noticed that there were several auxiliary bishops greeting the mourners along with Sister Rayday in a smart black dress covered by a well tailored jacket. She was the picture of perfection as she greeted the mourners and thanked them for their prayers. Dan walked up to the casket and reached down to touch the hand of the dead Archbishop. Death did not scare Dan, he was raised a Catholic and had been to countless wakes by the time he was 10 years old. He moved past the casket and reached out his hand to the two other bishops and then to Sister Rayday.

"Thank you for coming today," she said.

"I am very sorry Sister," Dan said. "I know this is a personal loss as well as a loss for the Archdiocese."

"Yes, Dan, it truly is. Thank you for your prayers."

Dan loosened his grip and made way for the other mourners. He was about to walk down the side aisle of the massive building when the nun reached out and grabbed him by the shoulder.

"Dan, I want to talk to you."

Dan turned toward her. "Of course Sister, what is it?"

"Not here, let's go to the sacristy where we can have a little privacy."

Dan followed the nun to the sacristy of the Cathedral. The room was as big as some churches he had been in. Everything was immaculate and there were mass vestments laid out on the table for the concelebrating priests who would arrive soon. She motioned for Dan to take a seat and she closed the massive door through which they had entered.

"Dan, I know that we did not leave one another on the best of terms the other day."

"That's my fault Sister," he said. "I should have been a little bit more sensitive to your grief."

"No Dan, it was my fault. I was just so worried about the press and about what would be said that I could not even contemplate right from wrong. Of course I am glad that the department wanted an autopsy. It is in the best interest of everyone, I just could not see that at the moment."

"The results will be in sometime today," he said.

"Yes, I know, the coroner has asked for several of the members of the cabinet to be present when they are released to us. I was hoping that you would be there with us. I'm sure that all the stress he was under caused the stroke, but what if it were something else? I want a cop I can trust to be there with us."

Dan nodded in compliance. "Of course I'll be there Sister. I also have a truly vested interest in what that report says." Dan had every intention of being there anyway. The Captain had already told him the time and place that the results would be released.

"Sister, I was wondering if you could answer a question for me," he said.

"I can try Dan."

"Why did the Archdiocese decide to use a south side funeral home to make the arrangements. I know there are plenty of undertakers, good Catholic ones right here in the downtown neighborhood."

She looked up at Dan and smiled. "It was in his will, his arrangements have been made for years. He was quite close with Mr. O'Connor and his daughter Shannon when he was assigned to the
seminary. I think he used to help at St. Edmund Campion on weekends in those days. He got close to the people of that parish and he
always wanted that funeral home to take care of him when the time
came. The funny thing was, even when he moved to another diocese
after his term at the seminary, he never changed that part of his will.
I guess if he had died down south, then they would have had to fly
there to make his final arrangements."

Dan nodded his head. "Do you know the daughter of Mr. O'Connor? I think her name is Shannon Wallace."

The nun looked at Dan in surprise. "Yes, I know her, she's in the
back of the Cathedral welcoming people and seeing to the details of
the day, but how do you know her name?"

"Just a little detective work," Dan said.

"Do you wish to meet her?" she asked.

"Very much so. I know this is a very hectic time for her, but I
would like to see if I can somehow speak with her."

The nun began to walk out of the sacristy and motioned for Dan
to follow her. She opened the large door and walked down the side
aisle to the back of the Cathedral. The crowd has doubled since Dan
and the nun had been in sacristy and the activity in the Cathedral
was beginning to get busy.

As they approached the back the Cathedral the nun stopped and
placed her hand on an attractive woman in a dark blue blazer and
knee length skirt. "Detective Gill, this is Ms. Shannon Wallace."

Dan reached out his hand and looked at the attractive woman. He
knew that he had not met her before but she seemed familiar to him.
"Ms. Wallace, we talked on the phone last week, I was inquiring
about the death of Mary Riley."

The woman extended her hand out to Dan. "Yes, Detective Gill, I
remember it well."

Dan noticed that she had been crying and the her mascara was begging to clump up under her eyes. "I know that this is not an opportune time to talk, but I have so many more questions that I need to ask you."

"Actually, Detective," she said. "This is not the worst time to help you. I mean in a half hour I will be of no use to you. But I have a few minutes to spare now if you need my help."

She walked in front of Dan and motioned for him to sit in the last pew closest to the door.

Dan sat down and reached in his pocket for a pen and the piece of paper he had torn from his notebook that morning.

"I was telling Sister Rayday that I found it unusual for a south side funeral home to be conducting the services for the Archbishop."

She smiled at Dan. "Actually Detective, I have known the Archbishop for many years, since I was in high school. He used to help at my home parish and would occasionally come to wakes at the funeral home. He became quite close with my father and always wanted him to do his final arrangements. Of course that wasn't to be, but it was still in the will for O'Connor and Sons to do the arrangements, so here I am."

"I see. So you would have known the Archbishop when he was a teacher at the seminary."

"Oh, yes. As I said he spent weekends at the parish and I was always at the rectory visiting Mary while she worked or even filling in for her when she couldn't be there."

He jotted down a few things on his piece of paper. "I really need to know about Mary's brother, Jerry. I would like any lead you can give me to his whereabouts."

"Now Detective, you know as well as I do that I don't know where Jerry is, even if I did I couldn't tell anyone. It's well known that he is a fugitive from the law. Never showed up to his trial. I believe that if I knew where he was, then I would be obstructing justice."

Dan smiled at her. "That may or may not be the case Ms. Wallace. There are statutes of limitation in Illinois. He may not even be wanted for a crime anymore."

"Nonetheless, I don't know where he is. I have not seen him or heard from him since he jumped bale many years ago."

"How about family or friends, I'm not looking for him because of his past crime, I just need him to fill in some puzzle pieces for me. He is one of several leads in a case I am working on."

"I thought I had mentioned that his parents are dead when we talked on the phone. Oh well, even if I didn't that doesn't change the fact that they are. Not long after Mary's death her parent's died. There were no other siblings, rather unusual for an Irish Catholic family, I know, but true nonetheless."

Dan was still taking notes. "How about cousins, friends, school-mates, anyone who might help me."

She leaned forward placing her hands on Dan's. Her long blonde hair fell forward and her blouse loosened a bit so that her cleavage could be seen in spite of the jacket. "There was no one else, Detective. They were a very small family. Jerry was a loner with the exception of his sister and a few seminary friends. When he was arrested all those friends forgot about him and erased him from their minds. He simply did not exist to them anymore and now he doesn't exist to the rest of us. He's gone, he'll never be found, there is nothing that would bring him back here now."

Dan looked up at her soulful eyes and then by habit down at the cleavage that was showing under the coat. As she leaned back to compose herself he could not help but see the gleam of silver as it slipped back under the blouse. The pendant that she was wearing, it was round with a small engraved heart.

CHAPTER 18

※

*I*t was very rare that a member of the police department needed to be at a reading of an autopsy report. But it was also very rare that an autopsy be done on the Archbishop of Chicago. This was not Los Angeles where the coroner was as famous as the stars he worked on. In Chicago celebrity was pretty rare, so those who attained that status were closely guarded by the local community. The man who held the office of the Archbishop became an instant celebrity regardless of who he was. He was expected to be available to the media and rub shoulders with the upper crust of Chicago.

Dan came into the office of the medical examiner of Cook County and greeted Sister Rayday in the waiting room. They exchanged pleasantries as they waited for the medical examiner to call them into his personal office. They were both a little nervous, neither one knowing what to expect from the report. Dan knew that there would be something revealing in the report, he just did not know what it would be.

The Medical Examiner opened his door and beckoned the two to come into his office. He was an impressive man in his twelve hundred dollar suit. Standing at six foot two with a dark tan and shining white teeth. He was not what Dan had expected at all. He thought the medical examiner would be a pale, sickly guy who worked in the lab all day, never seeing the weather outside of the County Morgue.

The medical examiner greeted both Dan and Sister Rayday and invited them to be seated at his desk.

"Sister Rayday, Detective Gill, I am Dr. Cross, the chief medical examiner for Cook County." Both Dan and Rayday shook his hand and took their seats on the opposite side of the large desk in the office. "I must admit that it is rather unusual to have a member of the CPD here for an autopsy report, you guys generally just have us send the file over to the precinct."

Dan smiled at the medical examiner. "Yes, Dr. Cross, I realize that, but this is a pretty special case."

"Indeed it is, I know that you are both anxious to receive the report, so I'll get right down to it." Dr. Cross opened a manilla file folder that was on his desk and began to peruse the contents. He glanced up and down and flipped a few pages. Dan thought that it was very dramatic and all put on for the benefit of the two guests.

"Something shocking in there Doctor?" Sister Rayday asked.

"Well, yes there is Sister. I have to say that I was surprised at first that we even had to do an autopsy on this case. It seemed from the doctor's report at the hospital that it was definitely a stroke that had caused the death. And even though the Archbishop was not under doctor's care and he technically should have had an autopsy, I thought the diocese would see that it would never happen. The Church still does have some power at City Hall." The doctor sat up a little straighter in his chair. "But I am very grateful that someone had to the insight to insist on this autopsy and that the orders came down that we do a full run of tests on his organs and blood."

Dan squirmed a little in his chair. "We thought that would be best in this given situation Dr. Cross."

"Yes, Detective, well it was a wise call. Although the Archbishop had all the classic signs of a stroke it seems that there was a toxic substance in his bloodstream that would certainly have caused the same symptoms. An emergency room doctor would naturally make the diagnosis of a stroke given all the information that he had at the time. But there is no way a thorough autopsy could miss what was the real cause of death."

"I knew it," Dan said. "It just wasn't right, he even knew it himself, something was really wrong."

"Well it seems that somebody had it in for the good Archbishop. His toxicology report shows more than trace amounts of a deadly drug known as coniine in his system. Now this is very rare, I have never personally seen a case of coniine poisoning myself and I had to do a little research to find out exactly what it was." He glanced down at the report again. "Coniine is a very powerful by product of the plant hemlock. As you know from history hemlock is a poisonous plant that has been used for thousands of years. It was mixed in with the potion that Socrates was given at his execution. We don't see too much of it anymore, in fact we don't see too much poisoning anymore in general."

"Why is that?" Dan asked.

"Because Detective, poisoning is very easy for us to detect. If there has been a poisoning, and there is an autopsy, then we will catch it. It is a very efficient form of murder, but not a very anonymous one. We almost always catch a poisoning unless the victim was under a doctor's care and no autopsy is required."

Sister Rayday sat at her chair speechless. She was visibly shaken by the news that the Archbishop had been poisoned. She stared blankly at the doctor not saying a word.

"Sister, I realize this comes as shocking news to you. I know that you did not hold the same suspicions as the Detective here, but we cannot deny the truth. This man was poisoned."

She looked down at the desk and then directly at the medical examiner. "Yes, I , I was so sure that it was a stroke, I saw him and he had all those symptoms."

"The symptoms caused by coniine poisoning are very similar to those of a stroke. Because coniine is an alkaloid it directly affects the central nervous system. It can induce trembling, loss of coordination or speech and paralysis, particularly of the victims respiratory system. You can see why even those who were very close to the Archbishop at the time would have thought that this was a stroke, particularly given the immense stress that he was under the past few days. The effects of this drug can work very fast, anywhere from 15 to 30 minutes depending on the dosage. And it doesn't take much to kill someone, less that one gram of coniine mixed with alcohol or even water will be fatal."

"But how? How could he be poisoned at a mass with seven hundred people in attendance?" Sister Rayday was now wiping her brow with a hanky she pulled from her suit pocket.

"That's for the Detective to figure out Sister. But I do know this, he was poisoned at that mass. The affects of the drug, and the amount we found in his system would indicate that he would be showing signs of the poisoning within 30 minutes at the most. Death generally comes no more than 60 minutes after the initial dose is given. He had to somehow ingest it at the mass."

"We'll figure this out Sister. I'll get over to the church right away and start the investigation."

She looked at Dan and nodded in agreement. "I know you will Dan, we have to find out who is doing this. We have to stop this craziness."

"We will." Dan stood and asked the medical examiner for a copy of the report. He took his copy and Sister Rayday took hers.

"How is this going to look to the public, we now not only have two priests blatantly murdered but the Archbishop poisoned. This is too much for them to handle, we can't let this information out!" The nun was frantic in her tone.

The Medical Examiner walked towards the door. "I'm afraid that the Medical Examiner reports are public record Sister, even for the Archbishop of Chicago."

"Well in this case they are not going to be public record doctor. I have a court order here for the file to be held confidential until further notice. It is to be a closed file and you are not to discuss it with anyone."

The doctor was shocked as he took the court order from the nun. "Very well, Sister, the case will remain closed, and no one from my office will leak out any information. I can assure you of the that."

The doctor held open the door and shook hands with both Dan and the nun. They exited into the outer office as the doctor's door closed behind them. Dan took Rayday by the arm and walked her over to the corner of a the outer office away from the receptionist. He was intent on speaking frankly to the nun and trying to get to the bottom of all that had happened.

"Sister, how did you get that court order so fast?"

"I worked on that order the day the Archbishop died and you were determined to have an autopsy done Dan, I was hoping it could be tossed away when we learned his cause of death, but now I am very happy that I had the foresight to get it done."

"I suppose that I agree with you. I mean this will make it easier for us to do our investigation if we don't have the whole city breathing down our necks about a murder."

"Well, that was part of my motivation, but the other part was for the Archdiocese, we cannot take much more of this Dan, we cannot have people targeting our clergy. This last death would just add to an almost mass hysteria among the Catholics of the city."

"How do you suppose that the poison was given to the Archbishop Sister, I mean there was a huge crowd in that church."

"I was thinking the same thing. It had to be done before the mass started, but that doesn't seem to add up with the time frame painted by the medical examiner. If he were poisoned at home or even before the mass started he would have been dead by the time the mass was over."

"Exactly," Dan said. "So it comes to reason that he must have been poisoned during the mass, I was trying to remember if he stopped to have a drink of water during the mass. I was watching him but not that intently. He could have asked for a drink after the homily and I missed it."

"I don't think so Dan. He was a stickler for the rules, he would not have had anything to eat or drink before he received communion. He was very worried about his image. Even if he was feeling nervous or sick, I am sure he would not have had any water during the mass. And even if he did I would have noticed it because it would have been so out of character."

"Then the only time that he would have been able to ingest the poison would have been at communion. Somehow the poison was put in the communion wine. Didn't the doctor say it was often mixed with water or alcohol?"

"Yes, he did, but then if it was in the wine wouldn't someone else have gotten sick too? All the priests partook of the Precious Blood, they all would have drank from the same bottle of wine."

Dan scanned his memory back to the sacristy just before the mass had begun. What was it that the sacristan had said to the Archbishop while they were talking? Thinking hard, his eyes closed in concentration. "They may have all drank from the same bottle of wine Sister, but they didn't all drink from the same chalice. Just before mass started I heard the sacristan tell the Archbishop that he set up a special chalice for him as he requested. He mentioned something about having a cold."

"My God Dan, could that sacristan have put something in the chalice?"

"Doubtful, the guy was about 90 years old and could barely walk, hardly the type to poison someone or even more to put an ice pick through someone's ear."

"Then there must have been someone else in the sacristy with them. Someone else who would have had access to the chalices."

"I was in the sacristy before the mass began Sister, the only people in there were the altar boys and a few priests. The sacristan said they were coming in there all morning hanging up their coats and putting on vestments."

"The sacristy is very open though Dan, almost anyone could have been in there. I don't envy your job right now."

"Nor I yours. You know as well as I do that this is going to eventually leak out Sister, the Medical Examiner can assure you all he wants that he won't talk, but his staff will, this is just too big to keep it quiet."

"All the more reason for you to find out who killed him Dan. You've got a big job ahead of you and of course I'll help in anyway that I can. "

"I'm counting on that Sister, I'm counting on you getting me into the mansion and into some of the Archbishop's papers and personal effects."

The nun looked at Dan hesitantly, she was still protective of the Archbishop even in death. She did not let anyone into the mansion while he was alive and she still felt the need to protect his privacy. "Exactly what kind of effects are you looking for Dan?"

"I don't really know. Pictures, old papers, jewelry. I know that this doesn't make sense right now, but I don't think that this is a recent vendetta against the Archbishop, I have a hunch, and a small bit of evidence that this goes back quite a few years. I need to know about his past and people that he used to know."

She stood up straight, defensive. "I won't have his memory sullied Dan. I won't just stand by and let the media and other people rip that man to shreds. He was a good man and he cared about people, he was the best thing to happen to this diocese in years."

Dan put his hand on her shoulder. "Chris, I know he was a good man. I've known him for years myself. But if we are going to get to the bottom of this and prevent any more killings you have to let me do some investigation."

She nodded in agreement and made her way to the door. She grabbed the knob and turned back to Dan. "He really was a fine man. I'll help you in anyway I can. I'll call you tomorrow and set up something at the mansion. Nothing has been touched, he didn't have any family so everything is still in order. You'll have no need of a warrant if I can be there with you."

"I was counting on you being there Chris" It was the first time he felt comfortable using her first name. "I am counting on your help."

The nun went out the door and walked down the hall. She stopped three doors down and leaned against the wall. She was overcome with grief and exhaustion and the tears flowed freely and she remembered all the good that the Archbishop had done, all the opportunities that he had personally given to her and to the people of the Archdiocese.

Dan sat back down on the seats in the waiting room. He strained to remember what had happened in the sacristy the morning of the priest's funeral. He was generally so observant never letting his guard down for a minute, but it had been such a confusing morning, so much activity. There was no way he would find every priest who had been in that sacristy and that sacristan was not going to be of much help.

Dan walked over to the receptionist and asked if he could see Dr. Cross again. There were a few questions about the poisoning that he wanted to ask without Sister Rayday present. The receptionist buzzed the doctor and informed Dan that he could go back into the office.

"I'm sorry to bother you again doctor, but there are a few questions that I have about this drug that killed the Archbishop."

"Certainly Detective, please have a seat. As I said before I have never seen a case of coniine poisoning myself and I had to do a little research to find out about it myself."

"Yes, well I was hoping that you would save me a little leg work and give me some insight into this thing." Dan opened his pocket notebook so that he could take notes on the doctor's comments. "For instance, how does one get coniine? I know you said it was from hemlock, what do you do go to the local alchemist and ask for a hemlock plant?"

"My research indicates that hemlock was introduced to this country from Europe almost two centuries ago. It wasn't cultivated as a cash crop, but somehow it seems to have spread wild to many parts of the country. I guess it kind of grows like a weed along many of the nation's highways. I doubt that it would grow here in the Chicago area, the zone might be too cold, but it certainly could grow in Southern Illinois, Indiana, Missouri, or Kentucky or really any state south of there. My guess is that most people would have no idea that the hemlock was growing there, and in fact there are some types of hemlock that are not poisonous at all. One would have to know what he was looking for.

"Not only that, but one would have to know that the poison lies very concentrated in the actual seeds of the plant. You probably couldn't just get coniine anytime of the year, you would have to wait for the plants to go to seed and then crush them up to a powder for it to be of any use."

Dan took copious notes as the doctor spoke. "So the person using the poison either knew a good deal about botany or perhaps bought it from someone."

"As I said, it's not my field of expertise. My guess is that you would have to know what you were doing to poison someone with coniine. It wouldn't be too difficult to do though, the seeds could be ground pretty fine, into a type of powder and then mixed with water or alcohol. The victim probably would never suspect anything since it takes just under a gram to kill a person."

"So conceivably the powder could be placed in a cup or glass and alcohol poured on top of it, thus making the poison mixture."

"Exactly, the powder would most likely mix nicely with alcohol, and it would be virtually undetectable if the alcohol were dark."

Dan nodded. "Like red wine."

"Sure, red wine would be the perfect mixture. It's dark, sweet and the victim generally takes a larger drink of wine than say a drink of gin or vodka."

"You mentioned that most people don't bother with poisoning anymore. I guess I never really thought about it, but your right, we have very few cases of this at the station."

"As I said, poison is very easy to detect these days. A mysterious death would be subject to an autopsy and the poison would be detected. There are very few poisons that cannot be detected today. My guess that the only real poisoning that goes on today is that of the elderly and the sick. A sort of euthanasia that probably would go undetected. I would say that someone who used poison like this was either very stupid or wanted it to be known."

"Exactly, this wasn't some kind of covert murder. This was done to be discovered, this killer wants us to know that he is killing and I don't think his game stops here."

CHAPTER 19

*D*an had an early appointment with Sister Rayday at the mansion of the Archbishop the next day. He got an early start, his usual routine of showering, coffee, and calling Maggie in that order. Maggie told him to be careful, just as she did everyday. He grabbed his file of copied evidence and headed to North Parkway to the mansion.

Dan pulled up to the semi-circle drive and parked his car behind a blue Ford Taurus that he assumed was Sister Rayday's. He glanced inside the car and noticed a briefcase, several piles of papers, a rosary, and a book about women's role in the church on the seat. He was sure that it was her car.

Dan rang the door bell and made his pleasantries to the little old nun who worked in the mansion. She told him that Sister Rayday was expecting him and that he should go up to the Archbishop's bedroom on the third floor. Dan climbed the large oak staircase, noting all the beautiful art that had been collected by the Archdiocese over the years hanging on the walls. The mansion was quite palatial and the bedroom of the Archbishop was no exception. The oak lined walls were covered with exquisite oil paintings and several crosses of different designs. The bed was a large mahogany four poster with a rich tapestry top and a brocade spread on top of the mattress. Everything was in order, it was not like the bedroom of Father Wysocki which was so disordered. Dan entered the room and saw Rayday sitting in a large leather wingback chair close to the fireplace. She was looking though a book and did not hear Dan enter.

Dan approached the nun as she perused the book. "Ahem, excuse me Sister, hope I'm not late."

She looked up from the book. "Oh, Dan, no not at all. I didn't even hear you come in, getting a little old I guess."

"Don't be silly Sister, I'm just good at sneaking up on people." Dan looked at what she was reading, it was a copy of the sesquicentennial book commemorating the 150th anniversary of the Archdiocese of Chicago. He thought that she was just tracing back memories of the Archbishop.

"I suppose you want to get started, Dan."

"Ya, that would be good, Sister. I don't even know what we're looking for but anything that might help find this nut will be helpful." Dan looked around the meticulously clean room, he had just the opposite problem of his previous search, this room was too clean, too orderly. "He was certainly a neat guy wasn't he?"

"Fanatical is more like it."

Dan walked over to the large desk that sat at the far side of the room. Like the room itself it was very neat and very orderly. He opened drawers and found everything in order. Envelopes, labels, personal stationary in one drawer. His personal bills, check book and bank book in another. One drawer filled with pens, pencils, a stapler, staple remover, whiteout, and notepads.

Dan went back to the drawer with the checkbook and pulled it out. He flipped though the pages and saw nothing unusual until he noticed that there were several checks made out to cash for $250.00. The same amount that Wysocki had made out several times in his own check book.

Dan walked around the room, there was no file cabinet, no disheveled papers, nothing personal like photos or notes. Dan scanned the top of the desk. There was an antique ink stand that looked like pure silver and in excellent condition. It was probably never even used by the Archbishop. On the far corner of the desk were two calendars. One marked official and the other marked personal. Dan reached for the personal calendar and began to flip though it.

It was amazingly empty. There were very few personal things going on in the Archbishop's life. An occasional dinner and an occasional lunch. He remembered that Sister Rayday had told him that the Archbishop did not have any family so there were no birthday parties or other gatherings marked. What Dan did notice was that every Thursday had a large X marked though it. He assumed that was the Archbishop's day off. He also noticed that on several of the Thursday's there was a small heart drawn at the top of the page, the same heart that appeared on the Wysocki calendar. Dan looked up and noticed that the nun was peering down at the calendar too.

"Did he take Thursdays off?"

"Pretty religiously. He never took meetings or appointments or confirmations on those days. He was smart to do that, the only time he had space to himself."

"What did he do on his days off?"

"I'm not really sure, he certainly did not spend them with me."

"Do you see this heart on some of the Thursdays? Did he ever mention anything to you about a club or a group he belonged to, or someone he met on a regular basis?"

She glanced down at the calendar and flipped a few pages and saw the heart that he was referring to. "No, I don't think so. I hope that you are not insinuating that he was in some kind of strange liaison or something."

"No, not at all. But what about bridge, did he talk about playing bridge?"

"As a matter of fact he did. He loved the game. Tried to get me to learn it on more than one occasion. But I could never stand the game. I guess he found it relaxing. I found it tedious."

"So he must have played with someone. Like a bridge club or something. You don't know who he got together with to play?"

She looked down again and then back up at Dan. "You know who he played with. He played with Wysocki." Her indignation coming to the surface once again.

"Should I have known this?" Dan asked.

"I know that you investigated Wysocki's room and that you know they were close to one another. I assume you found something similar to this in his room when you investigated."

"Well, Sister, perhaps you missed your calling. You should have been a detective."

The nun shuffled her feet uncomfortably. "No, Detective, I know my calling and it is not in your line of work."

"How about Danner? Did he join these games too?"

"I don't know. I didn't know Danner very well at all, only by reputation and his file. If he was part of the bridge games, I wouldn't know."

Dan reached for the manilla file folder that contained his copied evidence. He pulled out the cryptic note that he had found in Wysocki's room. He handed it to the nun and asked her if she recognized the handwriting.

"It is not only the Archbishop's handwriting but his cute little initials too. He always signed his personal notes TB, stood for the boss. A little inside joke, he wasn't very boss like and it was ironic that he should be called that."

Dan then pulled the photo he had found in Wysocki's room from the folder. "Do you recognize anyone in this photo?"

She glanced at the photo and held it a little closer to the green banker's lamp at the center of the desk. Her eyes widened as she studied the old photograph. "Of course, that's the Archbishop in the center, and I would say that the good looking one there is Wysocki and the other looks like a young Danner, although I can't be sure. Like I said I did not know him very well."

"Well your skills of observation are very good. That is the Archbishop when he was dean at the seminary and that one is Wysocki and the other is Danner. How about the other guys, know any of them?"

She looked at the photo again a little closer this time. "The only reason I even recognized Danner was because of his death, in all reality he had changed quite a bit. I don't really recognize any of the other men. There is no guarantee of course that they were ordained or that if they were that they remained in the priesthood. But it shouldn't be too hard to figure out who they are, the seminary should have photos of all their students from those years."

"Well I spoke with the rector on the phone, I am sure that he will gladly cooperate if I need his help. But I thought that maybe you could help me first."

"As I said, Dan, I don't know any of the men. But I do know one of the women."

Dan looked up at her, that was the last thing that he expected to hear. "Which one?"

"The same one that you know. You met her at the funeral the other day. That girl over to the side is Shannon Wallace."

Dan looked closer at the picture. How could he have not seen it? It was so obviously the undertaker he had spoken to on the phone and met at the back of the church. "Holy cow, you're right, I can't believe I didn't make the connection."

"Well her hairstyle has changed and she certainly looks a little older now, but her face hasn't changed much and she apparently has not put on a pound since she was a teenager. I'm no detective, but I would say that is her."

"There is no doubt in my mind. I guess it should n't really surprise me, she mentioned that the Archbishop had said mass at her parish on weekends and that he and her father were actually quite close. Sister you have no idea what a lead this is, she should be able to easily identify the others in the photo."

"If you don't mind me asking, Dan, what does this have to do with anything? I mean I hope that if I were murdered that the people in my personal photos would not be suspects."

"Well, Sister, if you were murdered and so were at least two others in a photo with you, I would hope the police would investigate it."

"Of course, how stupid of me."

"Now, I really believe that there are more personal effects of the Archbishop in this room that we are missing. I need to keep looking and this could take a while. I will lay money that he has a copy of this photo and a little silver medal with an engraved heart somewhere in this room."

Dan began to walk into the bedroom part of the room and went to the large dresser next to the bed. He opened the top drawer and saw a row of neatly rolled socks, the next drawer held underwear and hankies. The drawer below that had six t-shirts lined up neatly, but something seemed out of place to Dan. He opened the two top drawers again. They were shallow drawers and were quite full for their size. The third drawer was much deeper and only held six t-shirts, but also seemed to be rather full.

Dan took the t-shirts out of the drawer and laid them on the bed. The depth of the drawer on the inside did not match the depth on the outside. Dan knocked on the bottom of the drawer, it was pliable and gave back a hollow sound. He reached in his pocket and pulled his out his penknife, he gently inserted the penknife into the sides of the drawer and lifted. The false bottom came up with little resistance. Dan lifted the bottom out of the drawer and set it on the bed next to the t-shirts.

He peered inside the drawer. Under the false bottom there were two sets of keys. One looked like it would open a small box, the other was bigger, like it opened a door to something. Dan lifted the keys from the bottom of the drawer. "Well what do we have here?"

"What is it, Dan?"

Dan held the keys up for Rayday to see. "Keys, to what, I don't know, but my guess is that the answer does not lie very far from here."

Rayday glanced at the keys and then around the room. "Maybe a desk key or a strong box or something like that."

Dan also glanced around the room. He opened the one remaining drawer in the dresser. Nothing much in there but a few shorts and summer outdoor clothes. He lifted the clothes to check the bottom of the drawer, it was solid. He walked over to the closet and looked through the various white shirts and black pants, there were several suit coats in blacks and several Roman collars hanging on hooks. Dan looked up on the shelves of the closet. On the top shelf was a small black box. Dan reached up and grabbed the box down. The small key that he had found in the false drawer fit in perfectly. Dan unlocked the box and looked in.

There was nothing in the box with the exception of a piece of paper with the number 061575 written on it. Dan took out the paper and showed it to the nun. "This mean anything to you?"

She took the paper from his hand and looked it over. "No, its just a series of numbers, doesn't mean anything to me."

Dan took the paper back from her and looked at it again. "Wish I had studied my logic a little more in college. This could be anything."

The nun was putting the false bottom and the t-shirts back into the dresser. "How many digits, Dan?"

"Six."

"Too long to be zip code and two short to be a telephone number."

"Yeah, those were my first thoughts too. Could it be a date? June 15, 1975? Does that ring a bell for you?"

"Certainly not off the top of my head, that was over 25 years ago. I have no idea what that could mean to him. It isn't his birthday or an anniversary of anything in his life that I knew of."

"Where would he have been in 1975?"

"I guess he would have still been teaching at the seminary. I don't think he left there until a few years later. But I could be wrong."

"Well, maybe it will mean something to someone. I can't think of anything else it could be other than a date or maybe an account number on a private bank account."

Dan went back to the closet and poked around again on the shelves. They were completely in order, nothing out of place. As Dan reached up to peer at the contents of the top shelf he went on his tip toes to get a better look. As he did his feet slipped on a piece of loose carpet on the floor of the closet. He lost his balance and fell on his ass right next to the nun.

"Shit! Oh sorry, Sister."

"Dan, are you okay?"

"Just bruised a little in my pride." Dan stood up to look at what made him fall. He reached into the closet and removed the piece of loose carpet. As he did he saw the floor safe. He looked back at the nun and she nodded in agreement. The numbers were a combination, the combination to this safe.

Dan had long known how combinations worked. He asked the nun to read the numbers to him again. She read as he turned the dial, six to the right, fifteen to the left, seventy-five to the right. He turned the dial and the safe released its lock and opened for him. Dan opened the door and reached into the floor safe. He pulled out a large plastic bag and reached around for anything else. The safe was empty other than a bag. Dan handed the bag to the nun and stood up. She walked over to the bed and threw the bag onto the brocade spread.

"The mystery gets deeper," Dan said.

"Open it, Dan."

Dan opened the plastic bag and emptied its contents onto the bed. There was a manilla envelope, some photos, and a small ring box. Dan looked at the photos. The same picture he had found in Wysocki's room was in the pile. He held the photo up and saw that the faces of Wysocki, Danner, Mary Kate Riley, and one other man had Xs drawn through them. He showed the picture to the nun. "I guess we can add at least one more X to this."

Tears were beginning to well up in the nun's eyes. "Oh, Dan, what can this mean?"

"It means he knew a lot more than he was letting on, and that this photo is now a key piece of evidence."

He looked through the other photos, there was nothing very telling about them. Photos of himself at his ordination and his elevation to Archbishop. A picture of him and the Pope and a few pictures of a family taken many years ago. The manilla folder was the next item to be opened. It contained several letters addressed to the Archbishop, a copy of the one that was addressed to Fr. Wysocki and a copy of the one that was addressed to Fr. Danner. There was also a letter addressed to a Father Carmichael. Dan knew the name for some reason but could not place it.

"Who is Father Carmichael?"

"You mean who was Father Carmichael. He was the vicar for priests, killed years ago in a tragic car accident."

"That's where I know the name, the Archbishop had told me about him last week." Dan reached down for the photo. "Is he the unidentified man with the X through his face?"

She took the photo and looked at it again. "I'm not positive, I of course haven't seen Carmichael in years. But, yes, I think it might be him."

Dan looked at the letter addressed to Carmichael. It was similar in nature to the others, a slight threat, but nothing very telling. Then he looked at the letter addressed directly to the Archbishop himself. It was typewritten, sloppy in its style on very old paper. It read...

WE LOOK FORWARD, WE LOOK BACK. WE ARE SORRY FOR OUR SILENCE. OR ARE WE? WHAT ARE WE SORRY FOR? FOR NOTHING! FOR NOTHING!

Dan put the notes back in the folder. He then grabbed the small ring box and opened it. Inside, perched in the little ring slot was a small silver medal. The words NEVER TRUMP faced Dan as he stared at the box. "I would say that we definitely had a club going on here."

The nun grabbed the box and looked at it. "I don't understand."

"Neither do I, completely. But I know someone who will."

CHAPTER 20

*D*an headed back to the station to put more pieces of the puzzle together. He had to evaluate again what he had, and just as importantly what he did not have. He went to his desk and checked his voice mail for messages. There was one from his nemesis Bartly telling him that he was looking into the parish life of Father Danner. Dan was not pleased, Bartly was once again trying to squeeze his way into a high profile case. The next message was from Maggie confirming their dinner plans. The last message was from his young partner Raferty. Dan had sent Raferty to do the investigation in Father Danner's rooms at the rectory, he told Raferty what to look for and to bag any evidence he found. Raferty informed Dan that he found some of the things that he was looking for and that he would be in the station that afternoon.

Dan laid out everything that he had. The files on the priests, the photos of the men and women at the seminary, the hearts, the letters he found in the Archbishop's room, and the calendars from Wysocki and the Archbishop. Dan stared at the pile of evidence. In reality there was not much there. Some letters, some photos, two silver medals. He knew they all connected and that they would add up to something, but if all the key players kept dying, he would have nothing. Dan knew that the key was in the people in the photo. Of the eleven pictured he was sure of the identity of five and possibly six if one of the men turned out to be the brother of Mary Kate Riley.

Dan started to take notes, trying to make the connection when Raferty walked up to his desk. He was holding an evidence bag. "Got some of the stuff you were looking for." Raferty said.

"Let's see what you came up with."

Raferty dumped the contents of the clear plastic folder on the desk. "Five letters from parishioners I guess. One a copy of the one you got from his file and another one similar in nature. He also had the same photo that you found at Wysocki's, but no silver medal.. I looked all over the place, in jewelry drawers, in closets, desk drawers, everywhere I could think to look."

"It'll turn up if he had one. They all seem to have 'em."

"All?"

"We found one in the Archbishop's room and I'm pretty sure I saw one hanging on the chest of a certain funeral director." Dan pointed to the picture and picked out Shannon Wallace. "It seems that Miss Wallace was also a part of the gang in those days."

"Wow, well what do you know!"

Dan looked at the letters that Raferty had brought back with him. Raferty pointed to the letters and said, "For the most part these are just run of the mill letters, but there's one here that's very similar to the other threats."

Dan picked up the letter that stood out with a pair of tweezers he had on the desk. "I'll send this down to forensics and see what they can get off it, but its doubtful." Dan placed the letter in its own plastic bag. Dan laid the bag on the desk and read the type written letter.

> ITS ALL COMING TO A CLOSE MY FRIEND. OUR SINS FOLLOW US DON'T THEY? WE DON'T LOOK BACK ENOUGH. THAT'S THE PROBLEM ISN'T IT?

"What the hell are these letters all about? These guys really have an enemy." Raferty said.

"Obviously, Raferty, the murders would tend to indicate that."

"I mean they must have done something pretty bad to get threats like this."

"I agree, I mean what they hell did they do? Tease a guy? Take someone through a bad hazing? Do you think they did things like that in the seminary?"

"My cousin was in the seminary a few years ago, some of those guys were crazy. They had some sort of ritual to 'welcome' new guys. Nothing sanctioned by the faculty, but kinda like hazing nonetheless."

"That's interesting, why don't you give him a call and see exactly what happened. Is he a priest?"

"No he left his third year. Just wasn't for him."

Dan looked through the other things that Raferty had brought in, careful not to contaminate anything. "His photo of the gang is so worn. Like he was holding it in his hands a lot."

"That's what I thought too, all dog eared and stained. He must have spilt some coffee or coke on it or something."

"Yeah well I'll send it down to forensics with the stuff I found at the Archbishop's. I don't expect to find much."

Raferty helped Dan to put the evidence back in the bags and then set his butt on the edge of the desk. "By the way, your friend Bartly was at the rectory."

"I know, the asshole called to tell me. Was he in Danner's room?"

"No, he wanted to, I could tell, but I heard that the Captain told him only to interview people, not to touch any evidence."

"That's good. The farther we can keep that fat head away from evidence the better. I wouldn't put it past him to write a letter of his own and slip it in somewhere. But I will say that if he gets anything out of the rectory staff, he better share it. I'll remind the Captain just whose case this is."

The police station was filled with its ususal busyness. Phones were ringing and people were yelling over cubicles to one another. Dan heard names being called but didn't pay much attention until he hear his. He looked up from the desk and saw the mail boy pushing his cart through the narrow spaces between the desks and cubicles. "Gill, you got some mail today." The mail boy plopped some letters and a small package on the desk.

"Thanks" Dan quickly looked through the mail, nothing looked very pressing. He moved the letters aside and picked up the small brown package tightly bound with tape. "Well, just what I was hoping to get a little package from nowhere to brighten my day." Dan picked up the package, there was no return address but the post mark indicated that it came from the central post office downtown.

Dan reached into his desk drawer and pulled out a metal letter opener. He slid the opener around the edges of the package, slicing the tape open. As the paper came away from the package he could see that it was a small white cardboard box like you would get in a curio shop or a card store. He placed the package down on the desk and inserted the letter opener under the top of the box so that he could open it.

Raferty looked at him wide eyed. "What the hell are you doing?"

"What's the problem?"

"You can't open an unmarked box in here, what if it's a bomb?"

"Raferty, I know the rules, but this is way too small to have a bomb in it. If you feel more comfortable, why don't you just stand over there by Bartly's desk, I'm sure there are a couple of packages of potato chips you can hide behind."

"Fine, I will smart ass." Raferty moved across the narrow aisle over to Bartly's desk.

Dan continued to pry the lid of the cardboard box with the letter opener. The top came off and landed on the desk. No explosion. Dan peered into the box, there was a small package inside wrapped in tissue paper. Dan debated in his mind if he should unwrap the paper or call in forensics. The curiosity of the detective was stronger than his willingness to follow the rules and he carefully unwrapped the tissue.

He looked more intently at the box, the tissue giving way to the letter opener he was using. In the box, under the tissue was a severed thumb, there was no sign of blood on the thumb or in the box. "Shit!" Dan yelled.

"What is it, what is it?" Raferty asked.

"It's a frickin' thumb!"

Raferty rushed over to the desk and looked in the box. "Holy shit, who the hell would send you that?"

"My guess is our murderer. And, without using too much brain power here, I would say that this is the missing thumb from Father Danner." Dan reached for the tweezers still on the desk and gently lifted the thumb from the box. "Not a trace of blood, a very neat killer I guess."

As Dan held up the thumb he looked back into the little box, there was a small glint of silver at the bottom. He told Raferty to hold the thumb as Dan tipped the box over with the letter opener. Onto the desk tumbled a little silver medal with the words NEVER TRUMP engraved on it. "I told you it would show up."

"Ya, good for us, can you uh, take this damn thumb please?"

Dan took the tweezers back from Raferty and carefully placed the thumb back in the box. He then lifted the medal with the tweezers and placed it in an evidence bag sitting on his desk. "The boys in forensics are going to be busy tonight."

Dan reached into his desk and wiped his hands on a hanky that he kept there. He reached for the phone and rang the extension of the Captain. The Captain gave a gruff hello and listened while Dan explained what had happened. Dan heard the phone click down and waited for the Captain to round the corner from his office.

"Dammit Gill, why the hell did you open that, what if it was a bomb?" The Captain asked.

"Look at the size of the box Captain, it wasn't going to hold a bomb," Dan said. "Besides, it came to me, it was addressed to me, I had every right to open it."

Your rights don't really interest me at the moment Gill. Did you touch it with your hands at all?"

Just the outside brown paper, I never touched the box, but I can guarantee you that you won't find any prints, this guy is too smart for that. He wanted me to have this, to know that he knows I'm on the trail. It's not all that unusual for psychopaths to want to play cat and mouse with the police."

"I'm well aware of that Detective. But this is the first time this nut has made any attempt to make contact."

"At least contact with us," Dan said.

"What do you mean?"

"I mean he has contacted his victims before, the letters we found in Wysocki and Danner's files, there are more."

The Captain looked over the letters that Dan found at the Archbishop's and the one that Raferty found at Father Danner's rectory. "Get these down to forensics right now."

"It's next of my agenda boss," Dan said.

The Captain walked away from Dan and shouted over his shoulder as he moved down the hall. "And keep this under your hat!"

Dan gave a mock salute to the Captain and gathered all the evidence including the thumb and the medal into a pile on his desk. He carefully put everything into evidence bags and instructed Raferty to take everything over to the forensics department for further study.

"Why me, why don't you go?" Raferty asked.

"Because I have some serious investigating to do and I can't do that if my time is wasted running this stuff all the way over to forensics."

Raferty begrudgingly took the pile of evidence and headed for forensics. "Raferty do this, Raferty do that, I'm more than a gopher you know!"

"Yes, Raferty I know, please take this stuff down there for me. I would really appreciate the help"

Dan sat down at his desk. The thumb had actually unnerved him but he didn't want to let onto Raferty. He pulled the phonebook from his bottom drawer and looked up the phone number for Shannon Wallace's funeral parlor. He dialed the number and waited for someone to answer. He asked to speak to Shannon and was placed on hold.

"Shannon Wallace, how may I assist you?"

"Ms. Wallace, this is Detective Dan Gill, we met at the Archbishop's funeral the other day."

"Yes, of course Detective, I remember."

"Ms. Wallace, I really need to see you to ask you some questions."

"Concerning what?"

"Concerning the death of two priests."

"I didn't do those funerals Detective."

"I'm aware of that Ms. Wallace, but I believe that you knew those two priests pretty well." There was a pause on the other end of the phone. "Ms. Wallace, are you there?"

More silence. "Yes, I'm here Detective. I used to know them, and I am not speaking of them in the past tense because they are dead, I mean that I used to know them many years ago, before they were priests."

Dan took out his notebook incase he needed to take any notes. "I have come across some evidence Ms. Wallace that indicted just that. I just need to talk to you about how close you were to them and also to the Archbishop."

"I already told you that my father was very close to the Archbishop. He was almost like an uncle to my family, a kindly man who was always willing to give of himself."

"Can I ask how you knew Father Wysocki and Father Danner?"

"Mary Riley's brother was in the seminary the same time they were. They knew him and they knew her. They were also friends of the Archbishop when he taught at the seminary."

"Yes, I know that, too. But how close were you to them?"

Another pause on the other end. "We were casual friends, I would see them when they would visit the neighborhood, sometimes they would come with the Archbishop when he had mass here, I may have met them at the Riley's too. Detective what does this have to do with anything?"

Dan purposefully did not answer her question. "Were you ever in a club with them?"

"A club?"

"A social club or anything like that?"

"No, Detective, I was not in a club with them, they were in the seminary, girls couldn't be in that club."

"Yes, I realize that, but this would have been a club away from the seminary, perhaps just a group of friends who hung out together, not something organized."

"Look, Detective Gill, I was not in any kind of club with those guys. Yes, I knew them, I may have eaten dinner with them, but that was the extent of it."

"Yes, I see, well nonetheless I would like to still come by and see you, I have something I want to show you that you might be able to help me with."

"The picture?"

Dan fell silent this time. "Yes, the picture"

"It was nothing, I went with Mary to visit her brother, I had never been at the seminary before so I thought it would be interesting. Someone took a picture of a group that had gathered around us. Some of them were friends of her brother some of them just guys who wanted their picture taken with some girls. It was no big deal."

"But it was a big enough deal for you to know that the picture was still around."

"Well you see, it was, uh, kind of a joke with the Archbishop and my family. He would refer to picture over the years, telling me that I was the reason some of those boys did not become priests. It was not true of course, but it was a little joke. I know that the Archbishop kept the picture on his desk."

"On his desk?"

"Well the last time I visited him at the mansion it was on his desk, he even joked about it and told me I was the ultimate femme fatale, stealing good men away. It was all just a big joke."

"I really need to see you Ms. Wallace, I need you to look at this photo for me."

"Fine, when do you want to meet?"

"How about today?"

"No, that would be impossible. I can meet you tomorrow afternoon, you can come to the funeral home."

"Well, if that's the soonest you could meet me."

"Yes, I am not free until then, should we say 4:00?"

"That's fine , I look forward to seeing you then."

"It's a waste of time, that stupid photo has no meaning, none whatsoever." She hung up the phone.

Dan hung up the receiver and looked at his copy of the photo that he still had on his desk. "She's lying. She is definitely lying."

CHAPTER 21

❀

$\mathcal{I}$t had been a long day and Dan could not wait to get home and spend a little quality time with Maggie. This case was keeping them from spending enough time with one another. Dan drove to his cozy neighborhood, put the car in the garage and went into the house. He always loved this house. He spent countless hours trimming the lawn, tending to the flowers, making sure the garage was painted and the brick was cleaned. It was the showplace of the block and he liked it that way. Someday he and Maggie would get married and spend their retirement years nestled cozily in their dream house.

Dan walked in the back door and threw his keys on the kitchen counter. Maggie was standing at the stove stirring her world famous marinara sauce. The girl was Irish, but she could cook as well as any Italian in the city. Dan took in a deep breath and the aroma of stewing tomatoes, garlic, and basil filled his nostrils. It was the best of feelings, to be with someone you loved in your own home, sharing the basics of life.

Maggie turned when she heard the keys hit the counter. "Spaghetti marinara, garlic bread, Caesar salad, just waiting for you to get home."

Dan walked up to Maggie and gave her a kiss. "You're the best. Been thinking about this all day long."

"You've been thinking about dead priests all day long."

"True, but the sight of you and the smell of that sauce has driven that right out of my mind." Dan walked to the kitchen cabinet and pulled down two plates and two wine glasses. He set the table and pulled a bottle of good red wine from the rack in the corner of the kitchen. "How about a Mondavi 1998?"

"Sounds good, you pour and I'll be ready to dish up her in about five minutes."

Dan poured the wine and lit two candles that were already on the table. He sat in his usual chair as Maggie brought over the platter of spaghetti and the bowl of sauce. The garlic bread was piping hot and the salad crisp and picture perfect. "This is a wonderful end to a really crappy day," he said.

She sat down in her chair and began to dish the spaghetti onto her plate. "What happened?"

"After we eat, I don't want to talk about it now." Dan piled spaghetti on his plate and covered it in the wonderful sauce. "It's just a lot of evidence that is pointing to nowhere."

"You searched the mansion today, didn't you?"

"Yeah, and I found some stuff, but I don't know what it all means."

"Well, lets eat, do the dishes, make a fire and talk about it. You know it helps when you verbalize the case."

Dan ate heartily. The entire meal was perfect in its simplicity. They clinked glasses and drank their wine. After dinner Maggie brought out a beautiful tiramisu that she had made that morning before work. The lady fingers were perfectly moist and drenched in just the right amount of cognac and espresso, a recipe that she had learned years before. They cleared the table, did the dishes and put everything in its proper place. Dan went to the family room and lit a fire.

By the time he finished lighting the fire Maggie was sitting on the couch. Dan came over and sat next to her, drawing her close to him. "This is the best sweetie," he said.

She nuzzled up to him feeling his arms around her shoulders. "It sure is."

They spent an hour just watching the fire and being close to one another. Dan knew that they should get married. In his mind he always told himself that they would get married after his kids were out of college, or after the house was paid for, or after he retired from the force. There was always some imaginary deadline in his head. But tonight he knew that they should get married, that they should spend the rest of their lives together. Dan got up to stoke the fire and add another log.

"So what happened today?"

He got the fire roaring again and returned to the couch. He sat next to Maggie and put his arm around her shoulder, putting his feet on the coffee table. "Well, it was the first day in my career when someone sent me a body part in the mail."

"What?" She sat upright.

"The murderer sent me a thumb in the mail. I'm sure it's the thumb of Fr. Danner."

"Dan, that scares me, that means he knows that you are working on the case."

"Well its no secret Maggie that I have the case, at least he didn't send it here."

"Do you think he knows where you live?"

"Well our addresses and phone numbers are kept private from the general public, but it wouldn't take too much to find me. But don't worry, he's not after me, he wants me to know."

"Wants you to know what?"

"He wants me to know that he is a serial killer. He has a plan and he wants me to figure it out."

"So that he can get caught?"

Dan stretched out his arm. "No, I don't think so, I think he likes to play with the police, taunt us a little. He likes the publicity, likes seeing the murders in the paper. I'm pretty convinced that it's some kind of vendetta. I bet it's killing him that we haven't publicized that the Archbishop was poisoned." Dan had told her about the coroner's report the day before.

"Seems like the connection between the victims is stronger than ever."

"More than you know. I found a picture of 'the gang' in the Archbishop's room identical to the one we found in Wysocki's. Raferty also found one in Danner's room. But the Archbishop's picture had X's through the faces of everyone who was killed, or at least everyone who was dead."

"What do you mean?"

"There was one guy in the photo who had an X through his face who isn't one of our current victims. His name was Carmichael, he was a big mucky-muck with diocese, a vicar for priests. He was killed a few years ago in a car accident. Driving drunk, which was ironic since it was his job to get treatment for drunk priests."

"Do you think he was a victim of the same guy?"

"I don't know, it happened years ago and it wasn't the same kind of murder, the others were all killed directly and with violence."

"Except for the Archbishop. I mean he was poisoned, that's not too violent."

"No, but according to the coroner poison is almost always detectable, he wanted us to know that the Archbishop was killed. Killing someone in a car accident doesn't fit the profile of a serial killer."

"But it was years ago, maybe he was warming up for bigger events."

"I suppose that's possible. But how do you kill someone in a single car accident?"

"I don't know, you have to figure that one out." She nuzzled back close to Dan.

"The key to this thing is in identifying the people in that photo. I know who six of them are, Wysocki, Danner, the Archbishop, this Carmichael guy, Mary Riley, and Shannon Wallace."

"Shannon Wallace?"

"The funeral director. Remember I told you I thought I saw a silver medal around her neck at the funeral. I talked to her today and she claims that she wouldn't really know everyone in the photo, but I don't believe her. I have a meeting with her tomorrow at four to show her the picture."

"She remembers the photo?"

"Quite well, actually she brought it up before I did. I guess there was a little running joke between her and the Archbishop about it. She said that he kept it on his desk, but I found it in a floor safe in his closet. Maybe he had moved it there after the murders started."

"Well you said there were X marks through the faces of the dead people, I don't think he would have kept that on his desk."

"I guess that would look a little odd. He didn't have a lot of people upstairs, but yeah, how would you explain that to someone?"

"You know, Dan, I was thinking about how these guys were all killed. Don't you think it's odd that they were all doing their jobs when they were taken out?"

"How do you mean?" he asked.

"Well, Wysocki was hearing confessions and his brain was poked through his ear. Danner was on a sick call, and his thumb is cut off. The Archbishop is saying mass and he is poisoned, probably by the communion he received. They were all doing their priestly work. Maybe you can even stretch the point a bit and say that this other guy, Carmichael, was doing his work too. He was counseling alcoholic priests when he is killed in an alcohol related car accident. Sounds to me like your killer is sending a message."

Dan sat upright on the couch. "Wow, that's right, they were all doing priestly things. This guy has something against them in their priesthood. What could they have all done that would link them together as priests? This makes me even more convinced that this is a vendetta and that the picture links them all together. I hope that tomorrow Ms. Wallace will give me some insight as to who these other people are in the photo. If we can't catch this guy for what he has done, then maybe we can stop him from doing more."

"I would think that the other guys in this photo would start to be worried about that themselves. I mean I would think that maybe one of them would come to the police to tell you he was afraid for his life."

"Maybe they haven't made the connection, or maybe whatever they did was so bad that it precludes them from coming forward. Raferty told me that his cousin was in the seminary and the there was a fair amount of hazing that went on when you were new. I thought that maybe they took it too far and really scarred a guy somehow, either physically or emotionally. I mean, young men can be pretty vicious to one another. If they hazed someone who was already leaning towards being a psychopath, then who knows what could happen?"

"But why now, why wait all these years. You said the photo was taken almost thirty years ago, that's a long time to wait to get even."

"It sure is, but I don't understand the mind of all killers. Maybe revenge is sweeter when it is administered slowly. But I also think that the killer was blackmailing these guys."

"Why do you think that?"

"I found monthly checks in Wysocki's room that were made out to cash. Every month like clockwork. I also found the same entry in the Archbishop's checkbook. Why were they making out checks to cash for the exact same amount each month?"

"So this guy may have been making them pay to shut him up. He truly must have a criminal mind."

Dan stood up and walked over to the fireplace to stoke the fire. All these connections running through his head. He certainly had his work cut out for him. It was like a big puzzle, you know what the picture is supposed to look like, but when pieces were missing you couldn't really tell what the real picture was. Instead of concentrating on the pieces he had, Dan knew that it was time to concentrate on the pieces that were missing. He knew that Shannon Wallace would know more of the people in the picture. He knew that Jerry Riley, the brother of the dead girl had to be in that photo, after all he was the host that day at the seminary. If he could find out who the people were in the photo and find Jerry Riley then two more pieces of the puzzle would be in place.

Dan was sure that he would have to do some serious investigating of Jerry Riley, get a hold of his criminal record, get photos and do a computer search of the name around the country. He was hoping that he could find him in Chicago, but there was no guarantee of that. For all he knew the guy could be dead, another victim of the killer.

"Dan, I was just thinking about that photo," Maggie said. "Who took it? I mean wouldn't there have to be another person involved here?"

"I never thought of that. You don't think about the photographer when you look at a photo. I suppose there could be another person, or maybe a self timer on the camera, they certainly had the technology for that back in 1972. But now that you mention it, Shannon Wallace said that it was an impromptu picture, more like someone was walking around with a camera and wanted a group shot."

"Well, I don't mean to give you more to look for, but it does seem like someone actually took it then. Maybe this Wallace woman can give you some insight, she might remember who took it."

"It will be one of my first questions to her in the morning." Dan walked up to her and gave her a kiss. "You know I think you should be working as my partner. Raferty is so young and doesn't ask the right questions. No one can think things out like you."

As Dan was kissing Maggie the phone rang. "Crap," he said. Dan ran up to the kitchen to answer the phone. "Yeah, what is it?"

It was Raferty on the other end. "Dan, I was working late in the office and a call came in that you might be interested in."

"Raferty, burning the midnight oil, that a boy, what is it?"

"You know that Shannon Wallace, the funeral director?"

"Yeah,"

"She's dead."

Dan was in a state of shock. "What the hell happened?"

Raferty cleared his throat. "Well there was break in at the funeral home, she apparently caught the guy red handed and tried to stop him. She was shot."

"Shit, oh man, this is not good. Are you sure it was break in, I mean she may just be another victim of our friend."

"I talked to the uniforms who went there, they said there was forced entry, things were really a mess, they thought maybe he was looking for drugs or money."

"Drugs, at a funeral parlor?"

"They said it's not unusual for some undertakers to have sedatives on the premises, guess it's kind of an under the table thing when someone whacks out, they can offer them something to calm their nerves. But most of these places have alarms, theirs was shut off."

"So he shot her huh, they think he got away with anything?"

"They don't know yet, have to take some inventory. They'll never admit to there being drugs there anyway, but I'm sure if there is cash missing they'll let us know."

"You can't believe the wrench this throws into the mix, Raferty."

"I know, you said were going to meet her tomorrow, I think she was a key witness."

"Definitely, and it may be the killer who did her in, although this doesn't fit his M.O., he likes to kill people while they're working. He doesn't shoot people during a robbery."

"Oh, one last thing, I don't know if it matters, but she was pretty beat up too."

"He smacked her around before killing her?"

"I don't know if they'll be able to tell, she was not only shot, but she was crushed pretty badly under one of the steel caskets. They said it looked like it was dropped on her from about three feet, probably after he shot her, but we'll have to wait and see."

Dan told Raferty he would meet him at the office in morning and hung up the phone.

"Crushed with a casket, not your usual occupational hazzard." Dan went back down to the family room and cuddled up with Maggie for the night.

CHAPTER 22

*D*an started out on the hour drive north to the major seminary. The sprawling campus had been built in the late 1920's, just before the depression hit. It was an opulent place in its day, the first seminary in the country to have an indoor swimming pool and a golf course. The Cardinal that built the seminary wanted his men to have the best and to be able to mingle with the finest people of Chicago once they were ordained. The seminary sat on three hundred acres of prime forested land that had been donated to the diocese earlier in the decade. It had its own lake and its own power plant. It was a completely self sufficient operation. Popular rumor was that this was to become the preeminent Catholic University in America, but when the depression hit in 1929 all those dreams were shelved. By the time World War II broke out there was a general distaste for the seminary by the local people and zoning laws were created to cease any further expansion on the part of the seminary. When the seminarians registered for the draft in 1941 they all registered in the town where the seminary was located rather than going home. Since they were all exempt from serving in the armed forces this virtually guaranteed that all the young men of the town would be drafted, which is exactly what happened.

Dan pulled into the massive iron gates of the seminary and proceeded to the administration building. The campus had certainly lost some of its opulence from the first part of the century, but it was impressive nonetheless. The buildings were showing their age but they were still massive in their structure and it illustrated a time when the Archdiocese held true power. As Dan came to the administration building and parked his car he noticed the engraving on top of the massive stone structure, "Faith, Honor, Duty". It looked more like a military slogan than one for a seminary. Dan walked through the large doors of the building and proceeded to the long mahogany counter.

"I'm here to see the rector."

The secretary looked up from her position at the phones. "Your name?"

"Detective Dan Gill, I have an appointment."

The secretary looked down at a calendar beneath the counter and then lifted the phone to call the rector. Dan noticed that there were pictures of ordination classes hanging in the hallway across from the reception area. They went back several years, but not to the 1970's. Each year the faces in the class photos were less and less. The most modern year revealed that there were only eight men ordained to the priesthood for Chicago. He remembered the days in the 1950's when the numbers were closer to fifty.

The secretary looked back up at Dan. "You can go down the hall to his office, it's marked on the door."

Dan thanked her and walked down the hall. He found the office and gently knocked. He was beckoned to enter and he opened the door. "Good morning Father Sheahan, I'm Detective Dan Gill."

The rector extended his hand to the detective. He was about 45 years old, very thin and pale as though he rarely saw the sunlight. His hair was grey and he wore a very conservative sweater vest over his clerical collar. "Good to meet you Detective, please come in and have a seat."

Dan sat on a long couch in the rector's office. "Thanks for taking the time to see me Father, I am in great need of your assistance in identifying some people from a photo that I have." Dan took the photo out of his manilla folder at handed it to the priest. "From what we know this photo was taken in 1972, since the men are all dressed in cassocks I assume that they are all seminarians."

The rector took the picture and looked it over. His smile immediately faded as he realized that he did recognize several of the men in the photo and that they were all dead. Dan could see the little color that the priest had draining out of his face. "Oh my, Detective, you of course know that some of these men are dead in this photo."

"Yes, Father, that's one of the reasons that I am here, I am trying to make a connection between at least two of them, Father Danner and Father Wysocki. When I spoke to you on the phone last week you had mentioned that they were friends with the Archbishop when he was Dean of Formations, so it's not really a surprise that he is with them. I also know that Father Carmichael is among the men here and that he too is dead."

Yes, well that's what shocked me, I mean four of the eight in this photo are dead, and one had at least some criminal history. This dark haired young man here, this is Jerry Riley, you had asked me about him last week."

Finally a real connection. Jerry Riley was in the photo after all, although it didn't come as a surprise to Dan, he certainly expected to find Riley in the photo with his sister. "Did you tell me that you knew Jerry Riley?"

The priest looked up at Dan. "No, not really, just by reputation. He was arrested after he left the seminary and word traveled pretty fast about that. I understand that he never made it to trial, I mean I heard he skipped his bail. He certainly has not made any contact with the seminary since I have been rector."

"How long has that been Father?"

"Five years. Not that I would expect him to make contact with us, I mean we do keep a database of former students both ordained and lay for fund raising purposes, but we have no current address on Riley, I looked after your call last week."

Dan glanced down at the photo that was still in the hands of the priest. "How about the other three guys, do yo know who they are?"

The priest looked down again and studied the three remaining faces. "Not off the top of my head, I didn't enter here as a student myself until 1974, so if they were upperclassmen I would not have really known them, and they could have been gone by the time I got here. But we do keep photos of every class when they come here in September, we could certainly look at those and try to figure out who they are."

"I would really appreciate that, I think that some of their lives may depend on it."

"Do you think the two priests were killed because they knew each other? I mean we were told they were random killings."

"We don't really know what to think, Father. It could well be that they were killed for some vendetta. I do know that they're not the only ones who are dead in this photo. Two of the women that you see here are also dead. Mary Riley and Shannon Wallace, the tall blonde over here." Dan pointed at the image of Shannon Wallace.

"Oh my God!" exclaimed the priest. "We really do need to find these other guys then!"

The priest stood up and walked over to the phone on his desk. He informed the secretary that he was going down to the basement of the building to go through some archives and that he was not to be disturbed. He then invited Dan to follow him out of the office and down the stairs to the dark basement where the records were kept.

"We have records here that go back all the way to 1880, before this campus was even built. They haven't been kept in the best order, but we should have little trouble finding things from the 70's."

Dan followed the priest into a room marked Archives & Records. The smell of dust and slight mold filled his nostrils. Apparently no one had taken the time to seal the files or to put them on microfiche.

Dan knew that it was an expensive process and one that the Archdiocese was not necessarily willing to pay for. "You mentioned that there were class photos taken every year?"

"Yes, we still do it today, gives the faculty a sense of who is who. Back in the 1950's and 1960's the faculty needed those sheets because we were taking in an average of one hundred twenty five students a year. There was no way to quickly learn who everyone was without a scorecard. Today we average about 20 guys per class, so it's a lot easier to identify everyone." The priest flipped on a light switch and began to walk around the large archive room. He worked his way past row after row of file cabinets and ran his finger up and down the drawers until he found one marked 1970-1974. He opened the drawer and flipped through the files until he found 1972. He pulled out a large file folder and walked back to Dan. "If these guys were here in 1972 we should have photos of them."

Dan was anxious to look through the folder but he realized that he was a guest and that he did not have a subpoena. The priest walked past Dan and laid the folder on a metal table at the far end of the room. Dan followed him and watched the priest rifle through the contents.

"Here we go, the master sheet of photos of all the students that were here in 1972. It looks like there were about 350 or so guys here that year."

Dan set his own photo on the table and began to look for matching faces. The first he came across was Carmichael. The photos were arranged alphabetically. The second he spied was that of Danner. As he looked at the photos there were a few that stood out, but without knowing the men himself it was tough to make positive identifications. They all seemed to have the same short haircut, the same cassocks, the same look in their eyes, like deer caught in the headlights. As he scanned through he saw one that was a definite match. The photo read Bradley Fiore, Class of 1974. That made him a classmate of Jerry Riley. The photos were marked with the intended year of ordination. The man in the class photo was definitely one of the men in the photo that Dan had found. He looked to be about 23 years old, red hair, cut short with very intense eyes and thick dark eyebrows. There was no mistaking that this was a match. Dan took the notebook out of his suit coat and wrote down the name. "Was this guy ordained?"

Father Sheahan looked at the photo and the name. "It certainly doesn't ring a bell, but we can check on the ordination class of 1974 photo to double check." The priest again rifled though the filing cabinet and pulled out the photo of the Class of 1974. There was no listing or photo for Bradley Fiore.

Dan continued to scan the photos, now he knew how it felt for crime victims to have to look through countless pages of mug shots. After about an hour of carefully looking at the photos and narrowing his search down to about ten guys he felt that he found the other two men in his photo. Their names were Anthony Martin and Francis Goetz. The rector looked up their respective ordination photos and informed Dan that Goetz had indeed been ordained in 1972 and that Martin appears to have left right before ordination since he was slated to be ordained that same year. So now Dan had at least a little more information. Two had not been ordained and one had. Dan felt that his priority was to locate Goetz right away since he was probably in the most danger.

As they walked back upstairs Dan asked the priest if he knew where Goetz was stationed. The priest informed him that he did not, but that the diocesan directory would hold that information. They went back into the Rector's office and looked up Goetz's name. He was stationed at Our Lady of Christians parish on the west side of the city. Dan jotted down the phone number and the address of the parish next to the information that had put in earlier. He then inquired if the database would have a current address on the other two men. The priest went to his computer and after about ten minutes came up with their phone numbers and addresses. Dan wrote down all the information and thanked the priest for his help. He got into his car and started his drive back to the city.

Dan called from his car phone into the precinct and checked his messages. He had sent Raferty to the funeral home of Shannon Wallace to see if there were any new developments in her case. Raferty had left a message saying that it looked like a typical robbery, but that the doors showed no sign of forced entry and that there was only a little petty cash missing from one of the desk drawers. Nothing earth shaking.

As Dan continued his drive into the city he picked up his phone again and decided to call Father Goetz at Our Lady of Christians parish. The phone rang five times before someone answered.

"Our Lady of Christians, Nuestra Senora de Cristianos" the heavily accented voice answered.

"Hello, I was wondering if Father Goetz was available?"

"I can check, please hold on."

Dan waited patiently on hold when a deep voice came back to him. "This is Father Goetz, can I help you?"

"Father, this is Detective Dan Gill with the Chicago Police, I was wondering if I could talk to you for a few minutes."

There was stark silence on the other end of the phone. "Um, of course Detective, what can I do for you, is this in regards to the recent break in?"

"No, I'm afraid not, I really didn't know there was a break in, I'm with homicide, and I have some questions regarding the deaths of Fathers Danner and Wysocki."

Again the silence on the other end was noticeable. "Well, uh, certainly, how can I help you?"

"I think that it would be better if we talked in person, are you by any chance free in the next hour?"

"Well, that could be difficult, I have a meeting that I really should attend. But if you think its important I can cancel it."

Dan had on his official police voice. "Yes, I think it is very important, and the sooner the better."

"Then, by all means come over, do you know where the parish is at?"

"Yes, I have the address. I'm on my way back from the seminary now, I should be to your place in no more than an hour."

"From the seminary? What were you doing there?" Goetz was nervous in his questioning.

"Just doing a little investigating. Actually that's where I got your name and address. I'm hoping that you can help me put some things together. I have lots of puzzle pieces, but a lot are still missing. By the way, do you mind if I ask about your break in?"

"Not at all, but I thought you said that you were homicide."

"I am, but it just interests me, that's all."

"Well, it was late last week. Someone forced their way into the rectory at night. I was on my day off so no one was here at the time. The creep went through all my personal stuff, took some loose cash and a couple of pieces of jewelry. Nothing to make a big deal out of, but when the cook came in the next day she insisted on calling the police to file a report. Personally I would have let it go, it's not like he's going to be caught."

"He went though your room, through your personal items?"

"Well, quite honestly my personal stuff would be the only things of any value. We don't have a lot of money here and there's not much else to steal."

"Did he take any personal items that would be considered worthless to a common criminal?" Dan asked.

"I haven't really noticed to tell you the truth, my room was pretty well ransacked, I'm just now getting it back together. He definitely took money from my desk, a watch, two chains and a pair of cufflinks. But I haven't noticed anything else missing. Except, now that I think about it…"

"Yes?"

"I seem to be missing a photo album or two. Although that doesn't make any sense. I didn't even think about it until you mentioned it. They were sitting on my bookshelf and I notice that they are missing now."

"An album with recent photos?" Again the silence on the other end of the phone was almost eerie. "Father, are you still there?"

"Ah, yes, I'm sorry, um, no not recent photos, photos from many years ago, family photos, pictures of my early days in the priesthood, and from my seminary days."

"Listen to me Father and listen to me well. I do not, under any circumstances want you to leave the rectory. Stay where you are, don't even go into the church, just stay in your room, I will be there as fast as I can."

"Detective, you are quite frankly scaring me, am I under some kind of suspicion here for something?"

"Not at all, I just don't want to add your name to a growing list I have on my desk at the office."

"And what list would that be?" Goetz asked.

"A list of people found dead because they all knew each other." Dan hung up the phone and put his mars light on top of his car trying to make it back to the city as fast as possible. He reached for his phone again and tried to call Raferty so that he could tell him where he was going. There was no answer at his desk, and when the voice mail picked up he hit 0 to be connected to the main desk. He told the Desk Sargent to be sure to leave a message on Raferty's desk, since he was not very good at picking up his voice mail. The Sargent told Dan he would do it right away. Dan looked at his watch, he knew if he sped things up that he could make it back to the city in no time at all.

CHAPTER 23

*D*an arrived at Our Lady of Christians in thirty-five minutes. The mars light helped him to hit speeds of ninety miles an hour with no problem As he pulled up to the church he noticed that the neighborhood was run down, unkempt, and poor. There was a mixture of blacks and Hispanics on the block, people going about their business. There was a line at the side door of the rectory where food was being distributed by volunteers. Dan walked up to the door of the rectory and rang the bell.

The door opened and a young Hispanic woman answered the door. "Can I help you?" She looked Dan over from head to toe, his sport coat definitely out of place in this neighborhood.

Dan removed his badge from his coat pocket and flipped it open for her to see. "Detective Gill, Chicago Police Department, I'm here to see Father Goetz."

She opened the door wide and motioned for him to enter. She took him to an office just past the entrance and asked him to be seated while she called Father Goetz. Dan took a seat and looked around the small office. It had not been painted in years and there were slices in the old worn carpet on the floor. The furniture was old and nicked, there was absolutely nothing modern in the office including the old dial phone on the desk. Dan could hear the muffled voices of the secretary and what he assumed was Father Goetz talking in the main office. The door to the office opened and Father Goetz entered the room.

The priest was in his mid fifties, the same age as Wysocki. It seemed that time had not been as kind to Father Goetz as it had been to his classmate. His balding head was covered in freckles or age spots and little flakes of dandruff could be seen clearly on his black clerical shirt. He was average height but overweight. Dan figured that he tipped the scales at about three fifty. The priest waddled in and extended his hand to Dan. "I'm Father Goetz Detective, I must say you have me quite worried."

"I didn't mean to scare you, but I did mean to put you on guard."

"I don't really feel threatened Detective, I mean I know there have been two priests killed, but I hardly think that you are visiting all the priests of the diocese to tell them to be careful."

"No, but I am visiting all the people that I can find who were close to Wysocki and Danner and the Archbishop for that matter."

The fat priest sat in a chair across from Dan." I wasn't particularly close to the Archbishop."

Dan took out his notebook and pen and began to write down what the priest was saying. "At least not in recent years?"

"Is that a question, Detective? It sounds like you've already made some assumptions."

Dan looked the priest in the eye. He decided he was going to play his hand a little more direct than usual. "You were close to him when he taught in the seminary, you were in a bridge club with him."

The priest stood up and opened the door to the office. "This isn't the place to talk about that Detective. Follow me to a more private place." The priest left the office and Dan followed him up a flight of stairs to the priest's room. The priest unlocked the door and motioned for Dan to have a seat on one of the chairs close to a window. The priest was still standing when Dan sat down. He paced back and forth in front of the set of chairs. "I really didn't want to talk about this in front of the secretary."

"What's that, the fact that you used to play bridge with the Archbishop, there's nothing wrong with that."

"I understand that, but I'm concerned about the murders, the entire staff has been on edge and I have assured them that there is no possible connection between me and the two dead priests. I don't need them walking on needles and pins around here, this neighborhood is scary enough to come to everyday without having to worry about a murderer."

"So you do feel threatened?" Dan asked.

"Not so much threatened, just a little on edge. I mean I did know those two guys quite well in the seminary. I've been running it over and over again in my mind, I mean what was the connection between the two of them? The only thing I could think of was the bridge club in seminary, but that was so long ago, I don't even know if they still saw each other. I know that I didn't see very much of them if I didn't have to."

Dan took copious notes. "Why is that?"

"We just drifted apart, that's all. After seminary we all went our own ways, the only thing we had in common was the bridge games and it was impossible to keep those going with our individual schedules. I don't know if they kept the games going or not. Once the Archbishop was reassigned I doubt that they kept meeting, he was the glue of the games. They may have started the games again after he returned, but I'm not sure. I know that I was never invited."

"Do you remember who was a part of the bridge club?"

The priest looked into Dan's eyes. "That was a long time ago Detective, I honestly hadn't even thought about the club until Wysocki and Danner were killed. Not only that, but there were new guys in and out all the time, new first year students would replace guys who were ordained or left the seminary. In my four years at the place there may have been as many as twenty-five different guys involved."

Dan reached into the manilla folder and pulled out his copy of the notorious photo. "Do you recognize this picture?"

The priest took the photo and looked it over. He nodded his head as he ran his finger over the faces on the page. "Yes, I recognize it, I haven't seen it in years, but I know that we each got a copy. It would have been the year of our ordination, 1972."

Dan took the photo back and held it so that the priest could still see the faces. "Do you remember this guy in particular?" Dan pointed to the picture of Jerry Riley.

"Jerry Riley, yeah I remember him. His sister overdosed that year and he lost it after that, went crazy and committed some crime after her death. The last I heard he was in jail."

"Well, not really, he skipped his bail, never went to trial. You didn't hear about that?"

"No, I don't keep up with gossip, sorry."

Dan put the photo back into the manilla folder and set it on the ground next to him. He noticed that the priest's eyes followed his motion, still looking at the folder when Dan spoke. "Tell me about 'never trump'.

"Never trump? I'm not sure what you mean."

"Come on Father, I can only help you if you help me. I know that each of you received a medal that said 'never trump' on it. I assume it was part of being in the club."

The priest's face flushed red. He never thought that anyone would ever bring that up again. "It was just a charm, something we wore when we played or laid on the table during a game, kind of a good luck charm."

Dan leaned back a little in his chair. "I thought the church frowned on talismans. Sound a little superstitious to me."

"It was more than a good luck charm, it was a…I don't know how to put it, like a merit badge for a boy scout. If you were lucky enough to get invited to be a part of the bridge club, then you got a medal. We were young guys, ritual was important to us then."

"Why 'never trump' what does that mean?"

"That was the idea of the Archbishop, it was kind of a code that bound us together. In bridge the idea is to get the trump card out, but when you do that you make your partner the 'dummy', that's just the name he's given, it doesn't mean anything. But the Archbishop thought that it was a cute kind of secret code, you know, never make anyone in the club the dummy. Like the musketeers, we were supposed to be one for all and all for one."

"I hope I'm not being too presumptuous but that sounds a little like mind control."

"It was mind control. Sometimes the club was all you thought about, it was somewhat secretive and definitely elite. We often felt that we were better than other people in the seminary, we looked down on those who were not smart enough to learn bridge. We really weren't a very nice group sometimes. That's one reason I was glad to get away from it at ordination. I just wanted to get on with my life."

"Would you say that there were others who resented your group?"

The priest nodded his head. "Definitely. We were talked about and somewhat despised because we got together with the Dean of Formations and often got to miss seminary events just to play cards. But they could never really say anything too loud. I mean if it got back to the Dean that you were slamming his boys, then there'd be hell to pay."

"Did anyone hate you guys enough to want you dead?"

The priest was shocked at the question, his jowls jiggled and sweat ran down his forehead. "No, we never hurt anyone, not really hurt them. I mean there was an exclusivity, but that was it. Do you think these are revenge killings?"

Dan put his pencil and his notebook in his pocket. He wanted to use his hands for dramatic effect. "Listen Father Goetz, I don't know what to think. Deep down I believe that all the people in that photo know something and one by one they are all dying. Now you inform me about this club, that's the first time anyone has even admitted to it. You tell me you guys were exclusive, and sometimes not too kind. I look at that photo and realize that at least six people in there are dead and one is a fugitive from the law. You tell me what to think, I'm at a loss."

The sweat was pouring down the face of the priest, his nose was running and Dan thought that he might cry. "I don't know what to tell you. Yes, we were at times hated by other students. We often played jokes and got away with it because we were special. It wasn't fair, but that's the way it was. But we never really hurt anyone, not physically. We were just a bunch of guys who played cards and got away with a few pranks."

"A bunch of guys? What about the girls?"

The priest was wiping his face with a handkerchief he found in his pants pocket. "The girls were friends or sisters of guys in the group. They came up on some weekends to visit, the seminary had just introduced visiting days in 1970. They watched us play cards on the weekends, but they didn't play, they certainly never got involved in any of our little pranks around campus."

Dan leaned into the priest. "So you cannot think of one single person who would want these women dead? Or for that matter the priests?"

"No, I'm telling you everything I know. Why would someone want to kill all those guys, it makes no sense. I...I can't tell you any-more, because I don't know anymore."

Dan stood up from the chair. "Do you still have your 'never trump' medal?"

The priest looked at Dan and continued to wipe his brow. "No, I tossed it away years ago, it was a reminder of someone I didn't want to be anymore."

"An elitist?"

"Yes, and not a very nice guy. It was me that I buried back in 1972. I swore then that I would never be like that again."

Dan walked around the room and glanced at the priest's desk by the opposite window of the chairs. He had enough time to glance down before the priest could get himself out of his chair. "Well I'm glad to hear that you've changed. Wouldn't want to be an elitist now I suppose, could get in the way of your ministry. Funny, though, I would not have called the Archbishop an elitist, I knew him for several years, seemed pretty down to earth to me."

"Maybe he opted to change too, once he stopped teaching he didn't really have access to that club mentality. I would agree that he was a very nice man, and a good leader."

Dan continued to look down at the desk, he scanned it quickly hoping to find something that would help him. As he looked he knew that he had to keep the conversation going. "So would you like to tell me about the break in last week?"

"Like I told you on the phone, it was no big deal. Some personal stuff taken, you can see that we don't have much here to steal. I think that whoever did it was disappointed when they got in so took my personal things just to piss me off."

Dan now walked around to the back of the desk. "Did they take anything off of here? It looks pretty orderly to me."

"Yes, they did, but I straightened the desk back up, I had work to do."

Dan scanned the desk, but nothing seemed to out of the ordinary until the water mark at the corner caught his eye. It was an outline from a time when water had been spilled on the desk and not immediately wiped up. You could see the outline of a large paperclip, a circle that looked like a coffee mug, a letter opener and a circle the size of the other medals.. Dan knew that the priest may have gotten rid of his 'never trump' medal, but that it didn't happen in 1972. "Father how long have you been here at this parish?"

"Ten years."

"Ever have a break in before?"

"Yes, a few times, but word is out on the street that this place doesn't have anything, and we try to be good to the poor, giving them food and clothes everyday."

"Yes, I saw that when I came in, quite commendable. Listen Father, you have been quite helpful, at least now I know there was a club and what the medal was all about. I do though wish that you would be careful and keep a low profile for the next few days, or until we can catch this guy. You have to admit that it seems more than a coincidence that people in that photo are dying at an astounding rate."

"I appreciate that Detective. But I have to go on with my life, I can't stay here in the rectory and not get any work done. I'm here alone, I have to say mass and administer other sacraments. But I can stay kind of low, I have desk work to do and my schedule is relatively free the next few days."

"I understand, but just to be safe, I'm going to call for a special car to keep watch outside your rectory for the next few days in addition to the one making rounds daily. Someone will be here tonight at the latest. Thanks for your help, I think I can see my way out."

Dan headed back down the stairs and out the front door. As he entered his car he looked up and saw the priest looking out the window, just peering behind the worn curtains. Dan started his car and pulled away from the rectory intending to head back to the station and make arrangement for a car to be stationed outside the rectory later that day.

The priest watched as Dan pulled away. He sat at his desk and picked up the phone receiver. He dialed a number and waited for someone to answer. "Hello, he was just here."

"What did you tell him?" asked the voice on the other end.

"Not too much, he wanted to know about the bridge club, he already knew I was a member, I don't know how, but he knew."

"Of course he knew, he has seen the picture and he was at the seminary this morning, it was only a matter of time before he put those pieces together."

"But he knew everything I told him. Do you think he suspects anything? I mean he really looked at me with intense eyes."

"It's mostly a bluff, he doesn't really know very much. Besides by the time he figures it all out, it will all be over."

The priest began to sweat nervously. "I think I want out of this, I mean I did what you asked, I put the poison in the chalice. What more can I do, I mean I think my debt is paid. All I ask now is to be left alone."

"What else did he say to you?"

"Nothing much, just that he was going to put a police car in front of the rectory later this afternoon, to watch over me."

"Senseless isn't it? I mean we both know that you aren't in any danger."

"Yeah, well regardless, I don't want anything else to do with this, I mean it, my debt should be cleared, you've gotten enough out of me."

"I agree my friend," said the voice. "Just relax, go about your normal day, you won't be hearing from me again. Unless of course you have double crossed me."

"I swear to you, I didn't tell him anything that he didn't already know!" The priest was emphatic.

"Alright then, your part is over. Just keep your mouth shut, I suggest that you take a couple of days off, get out of the rectory, relax a little."

"Easier said than done. But maybe you're right, I should get out a little. I can cancel a few things and get away, that would do me good."

"Of course, now that you have been such a good helper you can take it easy, I promise that you won't hear from me again."

The priest hung up the phone and reached into his desk drawer for a cigarette. He had quit smoking about twenty times, but always returned to them in times of high stress. He had smoked about sixteen packs in the last two weeks. He lit his cigarette and sat back in his chair he spun the chair around and looked out the window, pulling the drapes back again, wondering when the police car would arrive. It was the last thought he had when the bullet broke through the window and lodged directly in his forehead, killing him instantly.

CHAPTER 24

※

*D*an turned on the scanner in his car and listened to the police calls that were coming over the airwaves. He heard the usual calls for domestic violence and drug busts. He wasn't really listening too closely when he thought he heard the name Our Lady of Christians mentioned. He turned up the volume and listened again. The dispatcher had definitely said that an immediately response was needed at the address that he had left only ten minutes before. Dan put the mars light back on his roof and sped toward the rectory. When he arrived he saw that the ambulance and the police car were already there. He pulled up to the curb and jumped out of his car. He pulled his badge from his pocket and ran toward the rectory. When he arrived at the door he was stopped by a uniformed police officer.

"Dan Gill, homicide, what the hell happened here?"

The uniform glanced at the badge. "That was fast, you guys usually aren't here for a while. Guy was shot on the second floor, I guess it was one of the priests."

Dan pushed past him and ran up the stairs to the priest's room. He entered the room and saw the dead priest sitting in the chair, the bullet hole prominently displayed between his eyes. Dan glanced over and saw that the bullet had come in through the window. It must have been a very precise weapon, it was very neat and to the point. No other glass was broken and there were no other bullet holes in the priest.

Dan reached into his pocket and put on rubber gloves so that he wouldn't contaminate the scene, although he knew there wasn't going to be much evidence in the room. Dan walked over to the window and looked out. There were no buildings directly across the street, just a vacant lot. He looked down to the street and realized that it would be an easy shot to make if the victim was directly in front of the window.

As Dan looked around the room he heard voices behind him. The police photographer was entering the room, camera in hand, ready to take pictures of the dead priest. The photographer turned on his flash and started taking photos. Dan asked him to also take a picture of the window and the view to the street below. As he looked around the room he realized that there were more and more people entering the crime scene. He turned around and saw Bartly standing in the doorway.

"Well, well, look who's here. You certainly have a propensity for dead clergy Gill," Bartly said.

"Bartly, hope those stairs didn't do you in big boy. I'm amazed at how fast you got here."

"Well, I was in the hood when I heard the call, thought maybe I could actually beat you to the punch on this one."

"Well, I was in the neighborhood too," Dan said. "As a matter of fact, I was just here interviewing this priest in connection to the other murders."

"What? You thought this guy was connected?"

"I did, and now I know it. Unfortunately, I was too stupid to stop his murder. But that isn't going to happen again. I'm going to catch this guy and put a stop to this."

"Good luck, Gill. You haven't exactly been successful so far."

"Listen Bartly, I know you wish you had this case, I mean you could be in the paper everyday, but you don't have it, I have it. So why don't you just get the hell out of here and let me handle this."

"Didn't know that you were assigned to this case, Gill. Maybe I should call the Captain and let him know I'm here so he can relax, I don't think he's exactly pleased with your progress so far. Hell, at this rate we oughtta have about fifty dead priests by Christmas."

"Screw you, Bartly. Go ahead, call the Captain, let him tell you who is in charge here."

As Dan and Bartly were fighting it out Raferty walked into the room. "Boys, boys, boys, let's just stop this arguing huh? It's not going to help any one."

Dan looked over at Raferty and then glanced back at Bartly. "My partner's here, I think we can handle this, why don't you run along, I think there's a doughnut shop just down the block."

"You know Gill, one of these days you'll get yours. Always have a smart remark, always ready to put the other guy down. Damn, I hope that I'm not as insecure as you when things don't go my way. Bartly took a cigarette out of his pocket and lit it in front of Dan, blowing the smoke into Dan's face. Bartly motioned to his own partner that it was time to go and left the room.

Raferty reached into his own pocket and put on a pair of rubber gloves so that he could help Dan to investigate the room. "That fat shit always seems to show up at just the right time doesn't he?" Raferty asked.

"Yeah, well you can't get your name in papers if you don't show up. I'm sure he's outside right now waiting for the reporters to show up." Dan glanced out the window and saw Bartly and his partner standing on the front lawn of the rectory.

"What are we looking for Dan?"

Dan looked around the room and then over at the dead priest. "Probably not much Rafts, I mean it is pretty obvious how this guy was killed, but we're not much closer to knowing why about any of this. I was just here twenty minutes ago, talking to this guy about the bridge club. He was a little evasive but he did put some things into perspective for me." Dan explained to Raferty what he had learned from the priest.

"So, there really was a bridge club huh? It sounds like they did more than play bridge."

"Yeah, I was thinking about that, he said that they played pranks, but it didn't sound like they did anything crazy enough to merit murder as a payback. Did you talk to your cousin to ask him about the hazing that went on while he was in the seminary?"

"Yeah, I talked to him this morning. He said that it was nothing more than it would be at any other college. Some forced drinking, moving statues in the church, scaring guys in the cemetery, stuff like that. He said that it was harmless for the most part and that anyone that had it done to them always turned around and did it to the new guys the next year."

"Yeah, my feeling is that these guys in the club were a little more organized than that. This priest told me that they sometimes took it a step further, but didn't give me anything specific."

"Did you ask him who took the picture?"

"Shit, no, it completely left my mind. Dammit! I had the chance to link one more person, and I blew it."

"It's alright Dan, I'm not sure I would have even thought of it if you hadn't mentioned it yesterday. You never give much thought to who takes a picture, just who is in them."

Dan walked around the room, he didn't even know what to look for anymore. At best he might find some things to link him to the other priests, but it wouldn't be any new information. He knew how they were linked. He went back to the desk and looked again at the watermarks that were left. The medal had definitely left a mark. Dan ran his fingers over the mark, the desk was very dry, it hadn't been tended to for many years. There was no way for Dan to tell how long the mark had been there, although the forensics team might be of some help. Dan looked over the other items on the desk. He saw the priest's checkbook at the far end of the desk and picked it up. He flipped through the entries and saw that he too was making out a check every month to cash for $250.00.

He then scoured the desk for a calendar, there was none there, but he found it when he opened the desk drawer. He gently took the book from the drawer and opened it to that day. He saw that the priest did indeed have an appointment that day that he must have canceled when Dan called. It was with a Mr. Lopez. Dan could ask the secretary about that later. He flipped back a few weeks and noticed that every Thursday was marked off with an X, it was apparently his day off too, and Dan wondered if he was still playing bridge after all. He noticed that he had marked the funerals of the two murdered priests and the Archbishop on his calendar, so he must have attended all three masses. Other than that, there was very little of interest in the calendar.

Dan continued to look through the room, it was still a mess from the apparent robbery the week before, and Dan had no expectation of finding the famous photo. Dan was convinced that it was the murderer who had robbed the place and he was pretty sure that the murderer would have taken the photo. Near the chair where Dan had been sitting earlier was a large ottoman piled with books, Dan had noticed them earlier but didn't think much about it. He now looked at the books more closely.

The first book was the Archdiocesan Directory, the same one he had seen that morning in the rector's office. The next two were books on the sacraments, they looked like professional books meant to be read by priests or theology students. The next book was a self help book entitled "Letting Go: Making Peace With Your Past". Below that there was a book that definitely piqued Dan's interest. It was called "The Suicide Club". Dan moved the other books to the side and picked up the thin blue book. He began to flip through the pages and realized that it was a book about how to commit suicide.

Dan noticed that there were three chapters dedicated to methods of suicide; Painful, Painless, and Undetectable. It amazed Dan that a book like this would even be published, let alone that anyone would buy it. He flipped again through the pages and could see that the book had been read, there were several pages that were dog-eared. He flipped to each of those pages, wondering if they held a clue or if these just happen to be pages where the priest had stopped reading when he was bored.

The first dog-eared page was in the Painful chapter. The priest had marked the page that contained various ways to do yourself in with a certain degree of pain. Dan scanned the page with his eyes and noticed that self stabbing had been underlined in the book. Dan thought that it would be a pretty terrible way to do yourself in. He continued to flip pages and came across a section in the Painless Chapter concerning poisoning. The chapter was heavily underlined and gave specific doses of certain drugs to take when you wanted to do yourself in. The chapter had noted that poison was not a good idea if you wanted your suicide to look like something other than a suicide, because poison was always easily detectable. That certainly rang a bell for Dan, that was the same thing that the coroner had said when he read the autopsy of the Archbishop.

The third place that was marked was at the back of the book. It was a glossary of terms relating to suicide. Dan looked over the page and saw that there were several entries underlined. The first was for barbiturates. The book did not recommend this as a method of suicide because there was always a chance of survival if you were found in time. The second underlined entry was for strychnine. This method was not recommended because the poisoning would be painful and could actually take a long time to work if the right amount was not administered. As Dan turned the page he noticed that one of the entries had been underlined, but that it was later erased, he could still see the little reddish flakes of rubber on the page.

Dan looked at the entry, it was for hemlock. The blood rushed from his face as he read the entry. The book noted that hemlock was readily available in the United States if one knew what to look for. It also noted that it was quite easy to administer and although it was readily detectable in an autopsy, it did not attack the body in the same way as many conventional poisons. This form of suicide was recommended for those who were dying of cancer or another terminal disease and were under a doctor's care anyway. Dan could not believe his eyes. Could this priest have killed the Archbishop? Could he have even killed the other two priests? Was he somehow the one who had been hurt by the group?

Dan turned to Raferty. "Rafts, don't touch anything else. We have to tear this room apart after the body is gone. I want you to go downstairs and inform the secretary the parish is closed until further notice, not to take any calls and not to talk to the press. Then call the Captain and tell him to get a forensic team over here stat! We may finally get a break in this case."

Raferty left the room and did as Dan said. The Captain informed him that a forensic team would be there in twenty minutes at the most. Raferty didn't know what else to tell the Captain and Dan didn't seem to be offering much more. Raferty came back up to the priest's room and looked at Dan who still reading the thin blue book. "What did you find in that book Dan?"

"It's a book on how to commit suicide."

"That's sick," Raferty said.

"That's not really the worst of it, Rafts. I think that this book could be used to get ideas for murder too. I mean the methods in here could easily be transferred to another person, and that just may be the case here."

"What do you mean?"

"Look here, this entry under Hemlock, it was underlined and then erased. We know that the Archbishop was killed by coniine, which is byproduct of hemlock. It may just be a coincidence but I don't think so. I told you this guy was helpful while remaining elusive. He claimed to have no part of the bridge club after 1972, but you can clearly see the outline of his 'never trump' medal on his desk. He's only been here for 10 years, so he was still holding onto that medal long past 1972. He also has monthly checks made out to cash for the same amount that the other priests did. He was in this deep. Maybe he was the one they hurt, maybe he was the one seeking revenge."

"You mean, you think he killed all three of them?"

"I don't know, I think that he had something to do with the death of the Archbishop. He certainly had access to the chalice, the sacristan said there were priests in and out of there all morning."

"Wow, what do you know! I mean, he was fat, maybe they used to make fun of him for that or something."

"Well, we better all pray that people who are overweight don't decide to take revenge on everyone who ever made fun of them, our caseload will never end."

"It was just a thought. What do you think the forensic guys are going to find?"

"Honestly I don't know, but I'm hoping they find some residue of coniine in here. At least then we could trace him to one murder, and from that maybe the other two. I wish I knew if these guys were mean to him when he was in the seminary. I'm not saying teasing you know, but really cruel somehow. I'm going to have to get hold of the other two guys in the picture and see what they know. They're not priests, but they were there when the picture was taken."

Dan and Raferty turned when they heard a knocking on the jamb of the door. "Detective, I am so sorry that we must keep meeting under these circumstances." Dan met Sister Rayday's eyes as she entered the room.

"Sister, you're here already."

"Yes, the diocese was called by the secretary right after she called the police. She's a rather astute staff member. What the hell happened here?"

"Well, Sister, he was shot while sitting at his desk. The shot apparently came through the window, from someone who was a pretty good shot."

The nun looked at the dead priest and then turned away. "Can't he be covered up or something?"

They're just about to take his body out now. We had to get photos and some evidence before we could move him."

"Dan, how much more of this do we have to take? When are we going to find out what is happening. At this rate, I won't be able to get the priests to even say mass. This will terrify them."

"I agree, Sister, but I don't know what we can do. I think we are very hot on this guy's trail, but I think that he knows that. I was here this morning talking to Father Goetz. He was killed only ten minutes after I left."

"Why were you talking to him, was, he one of the men in the photo?"

"Yes, the only one left who was a priest. How well did you know him?"

"I didn't know him at all, that's probably why I didn't know who he was in the photo. I don't know every priest in the diocese."

"Yes, I realize that. But you also don't know anything about him, no file on hand that has nasty letters in it or anything?"

"I resent you tone, Detective. We don't keep nasty files on the priests. I have not however had a chance to look at his file. I rushed here as soon as I heard."

"Sorry about that Sister, I simply meant, that we will have to look at this file to see if there is anything in there that connects him to the other murders. By the way, even though you didn't know him, you have seen him before haven't you?"

"I suppose, at diocesan functions or at the cathedral, why do you ask?"

"Do you remember him at the funeral of Father Danner?"

"There were a lot of priests there Detective, I don't recall if he was among them."

Dan nodded at her in agreement. "I wouldn't necessarily expect you to remember, it was just a stab in the dark. But I suspect that he was there."

The nun excused herself and said that she was going to the kitchen to make a pot of tea. She offered to bring a cup of to Dan and to Raferty, who both declined her offer. They excused her just as the forensic team entered the room. Dan explained what he was looking for and they began their search of the room. One of the team members suggested that Dan be sure to have the Medical Examiner check the fingers of the dead priest, because there could be residue there. Dan took out his notebook and wrote the advice down. As the team began to look for clues, Dan and Raferty went downstairs to talk to the secretary.

They questioned her about the priest, about his habits his schedule. She said that she hadn't noticed anything unusual that last few weeks, except that the priest had gone to three funerals at other churches within a two week period. She noted that it was unusual for him. Dan knew what the there funerals were and did not push the issue.

Dan continued to question her. "Did you notice an unusually large number of calls to Father Goetz in the last two weeks?"

"No, nothing out of the ordinary, of course I'm only here until 4:00, he answered the phone himself in the evenings." She was visibly shaken by the events of the day.

"How about unusual visitors?"

"No, just the regular appointments. We don't get too many visitors in this neighborhood." Again she sniffled and blew her nose.

"So, in the last two or three weeks, there was nothing out of the ordinary?"

"No, nothing out of the ordinary. You know though he was gone for five days three weeks ago."

"No, I didn't know that. Where did he go?"

"You know, I'm not sure, he just called it a mini vacation. He liked to drive, to get out on the road, but I'll tell you I think he got off the road this time."

"Why do you say that?"

"His car was covered in mud when he got back, from the tires all the way up to the door handle, like he was driving through a mud trail. He said it was just rainy a couple of days. What a way to spend your last vacation."

"I'd like to see the car if possible."

"It's in the garage, but it's been cleaned since then. He took it in the next day and had it completely detailed, from head to toe."

Dan thanked her for her cooperation and told her that she could leave after the forensic team was done.

"I'm glad to help," she said. "I just hope you guys can find out who is doing this to our priests, this can't go on."

Dan extended his hand to her to offer comfort. "I agree, we are doing all we can do, and with help from citizens like you, I'm sure we will catch this guy. By the way, that was very smart of you to call the diocese after you called us. They needed to know as soon as possible."

"Im sorry?" she asked.

"Your call to the diocese, I was told that you called to tell them what had happened."

"It wasn't me, Detective, after I called the police it was all I could do to answer the door when they arrived. Maybe someone else called, maybe they heard it on the scanner, lots of people in this neighborhood listen so they can tell when the police are coming."

"I see, well, then thanks for helping us now. I may have to come back later in the week to ask you a few more questions."

Dan walked toward the kitchen to talk to the nun. She was sitting at the table drinking a cup of tea. "I thought you said the secretary called the diocese after she called the police."

The nun looked up from her steaming cup. "She did."

"She says that she didn't."

"Well someone called, I'm not psychic, I don't know when a priest is going to be killed!"

"Do they keep a log of incoming calls at the Pastoral Center?" Dan asked.

"I don't think so, I mean that's an expensive piece of equipment. I know that we do not have caller i.d., it's cost prohibitive."

"Well someone called you guys and it didn't come from here." Dan sat down with the nun and placed his head in his hands, exasperated at what was happening.

CHAPTER 25

The ride back to the station seemed like it took forever. Traffic was terrible and Dan contemplated using the mars light once last time for the day. But he never used the light unless there was a real emergency. Besides he knew that Bartly was back at the station by now and was bending the Captain's ear about the case. Dan wished that something else would happen in the city so that Bartly could get involved in another case, but other than the priest murders, the city was unusually quiet the past three weeks.

Dan came into the office and walked gingerly past the Captain's office. He was about six feet down the hall when he heard his name called. Dan spun on his heels and walked back to the office. He saw Bartly sitting in a chair in front of the Captain's desk, his hands linked behind his neck like he owned the place.

"You called me, Captain?" Dan asked.

The Captain motioned for Dan to come into the office and take a seat. "Wanted to talk to you about this case, please sit down and join us."

Dan glared over at Bartly. "I suppose you've already been filled in on our latest development."

"Yeah, Bartly told me what happened today. I'm sorry Dan, this really seems to be going down the toilet fast."

Bartly stretched his arms. "Well, what do you expect Captain? You put Gill in charge and the shit's gonna rise."

The Captain gave a stern look to Bartly. "That's enough of that, we're here to solve murders, not fight with one another. But Dan, you have to admit that we are losing ground on this one, I mean we have at least five murders in three weeks that are connected. The Archdiocese is going to be up in arms about this last one. I hear that the priests are planning a demonstration at the Daley Center later in the week, and they don't even know about the Archbishop."

Dan nodded in agreement. He knew that a planned demonstration, even if it wasn't aimed at the police, would be disastrous. The press would pick it up and run with it. The papers would be merciless to the department, they always were. "Well, I haven't heard anything from the press yet."

"Yeah, but that won't last, in fact, after this next killing hits the news, you can expect the phone to ring off the hook. I want you to handle this Dan, I want you to talk to them and assure them that these are isolated incidents. In their eyes we have three killings, they don't know about this Wallace woman or about the Archbishop, let's keep it this way until we catch this nut."

"So you think that Shannon Wallace was killed by the same guy?" Dan asked.

"I do, I know the M.O. doesn't exactly match, but she was connected, you've shown me that much, she must have known something that was about to be revealed."

"There's more that I found out today, but I'd rather talk about it in private," Dan said.

"So what, I have to leave? Maybe I can be of some help here," Bartly boasted.

"Fine, stay, just try to be actually helpful for a change," Dan said.

Bartly sunk back in his chair, pouting like a child. "Don't worry Dan, I won't steal your thunder. Go ahead tell us what you found."

Dan cleared his throat more out of desperation than an need to get a hold of his voice. "Okay, for starters, this guy Goetz was definitely in the bridge club. He explained the 'never trump' thing to me, it was kind of a motto to keep them together, a sort of loyalty oath. But Goetz said that he left the group in 1972, right after ordination. However, I think that was a lie. I found a water mark on his desk in the outline of a circle, an exact fit of the medals we found on the other victims. He also was writing checks every month to cash for same amount as Wysocki and Danner."

The Captain interrupted. "So, he was basically another victim, just another pawn in this guy's game."

Dan nodded. "Maybe, but there's more. I found a book in his room about committing suicide, but I don't think he had that in mind. He folded over a couple of pages dealing with poisoning, and there was a definite mark, that was later erased under the section on hemlock. Hemlock is the plant that contains the coniine that killed the Archbishop. So either it is purely coincidental that he was researching coniine poisoning and that's what the Archbishop died from or...."

"Or, he was the one doing the killings and someone from one of the priest's families found out and did him in," said Bartly.

"I don't think so, I mean how would they have found that out. I do agree that he was probably the one to put the poison in the Archbishop's chalice. He was at the Danner funeral and he had access to the sacristy, but if you saw him you would know that he didn't have the physical strength to pull off the Danner murder, or even the Wysocki one for that matter. We know from the angle of the entry wound into Wysocki that the murderer was pretty tall and very strong. And Danner was brutalized, this guy could never have done that, he didn't have it in him. I can see using poison, it's a wimpy way to kill someone and hard to trace in this situation."

The Captain put his hands on his eyes and rubbed them. "So what's the theory here Dan?"

"I don't know. I'm hoping that the forensic guys are going to find some trace of coniine in Goetz's room. At least that way we'll know that part of the theory is right. But why would this guy kill the Archbishop? What was his motive? I can tell you that he didn't speak affectionately about the Archbishop. It struck me as strange that so soon after his death that he wasn't gushing over him like people tend to do. He said that the experience of the bridge club was not a good one, he was flustered when he spoke of it."

"So something happened in that club. Something that really pissed someone off," the Captain said.

"That's what I think. Something bad happened and someone wants to pay back the guilty parties. The notes we found in the priests' files certainly indicated that someone was unhappy with them. We haven't gotten a thing off those notes from forensics, but I didn't expect anything."

"So what's next?" asked the Captain.

"I have two more names to track down, neither of them priests. There is also another woman in the photo that I have no way of identifying and the person who took the photo."

Bartly jumped in. "What didn't you ask Goetz who took the picture, he would have known."

"I forgot to, I was so taken aback by the 'never trump' thing that it left my mind. I know I blew it."

"Well, at least you're consistent."

The Captain interrupted before anything could start. "It's okay Dan, it happens, at least you know who the other two guys are, maybe they can tell you who the other girl is and who took the picture."

"That's my hope. I'll get on it right away. Raferty and I will get out to see these two guys today if possible." Dan stood up and left the Captain's office and walked to his desk. Raferty was already there sitting on the edge of the desk. Dan acknowledged Raferty with a nod when he noticed that he was on a phone.

Dan sat at his desk and tried not to listen to Raferty's conversation but he couldn't help hear him make plans for the evening with his girlfriend. Dan tapped him on the shoulder and waved a finger at him and shook his head. Raferty informed his girlfriend that he would have to take a rain check, because he was going to be working tonight.

"Come on Dan, I haven't been with her in a week!"

"Easy there, stud, we have some work to do and if we get done early, you can be home by 9:00. That should give you plenty of time to go out for a little Chinese and a little nookie for dessert."

"Gee thanks, what a fun evening. I don't know how Maggie puts up with your schedule."

"Oh please you're worse than I am, you work extra hours all the time."

"I know, but I'm hoping that by the time I'm your age I learn to settle down a little and spend some time at home."

"Yeah yeah, that's what you say now. Listen, I want you to go down to records and see if you can find anything on these two guys." Dan handed him a copy of the names of the two men he had gotten from the seminary. "I'll try these numbers and see if they're still at these addresses, then we can make arrangements to see them tonight if possible."

"What am I looking for in records?" Raferty asked.

"Arrests, minor traffic scuffles, tickets, just the run of the mill stuff." Dan watched Raferty walk down the hall and then picked up the phone to dial the first number the one for Bradley Fiore. The phone rang but there was no answer and no answering machine. Dan swore under his breath, incredulous that people didn't have answering machines in this day and age.

He looked at the number for Anthony Martin and dialed it. This time there was an answer, a young woman or very young boy answered.

"Hello, can I please speak to Mr. Anthony Martin please?"

"Uh, wait…wait just a minute."

Dan could hear the young voice calling for mom in the background. The phone was then picked up by a woman who sounded like she was the mother of the house. "This is Lisa Martin, can I help you?"

"Mrs. Martin, my name is Detective Dan Gill, from the Chicago Police Department, I was hoping that I could speak to Mr Anthony Martin. Is this the right number?"

There was a brief pause on the other side of the line. "Uh, Detective my husband has been dead for a year. I would think that the police would have known that."

"I'm very sorry Mrs. Martin, I didn't know. Can I ask you what happened?"

"Look, Detective, I have been through this time and time again, if you're not calling to follow up on the investigation into his death, then what do you want?"

"Mrs. Martin, I assure you, I just didn't know that your husband was dead. I assume from our conversation that he was murdered."

Again silence on the other end, then a slight sniffle into the phone. "Yes, Detective, I believe you would call it murder. He was a salesman for a local janitorial supply company, he sold to a lot of schools, churches, small businesses and was all over the city everyday. He was robbed at gunpoint and shot as he was unloading his car with samples. They never found out who did it."

"Mrs. Martin, I cannot apologize enough. I had no idea."

"Then why are you calling?"

"I'm actually investigating several other murders and your husband's name came up. Actually it was a long shot of a connection, had to do with his days in the seminary."

"That was a long time ago Detective, are you still trying to solve murders from the 70's?"

"No, these are recent murders. But they involved some people that your husband would have known in the seminary. Is there a chance that you knew him then?"

"No we, didn't meet until twelve years ago. He came to the pre-school where I taught to sell us some supplies, it was love at first sight."

"I hate to continue to bother you, but you might be able to answer some questions for me."

"Go ahead, I'll help in anyway I can, at least one murder might be solved."

"That's my hope. Did your husband by any chance play bridge?"

"No, he hated the game, would never play it. Some of the neighbors had a club going when we first moved here. He was repulsed by it for some reason. In fact he had told me that his parents were big bridge players and that all they did was fight during the game and he wanted nothing to do with it."

"Were you aware that he was in a bridge club when he was in the seminary?"

"Impossible!"

"No, I think my sources on this are pretty on target, he was definitely among an elite group that played bridge at least once a week. I take it he never mentioned it to you."

No, never. He never talked about the seminary and I never asked him about it, I think it was a painful time in his life."

"When you husband died…"

"When he was killed," she interjected.

"Yes, when he was killed, did you by any chance have an opportunity to go through his personal things and sort out stuff?"

"It's been a year Detective, that has all been done many months ago."

"Well, did you by any chance come across a small silver medal with an engraved medal that could be worn on a chain, or as a charm?"

There was silence on the line. "How did you know that?"

"I'm sorry Mrs. Martin, I can't really say, but it can tell you that it was a symbol of the bridge club from the seminary. Anyone who was in the club had one of these medals."

"I'm telling you that's impossible, he hated the game. He would never have played it."

"Or maybe he just stopped playing it."

"I suppose, he never talked about those seminary days."

"One last question if I might. Did you husband have a propensity to write monthly checks out to cash, maybe for $250.00 or an amount near that."

"Detective, you're scaring me. I think you did call here to look into my husband's murder, I think you know something and your not telling me what it is!" She was now crying and screaming on the other end.

"Mrs. Martin, I honestly did not know that you husband had been killed, but I promise you I will look into his case. Can I assume from your reaction that he did write checks to cash every month?"

"Yes, but I never knew about it when we were married. I mean I didn't even know that he had a separate account until he was killed. I took care of all the money, so when I found his secret account it took me by surprise. For months after his death I let myself think that maybe he was having an affair, that maybe he had a child somewhere that he was supporting. I never knew what to think and I still don't know."

"Well, I don't know either Mrs. Martin, but I'll do my best to find out for you. Did he by any chance have friends who were priests?"

"Definitely not, he left the Church when he left the seminary. That much I know. He wanted nothing to do with it anymore. We weren't even married in a church, we had a ceremony at City Hall in front of a judge. I don't know what happened to him in the seminary, but it was something that completely turned him off from church."

"I see, well thank you for you help and again I am very sorry if I upset you in anyway. I want to assure you that your husband's case file is going on my desk as soon as I hang up. I'll look into this and if I find out anything, I'll let you know."

"Thank you Detective, I appreciate that." She hung up the phone and cried uncontrollably into her hands.

Dan hung up and knew that the next thing he had to do was get a hold of the file on Anthony Martin. He looked at his watch. Raferty had only been gone a few minutes, not nearly enough time for him to find any information and get back to the desk. Dan looked at his desk and found the Rolodex card he kept taped to the corner with frequent numbers written on it. He looked for Raferty's pager number and quickly dialed and left him a text message to either call him or get up there right away.

Dan's phone rang in the next minute, it was Raferty. "What's up Dan?"

"I need you to pull a file and an active case for Anthony Martin."

"I was running the other guys name through the computer down here first, but nothing has come up yet. You want me to stop that search?"

"Yeah, I need the hard copy file on this Martin guy, he was killed a year ago and it hasn't been solved."

"Okay, will do, I should be back up there in ten minutes at the most."

Dan hung up the phone and again tried to call the number he had for Bradley Fiore. Again there was no answer. He slammed down the phone in frustration. He knew in his heart that there was a connection between the Martin murder and the other killings, but how would he prove it? A murder that happened a year ago was almost impossible to solve, Dan knew that if you hit the ninety day mark that the chances of solving a crime dropped to about five percent.

As Dan was looking over the files on his desk Raferty came up to him with a folder in his hand. "Here's the file on the Martin murder."

Dan took the file and began to read through it. The report was made by another Detective who Dan did not know. The detective summarized that the killing was a simple robbery, the victim had been shot and his wallet was missing. There were no witnesses and Dan knew the area where the murder took place. He also knew that no witnesses would come forward at this late date. The contents of the trunk were left behind, but that wasn't unusual, who wanted janitorial supply samples? But what was shocking to Dan was the coroner's report. The gun wound was direct and to the head. There was only one shot and it was not done at close range. Ballistic tests were done on the bullet but there was no match on file for other crimes.

"Look at this Rafts, it says here that the killer was not in close range when the murder was committed. He took a pot shot at the guy from at least across the street. Kind of bold for that neighborhood and certainly not in character for your usual perp. This guy was killed first and robbed later. For all we know the gunman might not have even been the one who took the wallet."

"What do you mean, his wallet was missing."

"Yeah, but we've seen this before, a guy gets killed in a drive by or something and someone else comes by and takes the wallet and then makes an anonymous call to the cops. It says in the report that the call came in from a pay phone down the street from the scene. No one in the neighborhood came forward to say they saw anything."

"So this guy wasn't robbed?"

"I don't think robbery was the motive. I think he was assassinated, just like our friend Father Goetz. And if I were a betting man, I would bet that the gun used on Martin was the same gun used on Goetz. Call forensics and tell them to rush that test, I want to know if we have a match here."

CHAPTER 26

*D*an knew that Raferty would not have much luck getting forensics to hurry the ballistics test so he called the Captain and told
him about the latest development. The Captain assured him that he
would do everything in his power to get the test moved along. With
that done Dan took to calling the Fiore residence again. He was worried that he was the next target for the murderer and it caused him
great anxiety that there was no answer at the number that he had. He
dialed about four times when it dawned on him that he could use the
automatic call back feature on the phones to allow the dialing to be
done for him. He set up the call and hung up his phone, he could
wait until the phone gave a special ring indicating that his call had
finally been answered. This was the one time that Dan thought modern technology was wonderful.

He looked again at the report on Anthony Martin. There wasn't
much there. The department had labeled it a robbery/homicide and
pretty much had closed the case. It wasn't that the department was
lax in its investigation, it was just that there were hundreds of cases
like this in the files. There wasn't much chance of solving this one.
Dan had his own share of cases just like this one. They were frustrating, but there was very little that could be done, with no witnesses,
and no other evidence to hold onto.

As Dan poured over the file his phone rang, at first he thought his call had finally gone through but it wasn't the special ring designed to indicate automatic call back. "Gill here."

"Dan, this is Sister Rayday."

"Hello Sister, how can I help you?"

"I just left a meeting with the members of the cabinet. They are of course quite upset about the latest developments. They want to hold a press conference, there's a lot of pressure from the newspapers and the television stations to come up with some answers. We thought it would be best if someone from the police were with us, we want to give the appearance that we are all working together on this."

"Well, we are all working together on this aren't we?"

She cleared her throat. "Of course we are Dan, but you know as well as I do that the media hounds are going to try and put a wedge between us, they see this as the third killing in as many weeks and they're chomping at the bit for a story. I also think the people of the Archdiocese are at their wits end. The phones have not stopped ringing here all afternoon."

"Yes, I understand, do you want me to be the representative from the police?"

"Of course, no one knows the situation better than you. I think you know even more than we do."

Dan sighed into the phone, he knew she was right. "I think we know about the same amount of information Sister. By the way, did you pull the file on Father Goetz?"

"Yes, I did, there was nothing unusual in there. He also had a tough assignment, but nothing out of the ordinary in his file."

"No letters?"

"No, nothing, just his academic records, and a notation about a six week trip he took to a weight clinic in Maryland about three years ago."

"That's surprising, it didn't seem to work.. I might still turn up something in his room when we do the final search."

"How's your search of the other people in the photo coming?"

"Fifty fifty. I know the identity of all the men, as far as I know there is only one still living, one of the laymen was killed last year in a robbery."

The nun gasped on the other end. "Killed? Do you think it was the same guy?"

Dan didn't want to play his hand at this point, no sense in panicking anyone else. "No, I doubt it Sister, I think it was a simple robbery. He wasn't a priest, so I don't think he would have been a target."

"I see, so we are limiting our investigation to just clergy."

"Seems logical at this point doesn't it?"

"Well, uh, certainly, like you said, as far as we know it's only priests that we can link to this maniac."

"What time is the press conference?"

"Tomorrow at 10:00 A.M. sharp at the Pastoral Center, sixth floor, same place we met last time."

"Okay Sister, I'll be there." Dan hung up the phone and waited for it to ring with his automatic call back. An hour passed, and there was still no call. Dan was getting frustrated and he paged Raferty again to tell him they were going to take a ride out to the house of Bradley Fiore.

Raferty showed up at Dan's desk, ready to go to see Bradley Fiore. He told Dan that there were no files on Fiore, he was never arrested, never even got a speeding ticket. His record was clear. Dan took the address off his desk and headed down to the parking lot to get his car.

As they drove along the expressway Dan realized that the whole day had gone by without a word from Maggie. He felt bad that this case was getting the best of him and that he had been ignoring her too much over that last three weeks. He picked up his cell phone and dialed her number. There was no answer at her house. He hoped that she was at his house and dialed that number. The answering machine picked up and after the message played Dan told her to pick up if she was there.

"Hi, I'm here, where are you?"

"On the road. I have to check up on one last lead before the night is over."

"So I should eat without you I suppose."

"Are you cooking?"

"No, I knew somehow that if you didn't commit to me this morning that you weren't going to be home for dinner. I think I'll just run to KFC or something and grab a bucket of chicken."

"Sounds good. Save some for me, ok? Listen, Maggie, I'm really sorry that this case has sucked up so much of my time that last three weeks." Dan really was sorry, he was a sensitive guy even if he didn't show it all the time.

"I know, Dan. This is your job, its not like you do this all the time, you're a good cop, that's one of the reasons that I love you so much."

"I love you too. And hey, by the way, I think you should, go to your house and eat that chicken, I'm not sure my place is the safest right now."

"Why, what's up?"

"This guys isn't stable, I don't know how close he thinks I am to solving this, but every time I get close someone dies. Just lock the house up and take your chicken home. I'll stop by your place when we're done here."

"Okay, if that's what you want. Call me when your on your way, then I can watch for you."

"It's a deal, love you."

"Me too," she said.

Dan closed the phone and looked at Raferty who was making eyes at Dan and puckering his lips like a teenage girl. "Shut the hell up, asshole."

"What? I didn't say a word. Wish I had someone as good as Maggie in my life."

"What about the girl your seeing now?"

"Not nearly as understanding as Maggie, that's for sure. Told me today that if I missed dinner tonight, not to bother about breakfast."

"She breaking it off with you?"

"No, just not gonna give me any for a while. She really knows how to punish me."

They drove the rest of the way to the Fiore house in silence, both of them thinking about the case and wondering where the final piece of the puzzle was. Dan turned off the expressway and pulled into the posh neighborhood where Fiore lived. The neighborhood was one of the newer ones in Chicago, that is to say it was built in the late 50's and had been a white stronghold ever since. It was completely different that the neighborhood that they had been to earlier in the day. There were no Blacks or Hispanics here, just young and middle aged white people, tending to their lawns and watching their kids play in the parkways. At first glance you would think that you were in a suburb rather than in an urban setting.

Dan looked down at the address that he had written down earlier. He found the house that belonged to Bradley Fiore and pulled into the driveway. This was one of the few neighborhoods in the city where every house had a driveway. The house was dark, except for one light in the front window. There were no cars in the driveway and the grass was getting a little long. Dan and Raferty got out of the car and walked to the front door. It was a modified Chicago Bungalow, not unlike Dan's house, but wider and with a more modern look to it.

They rang the doorbell, but there was no answer. Dan could hear the phone ringing in through the door and he figured that it was his office still calling. He had forgotten to take the automatic call back feature off before he left. Raferty walked around to the back and looked through the back door. There was no sign of life. As Raferty was walking to the front, Dan was walking to the back and they met on the side of the house, in an area that Chicagoans had traditionally called the gang way.

"Looks like no one is here," Raferty said.

"Yeah, but given the circumstances, we might have probable cause to break in."

"I don't know Dan, maybe we should check with the neighbors first."

"Well, of course we'll check with the neighbors first Rafts, I'm not stupid."

As Dan and Raferty turned to go back to the front of the house they were confronted by a large man with a rake in his hand. He held the rake high in his hand and yelled at the two policemen. "What the hell do you two thugs think you're doing?" he asked.

"Uh, take it easy mister, we're cops." Dan reached into his jacket to get his badge. "Here, look, here's my badge."

The man took the badge out of Dan's hand, the first time that had happened in all his years on the force. He looked it over and gave it back to Dan. "How about you, let me see yours," he said to Raferty.

Raferty reached to his belt and pulled his badge up for the man to examine. "Here you go, just like his, I'm a police officer too."

"Well, what the hell you pokin' around here for? Scared the hell out of my wife." The man pointed to the house next door. "Sends me out here with a rake to scare you two off."

Dan and Raferty both replaced their badges. Dan extended his hand to the man, hoping that would calm the man down. "We're looking for a Mr. Bradley Fiore, is this his house?"

"Yeah, this is where Brad lives. But he ain't home."

"Yes, we can see that, do you know where he is?" Raferty asked.

"Yep, sure do," said the man.

"Well, would you like to tell us?" asked Dan.

"I don't know, is Brad in some kind of trouble?"

Dan knew the ploy of a nosey neighbor a mile away. Maybe the man was genuinely concerned for Fiore, but he was just as likely trying to get information out of Dan so that he could gossip at the horseshoe pits later that night. "No, Mr. Fiore is not in any kind of trouble, actually we were hoping that he could help us in an investigation we were doing."

The neighbor looked Dan over again and squinted his eyes. "Hey, I know who you are, I saw you on television about three weeks ago when that priest was killed. Is this in connection with that?"

Civilian detectives drove Dan crazy, but this guy did have some good powers of observation. "Well, I am the detective you saw on television. But I'm not really at liberty to say what this investigation is about."

The neighbor nodded his head. "Yeah, that's it alright. You think Brad knows something about the killing, or should I say killings since you have three of them now?"

"Like I said, we can't really give out that information."

The man was now leaning on his rake, much more relaxed. "Yeah, yeah, whatever, but that's it, Brad was in the seminary years ago, my wife said we should ask him about the killings, but I told her to mind her own business. She's a nosey one you know?" Anyway, Brad isn't here, he's on vacation with his fiancee, Laura. Nice lady, not her first marriage though, a divorcee, you know. But that don't matter, like I was telling the wife last month, Brad is lucky to have found her, help him to settle down and get his life in order. Here he has this big house and no one to share it with, she'll move in and fill the place up before you know it. If I know women, and believe me, after forty years of marriage, I know women, she'll have her clothes and makeup and all her doodads all over the place in about a week."

"Do you know when they'll be back?"

"Yep, day after tomorrow, coming in at 5:15 at O'Hare, I figure they should be pulling in the driveway by 7:00 at the latest, that is if the airline doesn't lose their luggage. Last time I went on vacation I had to wait two days to get my luggage back. Don't have a clue what they do with the stuff, but it showed up. When I was a Marine in

Korea I traveled all over the place with my duffle bag and not once did I lose it. Got all these computers and fancy bag handlers today and they can't even get bags from here to Cleveland."

Dan shook his head in disbelief, this was like having a conversation with his father ten years earlier. "Is that where they went, Cleveland?"

"No, why would you think that, are they murdering priests in Cleveland too?"

"No, it just that you said, never mind, do you know where they went?" Dan knew full well that the neighbor knew where they went.

"Took a little trip to Las Vegas, they thought it would be good to go and relax a little before the wedding. They needed to get away, her mother is always telling them what to do and she's about to drive them both to drink with this wedding planning."

"Well, uh Mr...? I'm sorry I didn't catch your name," Dan said.

"Well, that's cause I didn't throw it. Ha ha . Anyway, its Mr. Hapton, Gene Hapton. You need me to spell that for you?"

"No, that's okay Mr. Hapton, but thanks for your help. It's good that Mr. Fiore has a friend like you. You haven't seen anyone else around the house have you?"

"No, I haven't and I 'm sure if the wife did, she would have shagged me out here to investigate. As far as I know you're the first ones to come snoopin' around since they've been gone."

Dan again thanked the man and shook his hand. Raferty also extended his hand and thanked the neighbor for his help. They headed back to the car and got in. Dan took out his notepad and wrote down that Bradley Fiore would be flying into O'Hare at 5:15 in two days. He would plan to be at the house to meet him and his fiancee when they arrived home.

Dan started the car and drove back to the station. He dropped Raferty off and decided to call Maggie to let her know that he was on his way in. It was earlier than he thought and she was probably just finishing her chicken. The phone rang five times before her machine picked up. "Maggie, it's me pick up." There was no answer.

He thought it was strange but she might still be at his house, so he called there and waited for the phone to pick up. The answering machine once again greeted him. "Maggie, if you're there pick up." Again no response.

Dan thought of everything bad that could have happened, was she taken? Was she in an accident? Did she get mugged on her way to the restaurant? He was trying to stay calm but his heart was racing at ninety miles and hour. He was tempted to put the mars light on, but realized that he was only about five minutes from her house anyway.

As he waited at a red light his foot was getting anxious to press the accelerator. As he was waiting the cell phone in his pocket rang. "Gill here, what is it?" he snapped.

Dan, it's me, I'm sorry, I was in the bathroom when you called. Did I worry you?"

"Hell yes, I told you I was going to call."

"I'm sorry, I didn't realize it was so dire. This guy is really getting to you isn't he?"

"It's okay honey, I was just worried, you know, I wouldn't ever want anything to happen to you."

"I know sweetie, and nothing will happen. Now get your butt over here and have some chicken. It's finger lickin' good and I intend to lick every one of those fingers tonight."

Dan clicked off the phone. The light had changed and Dan smiled to himself. "The hell with it," he said as he pulled out the mars light and sped to Maggie's house.

CHAPTER 27

❀

The next morning Dan pulled his car in front of the Archdiocesan Pastoral Center and parked in a loading zone. Rank still had its privileges and he knew that his license plate would assure that he would not get a ticket. He saw the television news trucks parked all along the busy street with the antennas raised for a live broadcast. This was big news in Chicago and they all wanted to carry the press conference live. In many ways Chicago was still a small town, concerned with the day to day events that effected the city. Dan entered the building, flashed his badge at the receptionist and was directed to the conference room on the sixth floor.

As Dan entered the elevator, six other people jammed in there with him. From their suits and perfect hair Dan assumed that they were reporters ready to get their stories. As usual no one spoke on the way to the sixth floor. Dan knew that people were very protective of their personal space and that an elevator violated every rule about getting too close to people. When the doors opened Dan saw the sixth floor was in absolute pandemonium. There were television cameras and newspaper photographers everywhere. Dan scanned the room to find Sister Rayday, hoping that she would take him in a side room to get away from the frenzy. Dan saw her standing by the front of the room talking to one of the auxiliary bishops who had been given temporary control of the diocese.

"Dan, come on up here," she shouted.

Dan waved at her and walked to the front of the room. "Good morning Sister, quite a collection of vipers here today."

"They can smell blood, Dan." She turned to one of the auxiliary bishops and introduced him to Dan. They shook hands and it was explained that the bishop would actually be handling the press conference. The bishop told Dan that he wanted the police to make an official statement and not just answer questions. Dan assured him that he would keep it simple and explain that the leads were limited, but that they were working hard at finding the killer and looking for connections between the priests who were murdered. The bishop told Dan that he wasn't going to address the crime aspect of the case, but was going to concentrate on the structures that the diocese had put in place to keep order.

The press conference began right on time and Sister Rayday introduced the bishop who was now in charge of the Archdiocese. The bishop began by reading a letter from the Vatican concerning the death of the Archbishop. There was no mention in the letter made of the murders of the three priests. He then assured the media, and the people of the Archdiocese that the Church was in perfect working order and that life would go on as usual for the Catholics of Chicago. He then turned the microphone over to Dan.

Dan approached the microphone and pulled out a prepared statement on the murders. He wanted to read the statement because he did not want to slip up and give the impression that the Archbishop had also been a victim of the killer. After his statement he opened the floor to questions from the press.

A hand went up in the crowd and Dan pointed at a well known local reporter. "Detective, what has the police department done to assure that another killing will not take place?"

"We have done all that we can do. We have beefed up security in front of all the churches in the city, asking our patrol cars to go past each one at least once an hour We have also talked to our counterparts in the suburbs and asked them to do the same. We simply do not have the manpower to offer more than that."

Another hand went up and Dan pointed again. "Is there some kind of special connection between these priests? Or do the police believe that the only connection is that they were members of the clergy?"

Now Dan had to leave the script. "The only connection that we have been able to make is that they were all in school at the same time. But before you jump the gun on that let me assure you that at the time these men were in the seminary, there were over 350 men there. It is a connection, but the connection that they were priests is just as strong as link as their educational background."

The same reporter managed to get in another question. "But they definitely knew one another?"

"There is very little proof of that. In the 1970's there were many students at the seminary. so there is a chance that they may have known one another by name or face, but not on a personal level."

Another television reporter stood up and asked the next question. "There are some reports coming out of your department that these are revenge killings, can you substantiate that?"

Dan knew that Bartly had been talking to his friends in the press and he only hoped that he had not leaked the coroner's report to them. "We have no evidence that these are revenge killings, I suggest that you check your source and realize that you have been misinformed. I want to assure you ladies and gentlemen that we do not know what kind of killer we are dealing with. There have been three murders, all of them priests, we have the FBI doing a possible profile on the killer or killers. Please remember that we have found no evidence that these were all done by the same person. We have no DNA, no fingerprints, and an M.O. that is rather inconsistent. We don't want to throw the city into a state of panic. As the bishop mentioned, all the priests of the diocese have been put on alert, and all efforts are being taken to assure their safety. But I know that the diocese does not want everything to come to a stand still. Citizens can greatly help us in our investigation if they have any information relating to these cases. They should call the police and let us know what they may have seen or heard. I can take one more question."

The battle to ask the question was won by a short man from a small independent paper. "Have you investigated the death of the Archbishop? Is his death somehow linked to these killings?"

It was the question that Dan had hoped would not be asked. Very few people knew about the poisoning and Dan wanted to keep it that way. "Yes, we have investigated the death of the Archbishop and he died of natural causes. The Archdiocese has requested that this case be closed and all evidence points in the direction of natural causes. There were a thousand witnesses to his death, we know what happened to him."

The bishop stood up and interrupted. "We are quite sure that the stress caused by the murder of the two priests and the failing health of the Archbishop all led to his stroke. In many ways the killer or killers did have some thing to do with the death of the Archbishop, but we know it was not direct, it was a side effect."

Dan stepped down from the microphone and allowed the bishop to finish the press conference with a few more questions. Most were related to the structure of the diocese and how a successor to the Archbishop would be chosen. Dan stood next to Sister Rayday, he wanted to talk to her before he left. The reporters began to clear out and Dan and the nun went into a side room.

"What did you find in Father Goetz's room?" she asked.

"Nothing much yet, this one is even more mysterious than the others, I mean I was literally in his room only ten minutes before he was killed."

"My God the man was sitting at this desk when he was shot, how can you protect people from a maniac like this?"

"You know, Sister, I think that the murders of priests is pretty much over by this guy."

"Why do you say that?" she asked.

"Because all the priests in that photo are dead."

"What about the other guys, did you find out who they were?"

"We're working on that, I'll keep you informed," Dan lied.

"I just wish this was over, I can't see us having to bury one more priest and trying to explain that to the people of the diocese."

"I agree, I mean we're the one's under pressure here too, and I feel terrible that this nut is able to get away with this." Dan shook her hand and left the Pastoral Center, he headed back to his car and drove to the department to see how the forensic guys were doing with the coniine search and the ballistics test.

When Dan entered the office he saw Raftery once again sitting on the edge of his desk. "Hey Raferty, desks are made for glass not for you ass."

Raferty waved his hand at Dan. "Then get a chair that I can sit at."

Dan walked to his desk and sat in his chair. "So how successful were you down in forensics?"

"Not very successful at first, they told me I was crazy, that there were other cases in front of this one. But then late last night they left me a voice mail saying that they would have results this afternoon. I must have been more persuasive than I thought."

Dan smiled, knowing that the Captain, and possibly even the Mayor himself had seen that the job was pushed through. "Excellent work Raferty, you'll be known around here as the guy that can get things done. How about the tests for coniine, did they say anything about that?"

"They said that was going to take a couple of days even if they rushed it. They never heard of coniine and they have to send someone to the library to find out about it. I don't think they are too sure what they are looking for. But I did call the coroner and asked him to check the dead priest's fingers for the stuff, he said that he would do that this morning."

Dan's phone rang while they were talking. "Gill here."

The man on the other end identified himself as Gene Hapton, the neighbor of Brad Fiore. "Hey, I uh checked on Brad's flight and it will be in tomorrow on time. You want me around when you come to the house tomorrow night?"

"Thanks Mr. Hapton, but I don't think that will be necessary. How's the house, any more strangers come by besides us?"

"No one came up to the house at all last night and I've been watching all morning, no one at all. Hey, I saw you on the television this morning, you handled those guys pretty well."

"Thanks, chalk it up to experience. You've been very helpful, but please don't say anything to the other neighbors if possible."

"Hell no, I wouldn't say anything to them. Bunch of nosey people though, they'll be asking questions tomorrow night if you guys come back here. Plus, if you have to take Brad in or something the club will be wondering where he and Laura are when they don't show up Saturday night."

"The club?"

"The bridge club, we get together every other Saturday for a friendly game. No gambling or anything, just some neighbors that like to play bridge."

"How long have you guys been doing that?"

"I don't know a few years. Hard to find people to get together with, these young couples that move in don't know how to play, it's over their heads. If it ain't on one of those video games or on the computer they have no interest in it."

"Both Dan and his fiancee play?"

"Yep, good players too, work together like a team should."

"Well, I don't think that Mr. Fiore will have to miss his game, we have no intention of taking him in for anything." Dan thanked the neighbor again and hung up the phone. He looked at Raferty. "Seems like Brad Fiore is quite the bridge player."

"Surprise, surprise."

"Yeah I guess that was a given, but he didn't turn his back on the game like Anthony Martin did. I guess for most people old habits die hard."

Dan asked Raferty to give a call to the coroner again and see if he had found anything on the hands of Goetz. Raferty went over to his own desk to make the call. Dan walked down the hall to talk to the Captain. When he got to the office the Captain was on the phone and indicted to Dan that he should be seated until he was finished.

"You looked good on t.v. this morning Gill."

"Thanks, not something I would like to do all the time though."

"Well, you did a fine job keeping things under control and making us look competent. The Commissioner is quite please with your effort."

"We're doing all we can do, but all the evidence is so circumstantial. Forensics has been able to come up with very little to aid us in catching this guy. We're going to have to wait for him to make a mistake. By the way, thanks for calling forensics and asking them to rush the ballistic tests."

"Well, actually, I had the Mayor make the call. It's amazing the power he wields, my guess is that we'll have those tests after lunch."

"You know I hate to bring this up, but someone from the department leaked the information about our leads indicating that these might be revenge killings."

The Captain indicated to Dan that he should shut the door to the office. "Yeah, I already had a little talk with our friend Bartly. He claims that it wasn't him, that he never talks to the press. That was my confirmation that it was him, that guy has the newspaper's number on his speed dial for Christ's sake. I've pulled him totally off this case, he's not going to bother you or hinder you. He's working on the murder of a prostitute on the west side. He won't be making headlines anytime soon."

"I wasn't aware that you were wise to his tricks."

"Very wise to them, Dan, but with little recourse. It was never proven that he planted evidence, and I can hardly bust him for being around when the cameras are on. But believe me, I know how he works, he has definitely reached his level of incompetency here, he'll never see a promotion while I'm around."

The information gave Dan a little twinge of self satisfaction. He was never really sure that the big wigs in the department knew what a scum Bartly really was. "It's good to know that I won't have to deal with him for a while."

The Captain's phone rang and he answered it, holding up his finger so that Dan would wait until the call was over before he left. He ended the conversation and looked at Dan. "That was forensics, the ballistics test is over, the computer made a definite match on the bullet. You were right Dan, it was from the same weapon that killed Anthony Martin a year ago. How the hell did you know?"

"I don't know, Captain. It scares me sometimes that I think like one of these nuts, but it just didn't seem right to me that Martin was killed from so far away, that's not how things work in that neighborhood. But it doesn't put me at ease either."

"What do you mean?"

"Now we know for sure that we're dealing with a guy who is calculating and cold. He takes his time, he plans things out. We might not see another murder for a year or we might see one tomorrow. I really believe more than ever that this guy is taking out revenge on this former bridge club and in my mind I can narrow it down to three suspects."

"Who do you think it is?"

My prime suspect is this guy Jerry Riley. He is the only man in the photo that I can't find, he has a minor criminal record and is a fugitive because he skipped bail. Then there's Bradley Fiore, we know he was in the club, that he plays bridge to this day, that he left the seminary very close to ordination. Of course he was out of town when Goetz was killed, but its not that much of an effort to get on a plane and fly back to Chicago from Vegas, there must be twenty-five flights a day that go back and forth. My third suspect is the one that may be the hardest to catch, because we have no clue who he is. The man who took the photo.

"What about the girl in the photo that has yet to be identified? Is she a suspect too?" the Captain asked.

"I don't think so, these killings are not being done by a woman. Women are not typically serial killers, the FBI has only a couple on file in this century. Plus the first two killings were done by someone with incredible strength, she would have to be an amazonian to have shoved that icepick through Wysocki's head."

"But don't forget Dan, the killer probably isn't working alone. I mean I think your instinct about Goetz killing the Archbishop is pretty much on target. I really believe that we will find some of that poison either in his room or on his body. That was good insight on your part. And, if the killer isn't working alone, then we can assume that someone may have helped him or her with the murders of Wysocki and Danner."

"So, what you are saying is that it could be anyone."

"Not necessarily, I think your idea about this Jerry Riley is your best bet. But you have to keep looking for that other girl and the photographer, they may be the key that's missing."

"If they're alive, at this rate being in that photo is more deadly than being in a street gang."

CHAPTER 28

*I*t had been a long day. In some ways Dan was glad that the ballistics test showed the match between the two killings. But it also gave him cause to reevaluate the situation. This was a serial killer, but a serial killer with a specific mission. Dan was convinced more than ever that anyone who was killed by this guy had known him. This wasn't your typical serial killer who watched for a weakness in his victims, this was a man with a very definite goal, a propensity toward revenge. In his mind Dan was sure it was Jerry Riley, but how did he ever get Father Goetz to help him? And why didn't the Archbishop give Dan more insight into what was happening, what could have happened that would make the Archbishop keep his mouth shut. It was getting frustrating for Dan, even if it was Jerry Riley who was doing the killings he would have a hard time proving it, he had left basically no evidence.

It was Dan's turn to provide dinner for Maggie. He wasn't a gourmet cook but he knew how to grill. He had stopped at the store on the way home and picked up two steaks, two potatoes to bake, a small container of macaroni salad, and a frozen cheese cake for dessert. He had left the department a little early and he knew that he would be able to beat Maggie to the house and get things started before she arrived. Dan washed the potatoes, tossed them in the oven and went out to get the grill going. All his neighbors had long ago converted over to using gas grills, but Dan was a purist, nothing but charcoal for him. He wouldn't even use the self lighting charcoal, preferring instead to make a perfect pyramid of coals, dousing them in lighter fluid and then carefully tending to it until the charcoal was glowing red surrounded by a sea of grey ash.

Dan had just lit the grill and was waiting patiently for the coals to turn grey when the phone rang. "Gill here."

"Dan it's Raferty, just got a call from the coroner."

"What did he say, did he find anything?"

"Yeah, he found traces of coniine under Goetz's fingernails. Not a lot, but it's not a common substance. It's not something he would have ever checked for if you hadn't tipped him off. Good work Dan."

"Well, I guess it does prove that he was at least around the poison. Of course I believe that he was the one who poisoned the Archbishop, but I doubt that he killed the other two guys. I mean if he did, then why would he have been killed himself?" Dan asked.

"Exactly, but at least we know what happened to the Archbishop, and maybe it wasn't even connected to the other killings. I mean maybe Goetz had his own vendetta to settle and saw this as an opportune time to do the deed."

"I suppose, but I think he was working with this guy. He was nervous as hell when I interviewed him. He could have filled a bucket with all the sweat that was pouring off his forehead."

"Well, I just wanted you to know that the report came in. I'll be in early tomorrow, see you at the office."

"Okay Rafts, hey by the way, you're doing a good job on this case. We're gonna catch this guy." Dan hung up the phone and opened the refrigerator to take out a cold beer. He never grilled without having at least one beer going. He wasn't a big drinker, but he liked his beer when he attacked the grill. He went back out to the patio and watched the charcoals do their thing. The flame had died down and the red glow was just coming up. They would be ready in twelve minutes by Dan's calculation. That gave him time to get the steaks ready.

Maggie came into the back door of the house while Dan was tenderizing the steaks. She had a bottle of red wine in her hand and threw her keys on the table. She walked up to Dan and gave him kiss. They often met like this, no words exchanged, just a longing glance and a kiss at the end of a hard day. "So, Detective, how was your day?"

Dan stopped pounding the steaks so that he could talk to her. "I think you could call it productive. We learned that Goetz did have coniine under his fingernails and that the bullet that killed Goetz was from the same gun that killed Anthony Martin a year ago. We are dealing with a criminal mind that I have never encountered before. Calculating, cold, and patient. I'm sure that he did have something to do with the death of Father Carmichael, the car crash vicitm, remember?"

Maggie nodded in confirmation. "The killing of Father Goetz doesn't fit the pattern though."

"How do you mean?"

"Well, if you look at the other killings, they were all doing work of some kind. Wysocki in the confessional, Danner while he was anointing the sick, Carmichael was a counselor to alcoholics and he was killed in a drunk driving accident. And you said that the Wallace woman was crushed by caskets. And didn't you say that this Martin guy was on the job while he was killed?"

"Yeah, he was a salesman and he was making a call to a nearby school or something. But maybe it's not just employment or vocation."

"What do you mean"? She asked.

"The priests were all doing something with the sacraments, remember you're the one who pointed that out to me."

"Except Goetz, you said he was sitting at his desk."

"Yeah, he was, but I don't know what he was doing at his desk. I bet the photographer took pictures of his desk, I wonder if he was working on something sacramental when he was knocked off. I was so busy looking at the watermark of the medal that I didn't pay any attention to the papers that were on the blotter of the desk. But even if he was, it wouldn't matter. The shot came from outside, the killer would have no idea what Goetz was working on. I think he was killed to shut him up. The M.O. may not fit, but I don't think that matters in this case. I think we should focus on sacraments and places of work. Not that there are many people left to kill, the people in that photo are dwindling away pretty fast."

"What does this Fiore guy do? Can he go to work and not expect to be killed?"

"I have no idea what he does. The only thing I know is that he's out of town with his fiancee and will be back sometime tomorrow night."

"His fiancee? He's getting married?"

"I suppose, the neighbor said he was in Vegas with his fiancee."

"Dan, marriage is a sacrament of the Church. He's not in danger at work, he's in danger of receiving the sacrament of marriage."

"Holy shit, you're right! His neighbor said that they went to Vegas to get a break from the wedding plans. I would think that means that the wedding is pretty close."

"Well like you said, it doesn't really matter how close it is, this guy is pretty patient."

Dan went back to pounding the steaks. He opened the oven and realized that the potatoes would be done just about when the steaks came off the grill. He put the steaks on a plate and took them outside to the grill. He gave a final poke to the charcoals and placed the wire rack over them. He let the rack heat up a few degrees and dropped the steaks on. They sizzled as they hit the heat and the smell of grilling meat began to float up to his nostrils.

Maggie came out to the patio with a glass of wine and a fresh cold beer for Dan. She handed him the beer and gave him another kiss. "Smells good already," she said.

"Ah yes Miss Maggie, you are the queen of the kitchen but I'm still the Baron of the Barbeque!" Dan watched the flames jump up and occasionally lick the cooking steaks, the juices dripping on the fire.

By the time the steaks were done, exactly six minutes on each side, Maggie had set the plates and utensils on the picnic table. She had placed the baked potatoes on a small plate and the macaroni salad in a small glass bowl. She brought out two candles and lit them. The sun was just going down and the twilight bathed the backyard in a beautiful red glow. They ate their steaks and talked about their day. Maggie told Dan about the various clients that she had to deal with and all their quirky ways. He laughed at her stories and secretly gave thanks to God for having this woman in his life.

After dinner they went into the family room to watch a movie. It was a little too warm to have a fire so they just sat on the couch as Dan popped an old movie into the VCR. They loved to watch old movies and Dan had a great collection of Jimmy Stewart, Humphrey Bogart, and his favorite Hepburn and Tracy. Tonight they were watching Jimmy Stewart in "Harvey" an old classic that most people living today would have never seen. Dan and Maggie cuddled up on the couch and laughed out loud as Stewart talked to an imaginary six foot rabbit. Dan was always amazed at Jimmy Stewart's performance. He had the audience completely convinced that there really was a six foot rabbit and that it was not just a figment of his imagination. Even though you never saw the rabbit, you were sure that it was very real. That was great acting, too bad more people didn't see this movie.

When the movie was over Dan hit the rewind button and sat back on the couch. "It's too bad more people can't be like Stewart in the movie. So innocent and so trusting. That rabbit was really there for him."

"Yeah, I guess that some people would call him crazy, but he saw something different, something that comforted him."

"I think that's how it is for this killer, Maggie. I think he is out to prove something, some kind of payback. In his mind, he doesn't see these as killings or murders, he sees this as a mission. A way for people to atone for something bad that happened in the past. I bet that if you saw this guy in the street you wouldn't even know he was a killer. The FBI is supposed to come up with a profile for us, but I already know what it will say. He's probably a white male between 35 and 50, most likely a professional, probably obsessed with the police and crime prevention. He might be married, since the killings aren't sexual in nature he's probably not very aggressive. My bet is he's mild mannered. Probably even married with children. That's why they're so hard to catch. You'd never think to look for them in lineups or in a book of mug shots. In this case it wouldn't surprise me if he worked for the Church in some capacity. If it's this Riley guy, he would have changed his name, made up a new identity and just blended in. After more than twenty years, I can assure you that no one is looking for him anymore. Not enough money or manpower to keep those cases open this long."

Maggie put her arm around Dan. "I've been thinking about this Riley guy. You had said that his sister overdosed but that it didn't seem natural. Everyone you talked to said she was such a good girl, straight laced and all."

"Yeah, but now we know that sometimes it's the best kids that are involved in drugs. Remember Joe and Angie's kid? He was a straight A student when he overdosed his senior year," Dan said.

"I know Dan, but this was 1972, good kids went bad back then too, but those kids left home, they didn't lead double lives. I think something happened to her. Maybe it wasn't an accident, maybe the brother had something to do with it and that drove him over the edge. Maybe that's why he committed the crime and then skipped bail. I mean the guilt could have just driven him over the edge."

"Yeah, that makes some sense. He did leave right after she died and he was acting out of character when he was arrested. I never really focused on her death, I mean it happened so long ago and she was not a victim of the killer. At least I never thought she was a victim of the killer, but maybe she was after all. I would love to know what happened that night she overdosed. I don't even know where it happened or what the circumstances were."

"Well, there's one guy who might know."

"Fiore," he said.

"My guess is that he knows a lot about Miss Riley."

"And a lot about that night she died," he said.

CHAPTER 29

*D*an spent the next morning going through the evidence. He read the ballistics reports, he looked at the letters, read over the coroner's report on all the murders, including the reports on Father Carmichael and Anthony Martin. He had subpoenaed the bank records of the priests and all of them had written monthly checks to cash, which they had cashed at their various banks. This might not have been unusual, lots of people had direct deposit and then wrote checks to cash so that they could have liquid funds each month. But these checks were all for the same amount and written each month within three days of one another.

Dan had come to believe that Father Goetz had poisoned the Archbishop but he had doubts that he had killed the other two priests. There was no hard evidence either way, but it was in his gut that Goetz had been used as a pawn in this game of cat and mouse. Goetz had also been writing checks to cash each month and his bank account was not in any way padded with extra money, he had about the same amount of savings as the other priests. They never found the silver medal in the room of Goetz, but Dan was sure, from the watermark left on the desk that he still owned his medal.

After putting all the evidence together, Dan realized that the final piece of the puzzle would be found in the interview with Bradley Fiore. Dan and Raferty planned to be at the Fiore house no later than six, incase the flight was early or traffic was light. Dan told Raferty to meet him at the car by 5:30 for the drive to the well kept north side neighborhood.

When they met at the car Raferty asked Dan what the plan of action was for the interview. Dan explained all his theories and wanted to play good cop, bad cop with Fiore. Since Dan had more experience, and because Raferty was just too nice and too young it was decided that Dan would be the bad cop that night. Dan knew that Fiore knew something and he planned to squeeze it out of him one way or the other.

They pulled up in front of the well kept Fiore bungalow at five minutes before six. Just as before there were kids playing on the parkway, neighbors were cutting their grass, the smells of meat grilling filled the streets. This was a very low key neighborhood, lots of cops and firefighters lived here and they took good care of their houses and their kids. As they waited in their car they saw the nosey neighbor Mr. Hapton approaching them.

Mr. Hapton came up to the car and waived at the two detectives. "I don't expect them back for about an hour. You know how those airlines are with luggage and all."

Dan smiled at the neighbor. "Well, we just wanted to be sure that we didn't miss him Mr. Hapton. Besides, planes are early sometimes and maybe they only took carry on luggage with them."

"Nope, they took suitcases. Saw them leave, no way they could carry on those things. If Brad was going by himself he would have brought a small bag, but Laura travels with a whole shit load of stuff. Guess it's makeup and other doodads. My wife is the same way, we went on a cruise last year and she brought three bags with her. I would have been happy to throw my stuff in a shopping bag and be done with it."

"Well, we don't mind being a little early," Raferty chimed in.

"Suit yourselves, you want a glass of pop or something?"

"No, thanks, we're good. We'll just wait here and take in the sites," Dan said.

The neighbor made his goodbyes and walked back to his house. Dan could see the curtains in the living room moving back and forth as Mr. Hapton approached the house and would see them occasionally move during the next hour. Dan figured that Mrs. Hapton was the real nosey neighbor but never had the guts to actually go out and investigate things. She sent her husband out on reconnaissance missions who then in turn reported directly back to her.

At 7:00 a taxi pulled into the driveway of the Fiore house. Dan saw the curtains on the Haptons move and a sheepish woman peering through to see what was happening. Dan expected Mr. Hapton to come out again to greet Brad and Laura, but he stayed in the house. He probably figured that Brad would fill him in later, after the cops left. Dan and Raferty waited about ten minutes while the couple took their bags and went into the house.

"Okay, Rafts, let's go." They exited the car and approached the front door of the bungalow.

They rang the doorbell and waited for someone to answer. Bradley Fiore opened the door. He was in his mid fifties, with sandy blond hair. He was about six feet tall and had an above average build for a man his age. Dan recognized him from the photo, of all the men in the picture he had aged the least.

"Can I help you?" Fiore asked.

"Mr. Fiore? I'm Detective Gill, and this is Detective Raferty we're from the Chicago Police Department, I was wondering if we could talk to you for a few minutes."

"What's this about, am I in some sort of trouble?"

"No, not at all, we just have a few questions we need to ask you," Raferty said. This set the scene. Raferty was going to be the nice guy, the soother who would make Fiore feel comfortable while Dan would remain stern, never smiling, causing a degree of uncertainty.

Fiore led them into the living room and invited them to be seated. They could hear someone in the bedroom down the hall. Fiore looked over his shoulder in the direction of the noise. "That's my fiancee, does she need to be here?"

"No," said Dan. "But you might want to tell her who we are and that you'll be busy for a few minutes."

Fiore walked down the hall and the told his fiancee that she should stay in the bedroom and go about unpacking their things. He assured her that it wasn't a big deal and she had nothing to worry about. He returned to the detectives and took a seat in a large chair the was situated perpendicular to the couch where the detectives sat.

"You realize we just got back from vacation, we haven't even unpacked yet."

"We realize that," Dan said.

"Mr. Fiore, we really needed to speak to you as soon as possible, we would have liked to talk to you two days ago, but we know that you were in Las Vegas."

"Been talking to Gene Hapton huh?"

Raferty smiled, Dan did not. "Yes, he was quite helpful in assisting us to track you down," Raferty said.

"Well, what is this all about?" Fiore asked.

Dan removed his notepad from his jacket so that he could take notes. "Were you aware Mr. Fiore that three of your friends from the seminary have been murdered in the last three weeks?"

Fiore looked surprised. "Three? I only knew of two."

"Well, Father Goetz was killed several days ago in his rectory. Were you aware that other classmates of yours have also been killed or murdered over that last several years, including Father Carmichael and Anthony Martin?"

"I had heard about Tony Martin, but I didn't know about Carmichael. What does this have to do with me?"

Raferty needed to make him feel like he needed the police. "We're concerned for your safety Mr. Fiore, many people with whom you have had past friendships are showing up dead, most of them murdered. We want to be sure that you're taking every precaution to protect yourself."

"There were over three hundred guys in the seminary when I was there. I find it hard to believe that the police are visiting everyone of them."

Dan interrupted. "No Mr. Fiore, we are not visiting everyone that went to the seminary in your time, but we are visiting everyone whose face appears in this photo." Dan took the photo from its folder and handed it to Fiore.

The man's face went pure white, and his youthful appearance drained from his entire body. It was as if Fiore had aged ten years right before their eyes. "Are all these guys dead?"

Yes, except you and Jerry Riley, as far as we know. Two of the women are also dead. Shannon Wallace, and Mary Riley."

"I knew Mary Riley was dead, but I didn't recall the name of Shannon Wallace, which one is she?" Fiore asked.

Dan pointed to the face of Shannon Wallace the photo. "Do you remember who this other woman is, here over to the side?"

"I can't remember her name, she was a friend of the Riley's, just one of the girls his sister used to bring up with her when she visited the seminary."

Raferty showed real concern for Fiore. "You see why we're concerned Mr. Fiore. We don't want anything to happen to you."

"I don't think anything will happen to me, I mean I haven't been in contact with any of these people for years. Once I left the seminary I was considered anathema, they didn't call me and I didn't bother to call them."

"But you were all very close in those days weren't you?" Dan asked.

"Not that close."

"Come on, Mr. Fiore, we know that you were in the elite club, the Dean's bridge group. We know that you guys often found yourselves above the law of the seminary and had certain privileges that other students did not enjoy. Your club was so tight that you even had little medals made to commemorate your friendship."

Fiore looked down at the ground. "That was a long time ago, that ended when I left the seminary. I didn't want anything to do with them anymore."

Raferty leaned in toward Fiore. "Why is that Brad?" He used his first name to make him more relaxed.

"They weren't the nicest guys. You were right Detective when you said that we were above the rules. We never got in trouble and didn't have to do half the things that other students did. It just wasn't right. I didn't realize it at the time, but once I left, I could look back with a little more perspective. It wasn't a healthy situation."

"It certainly wasn't healthy for Mary Riley was it?" Dan asked.

Fiore shot his head straight up. "I don't know what you're talking about!"

Dan was stern in his response. "I think you do Mr. Fiore, I think that something terrible happened to Mary Riley and I think you know what it is. I also think that whatever happened made you leave the seminary and turn your back on that group. Now why don't you tell us what happened so we can help you avoid being murdered."

"You don't know what you're talking about, Mary Riley overdosed on drugs. It was the early 70's, lots of people did drugs, she just didn't know her limits."

"I don't think that you mean that Mr. Fiore," Dan said. "We know how shocking Mary Riley's death was. We know that she was not into drugs, it would have shown up sooner than it did. Why don't you just tell us what was going on up there in your club? Or does 'never trump' still mean something to you?"

Fiore had true intensity in his eyes. He was angry and was about to explode which is what Dan was hoping for. "Never trump doesn't mean a damn thing to me. That was a stupid saying that was supposed to bind us together. Never make your friend the dummy, never let anyone down. But that group let a lot of people down. They hurt people all the time in the name of unity."

Raferty looked at Fiore, trying to calm him a little and bring his trust level up. "Did they hurt you Brad?"

"Just being a part of that group was hurtful."

Dan saw his opportunity to jump in. "Did they hurt you enough to make you want to get revenge, to hurt them back?"

Fiore stood up from his seat. "What the hell does that mean? Are you accusing me of something? Because if you are I'm done talking to you. You want to arrest me, go ahead, but don't sit here and insinuate that I had something to do with someone's death. I didn't have anything to do with it, it wasn't me."

"Whose death are you referring to, Mr. Fiore?" Dan asked.

In the midst of the exchange Fiore's fiancee, Laura had entered the room. She stood by the archway at the edge of the hall. "Stop this, what the hell do you guys think you're doing, you are grilling the wrong guy!"

All their heads turned to look at Laura. "Be quiet Laura, you don't need to worry about this," Fiore said.

"No Brad, this has gone on long enough, it's time for this to stop. Tell them what you know and this nightmare can end. Its time for us to get on with our lives."

Dan looked at the woman in the doorway. She looked about five or six years younger than Fiore. Her hair was a golden blond, her eyes crystal blue, even with the stress that was on her face she was still an attractive woman.

"Why don't you come in here Miss...?"

"Walters, Laura Walters." She came in and put her hand on Fiore's shoulder so that he would sit back down into the chair. She sat on the arm of the chair with her arm over his shoulder.

"Excuse me for asking Miss Walters, but have we met?" Raferty asked.

"No, Detective, but you've seen me before."

"In the photo," Dan said. "You're the missing girl from the photo."

"Yes, I was in the club too. I was only a senior in high school, but Mary Riley would bring us up to visit her brother every couple of weeks. We started to get to know the guys little by little and formed quite a tight little group."

Fiore interrupted her. "Laura, I don't think that we need to say anything to these guys, I think they're accusing me of murder."

"No, Mr. Fiore, were not accusing you of murder," Dan said. "But we certainly could accuse you of lying. You said you didn't know who the other girl in the photo was. Listen, we simply want to find the guy who is responsible for all this. We really need you to tell us what happened, why would all the people in this photo be dead, the club is the only thing that links you all."

"Okay, its been a long time coming, and quite honestly I don't know how much more of this either one of us can take." Fiore sat up a little in the chair and brought his folded hands up to his mouth. He took a deep breath and began to tell the detectives what they wanted to hear.

"It was the early 70's, and we were a close group. We were hand picked by the Dean of Formations to be a part of his special club. All of us were very good at math and logic and he saw us as a kind of breeding stable for bridge players. It did have its privileges, we didn't have to attend certain meetings, we were given answers to certain exams, we really had full reign of the place. But for us, the most important perk was the free time. We were allowed to get together twice a week to play cards, smoke cigarettes and drink alcohol. No one else had gotten away with that. The other guys had to be in their rooms by nine, while we were in the faculty building learning the fine art of bridge.

"The Dean had already been friends with Jerry Riley, he knew him when he was still in college and probably talked him into coming to the seminary. Riley's dad and the Dean were good friends, so it naturally translated down to his kids. That's why Mary Riley was allowed to come and visit the seminary so often, even when it wasn't a designated family day. She would come up and bring one or two of her girlfriends with her. That's how I met Laura. She was one of Mary's best friends and came up almost every week."

"Along with Shannon Wallace," Dan said.

"Yes, Shannon was a regular too, there were other girls who would come and go, but they were never in the group, they weren't consistent visitors and I couldn't even tell you one of their names today. They were girls that Mary knew from school. Laura might have known some of them, but I never really bothered to learn their names.

"Anyway, we did a lot more than play cards together. We were real assholes around campus, we began to treat the other students with disdain and would get away with it. The other faculty probably suspected something, but they could never prove it was us playing the pranks around campus. The dean always covered up for us, always threw the blame in another direction. As time went on we started to move away from his control, got a little more cocky and started meeting without him. He was still our mentor, but we were all getting a superior attitude. Pretty soon we started meeting down by the boat house to plan our takeover of the school. I don't mean like we were going to capture the faculty or anything, but we wanted to find ways that we could control things even more. We figured out ways to get into the school records, how to manipulate grades and get rid of people we didn't like. You have to remember that we were the cream of the crop, the smartest guys on campus.

"I know this isn't an excuse, but we were caught up in the turmoil of the late 60's and early 70's. All over the country college kids were protesting things like the war and poverty. We were locked up in a private sanctuary never allowed to do the things we really wanted to do. It was like being in prison, except that we figured a way to get the keys and take what we wanted. It wasn't long before out intellectual gatherings turned into nothing more than excuses to get together and think of ways to make everyone else's life miserable. Our noble ideas turned into nothing more than vengeance parties.

"I remember late in 1971 someone had brought in drugs for the first time. We had already become big drinkers, the Dean would serve us booze while we played cards and someone would steal one of his bottles every week. He must have known what we were doing, he was missing an awful lot of alcohol in those days. Anyway, we started out with pot, and mixed it with the booze. We would get pretty high. Some guys wanted to try harder stuff so we convinced the girls to buy some stuff for us at their school."

Laura broke into the conversation. "Mary Riley knew everyone at school, the good girls and the bad girls too. She was able to get some speed to bring up with us and it became a weekly routine."

Fiore resumed his telling of the story. "Well some of the guys really got off on the speed. They liked the high and the crash the next day didn't matter because if we missed class it was no big deal. Pretty soon the parties started to get more friendly. The girls were there bringing us the stuff every week and we started to couple off. It wasn't very moral, but it was the decade of free love, we knew that everyone else was having sex in the real world and we wanted to try it. Some of us stuck with the same girl, but some of the girls had more than one partner. Mary Riley was the leader of the pack, she slept around during those parties. It always amazed me that she would do that with her brother right there, but it didn't seem to bother either one of them. She was sleeping with at least three of the guys and he was sleeping with any girl she happened to bring with her.

By 1972 we were thick as thieves. We had these superior attitudes and thought that the world was our oyster. Nothing was going to stop us from doing what we wanted to do until that one Saturday night. That's when our world came crashing in on us. We were at the boat house, smoking pot, drinking whiskey, some guys were doing speed. The girls were there and were strangely keeping to themselves that night. We asked what was wrong, but they all looked at us like we were devils. They gathered around Mary Riley, she was crying and they were all talking to her. I figured that she was just dumped by one of the guys, it wouldn't be the first time that the triangle romances went bust. But then she stood up and whispered into her brother's ear. He was pissed and walked up to two of the guys and started yelling at them and shoving them into the walls. Well we were all a little scared, you know, we didn't need a fist fight down there.

"Well, it came out that Mary was pregnant, but she wasn't sure which guy was the father. Some of these guys were about to be ordained deacons and they weren't about to give up everything for an unplanned pregnancy. One by one the three guys she was sleeping with denied that it could be theirs. I can't even be sure anymore who she was sleeping with, but I think one of them was Goetz, but I'm not even sure of that.

"So, Jerry Riley wanted to know what we were going to do about this. Things had gotten out of hand and someone needed to take responsibility. Jerry insisted that one of the guys have the balls to stand up for what he had done, but none of them would. Then someone, I don't know who, suggested that she have an abortion. I mean that was a big leap for all of us. Yeah, we were screwing around and we were drinking and doing drugs, but in our minds abortion was a whole different ball of wax. We were taught that abortion was taking a life, and how could we reconcile that? And you have to remember that this was 1972, abortion was still illegal in this country, the only way to get one was to bribe a doctor and have it done after hours. Since these guys were willing to break the law and perform abortions, they were real crooks, they weren't noble knights doing a favor for women, they were usually quacks who wanted the quick, tax free money.

So after a long discussion it was decided that we should pool our money and pay for the abortion. We were all scared, if anyone said no, then the group would turn against them, and we all knew what the group was capable of doing. Jerry was against the idea, he wanted her to have the baby and one of the guys to marry her. But it wasn't going to happen. Carmichael was the smartest guy in the group. He said that he knew a doctor on the south side that would do it, but it was a lot of money. I don't know how much we collected between all the guys, but I know that everyone chipped in. It was decided that this wasn't something that she could go through by herself, so over our next break, when we were all home we went with Mary so that she could have the abortion.

"Right up to the end Jerry was against it, he wanted her to have the baby even if no one would marry her. But she said that she couldn't take the pressure, she would be kicked out of school and never get into college. She believed that he whole future depended on that abortion."

Fiore stopped, there were tears beginning to well up in his eyes and he held tightly onto Laura's hand.

Laura spoke while Fiore composed himself. "Those three guys were such cowards, none of them would take responsibility and there were no DNA tests in those days. Plus, you just did what the group said, you know, 'never trump', never make anyone the dummy. It was a group mentality that had gotten completely out of hand."

Fiore spoke again. "So we went on a Friday night to this old empty store on Western Avenue. This doctor had kept a lease on the place, but kept it empty so that he could use it to perform abortions. The place wasn't very clean and he wasn't too happy to see so many of us accompanying this girl. The more people that knew about his little operation that greater chance that he could be arrested. He told us that there was no deal unless we all waited outside. Well, we figured we had no choice so we waited in the alley.

"It was the most awful hour of my life. You couldn't get in and you didn't know what was happening. A couple of times, I swear you could hear Mary crying out in pain. It was just killing Jerry that he couldn't be in there. I don't know how long it exactly took, but it seemed like it was the whole night. Eventually the door opened and the doctor told us that it was over, but that she had some unexpected bleeding. He said he had sewn her up, but that she should lay still for the rest of the night. He offered to let her stay in the abandoned store, but he had to leave, he couldn't explain his absence from his wife for much longer.

"We waited with her through the night. She was in a lot of pain and she kept bleeding, we kept replacing the sheets and trying to keep her comfortable. But it was no good, we were bright, but we were also scared. I mean we should have taken her to a hospital, but she kept saying no, she wasn't going to have some doctor find out that she had an abortion. By the time morning came she was dead.

"I had never been party to anything like that before. It was terrible. Jerry was out of his mind with grief and the rest of us were in shock. The last thing that Mary said before she died was to never let anyone know how she died. I couldn't believe that she cared at that point, but it was what she said. So there we were with a dead girl who had just had an abortion. All of us had excuses for not being home so no one missed us, we had the morning to think about what we were going to do. That's when Jerry decided to call the Dean and tell him we needed his help.

"He got there about an hour later and looked over the situation. He was beside himself. He knew Mary for many years and was close to her. He couldn't believe that they didn't come to him sooner so that he could have helped in the situation. He wanted to know who the father was, but no one could say for sure. Besides, at this point we were all in it up to our eye sockets. We told him that she didn't want anyone to know that she had an abortion. That's when the Dean suggested that we would have to make her death look accidental so that an autopsy wouldn't check to see if she had been pregnant.

"Someone suggested a car accident, but it was broad day light, how could we get her in a car and crash it? Then someone suggested the drugs. We had plenty, we knew how to use them and we knew how to get them into her system. We found an old syringe that was left by the doctor and one of the guys cooked down the powdered pills until they were liquid. Then they injected her in about five spots with the drugs. She was already dead, but they wanted the officials to find drugs in her system. In those days if you were found with drugs in your system that was going to listed as your cause of death. I don't think the coroners were very sophisticated then, it was pretty easy to make it look like she overdosed.

"We waited until it was dark and wrapped her in a sheet. We put all her clothes on her and put the left over drugs in her purse. Jerry drove her home and put her in the family car in the garage. When they found her the next day it looked like she had overdosed in the garage. It was an open and shut case."

Laura once again held tightly onto Brad's hand. "But that wasn't the end of it. Too many people knew what had happened and the group could no longer go on. I never went back to that seminary. I only got reacquainted with Brad about five years ago at an AA meeting. That night had ruined both our lives and we wanted to exorcize those demons. We've found a lot of solace in one another."

Dan had been taking notes the entire time Brad Fiore was talking. "A lot of people did know what happened and you were able to keep it a secret for a long time. But someone was blackmailing you, right?"

"Yeah," said Fiore. "It started about ten years ago, I thought the whole thing was over, but then I got letters every month asking me to pay for what had happened. I made my cash payment every month, dropped it off in a garbage can in Lincoln Park like clock work. It drove me to the bottle, it was ruining my life. I had no idea who was doing it, but now that I look at this photo, and realize that everyone is dead, I can only assume that it was Jerry Riley. And now, money isn't enough, he wants blood too, blood in revenge of his sister."

The realization that Brad and Laura were in danger hit hard. Laura began to cry and was being comforted by Brad. Dan knew that he had one more question that he had to ask. "This photo is very telling, we've finally been able to identify everyone in it, but I have to know, who took it, that's the person that's missing."

Fiore looked at Laura and she shrugged her shoulders. "It was some girl, a friend of Jerry's not one of Mary's high school friends. I don't remember her name, she took the shot early in the year and then we never saw her again. The Dean is the one who gave us the copies right after it was taken, he would have probably known her, but I can't tell you who she was. She wasn't in the picture because she wasn't in the club, just attached somehow to Jerry."

Raferty looked at the couple, they were torn apart by what had happened and he wasn't about to sit in judgement of them. "I understand your wedding is approaching pretty quickly."

"In two weeks," said Laura. "That's why we took the quick trip to Vegas, everyone is driving us crazy with the details."

"I really hate to be the one to break this to you, but I think you are in danger and I think it's going to happen at your wedding."

Dan jumped in. "We're not sure, but we think this guy likes to kill with some drama, during a sacrament of the Church if possible or while the victim is working. Since you're the last two in the photo, it makes sense that he'll try to take you out at the same time."

Laura began to cry. "But we can't cancel our wedding, there has to be a way to stop this guy, to catch him."

Dan stood up and reached out to touch Laura on the shoulder. "I'm not proposing that we stop your wedding, and what I am going to ask you to do might be dangerous, but it's the only way we can catch this guy."

"Okay," said Brad. "Tell us what you have in mind, and if we can we'll cooperate."

CHAPTER 30

*I*t was a busy two weeks for Dan and Raferty. They spent a lot of time compiling all the evidence. They had the police artist do an age projection drawing of Jerry Riley so that they could recognize him if they saw him at the wedding. They ran his fingerprints through the national crime database, but nothing came up. There was no sign of Jerry Riley since he skipped bail in 1972. They also spent a lot of time with Brad and Laura, getting the details of their wedding and figuring out a plan of how they could catch the killer if he showed up.

The hardest part was convincing the Captain to sign off on the expense of having twenty undercover officers at the wedding. Dan knew that this was an extraordinary request, and the Captain at first rebuked the idea, saying it simply was not in the budget. But Dan encouraged him to call the Mayor, who immediately approved the expenditure, he was anxious for this case to be closed, regardless of the cost.

Dan learned that Laura had received an annulment from the Church earlier that year and that the wedding would indeed be taking place in a Catholic Church. Dan was cautious, he didn't want too many people to know of his plan, so he was hesitant to even inform the priest who was performing the wedding. His plan was to have five men stationed outside the church, dressed as wedding guests.

They would look like men and women who were simply stepping outside the church for a smoke or to get some air. There were to be an additional five plain clothed officers planted in cars along the street of the church. They were to have their weapons ready to go. Each of them would be given the age enhanced photo of Jerry Riley. There would also be ten officers in the church, dressed as wedding guests. They were to watch all the doors and watch for anything suspicious. Dan reasoned that the killer was not going to go out in a blaze of glory so the chance that he would riddle the church with bullets was very low. Dan also planned to be in sacristy of the church, to watch the chalice and the hosts, to be sure that no poison would be somehow slipped into the mix.

On the day of the wedding Dan woke up and went through his morning routine. He had his coffee and read his paper. The wedding was scheduled at noon and the church was not too far from his house. He would leave about 10:30 to get everything set up. He called Maggie about 10:00 but there was no answer, he figured she was out doing her Saturday morning shopping. After he hung up he went upstairs to pick out a tie and finish dressing. While he was in the bedroom going through his wardrobe he heard the back door open and a set of keys hit the kitchen table.

"Maggie? Is that you?"

"Uh huh, are you trying to pick out a tie?" she asked, as she started to go up the stairs.

Dan turned around and saw her enter the bedroom. "Yeah, which one is better?" he asked as he held up two choices.

She shook her head. "Neither, let me pick one out, I swear you must be color blind, you can't wear an bright orange tie with a dark blue suit." She reached into the closet and grabbed a more conservative tie for him to wear. He put it around his neck and she began to tie it for him. No one could make a half Windsor knot quite like Maggie. She finished the tie and gave him a little kiss.

"What are you going to do today?" he asked.

"I'm going to do a little shopping, and then come home and get those weeds out of your garden. You've been a little too preoccupied to take care of it properly. Then I think I'll start a nice dinner. What time do you expect to be back?"

"I can't really say, the wedding starts at 12:00. If things go as I plan, then we'll have this guy in custody by 1:30, I should be able to book him and get the papers rolling by 6:00 at the latest. That's if things go the way I think they will."

"Do you think something could go wrong?"

"Something can always go wrong, its like an operation, you hope that everything goes as planned, but complications can certainly set in."

"I'm amazed that you got this couple to agree to all of this. I think I would have postponed my wedding if I were in their shoes."

Dan slipped on his suit coat. "Laura was adamant that the wedding go on, even before we suggested that we be there undercover. She was pretty clear that this was not going to put on hold. At least this way we can have twenty cops there to protect them, and hopefully catch this nut."

Maggie straightened his coat and brushed a few flakes of lint from his lapels. "I hope that you're a step ahead of this guy this time. He seems to have everything planned out, what if he suspects that you guys are going to be there."

"I've thought of that, he certainly knows that I'm on the case, otherwise he wouldn't have sent me Danner's thumb in the mail. But we've been very careful about talking to Brad and Laura, we haven't been back to the house since that first interview, so unless he was tailing them twenty-four hours a day, he doesn't know what we have planned."

"Well, you just be careful. I don't want to be eating dinner by myself!"

Dan kissed her passionately, and then brushed her bangs out of her eyes. You know I'll be careful. I have plenty to come home to, I know when I've got it good." He headed down the stairs and into the kitchen. He picked up his keys and headed out the back door to his car. He gave one last smile to Maggie and she waived to him from the back door.

Dan arrived at the church with plenty of time to spare. The team had gone over the operation a number of times back at the station. They had a map of the church grounds and knew every entrance, every way in and out for a pedestrian or a car. If Riley was going to show up at the church, he was going to be caught. Then this would finally be over and these people could get on with their lives.

Dan sat in his car and waited for the other officers to arrive. By 11:30 they were all there, but they did not acknowledge one another. The plan was for Dan to do a head count and make sure that twenty cops had shown up dressed as wedding guests. Some of them stayed in their cars, others went into the church to get a designated seat, and several stayed on the front lawn of the church smoking and talking as though they were couples. They seemed to blend in well. Raferty was already in the church when Dan got out of his car , carrying a small paper bag and went inside through a back door.

The church was beautifully decorated with purple and yellow flowers adorning the altar. The kneelers were in place for the bride and groom. It was to be a small wedding party, just a best man and a maid of honor. Dan went into the sacristy to look for the groom, it we decided earlier in the week that the groom would arrive with the best man by 11:00 and hang around the sacristy incase someone tried to drop some poison in the wine. Dan saw the groom and extended his hand. The priest performing the wedding had not arrived yet. Dan opened the bag and took out a fresh bottle of altar wine that he had purchased at a local religious goods store. He opened the sacristy refrigerator and took out the bottle that was already there and replaced it with the fresh bottle.

When the priest arrived in the sacristy to set up for the wedding, he greeted the groom and the best man and then introduced himself to Dan. Dan told him his name and said that he was the cousin of the groom, and he was here for moral support. The priest chuckled and welcomed Dan as he went about setting up mass.

"Hey, Father, let me help you with that, I used to be an altar boy in grade school," Dan said.

"Well, that's nice of you. You can take these two cruets of water and wine and place them on the credence table over to the side, and then place the chalice next to them on the same table. Dan took the freshly filled water and wine cruets and placed them on the table then returned to the sacristy to grab the chalice. This was the time that the groom was instructed to distract the priest. As he did so, Dan took a cloth from his pocket and wiped the inside of the chalice clean. There was no poison anywhere in that cup. Dan then placed the chalice on the table and returned to the sacristy. He stayed with the groom and best man as the priest went about testing microphones and making final lighting adjustments to the church.

"There's nothing in that cup, I can assure you of that," Dan said.

"That's good, I didn't think he'd try it the same way twice anyhow," said Brad.

The priest came back to the sacristy and informed the groom and the best man that it was time to proceed out. The groom was visibly nervous but Dan didn't know if it was the idea of marriage or the idea that a killer might be in the church. Dan excused himself and returned to the body of the church where he took a seat as close to the front as possible. As he slid into the second pew, the mother of the groom smiled at him and wondered who the hell he was. Dan smiled back and slid all the way over to the opposite end of the pew. He quietly slipped his gun from his pocket and began to look around the church. He didn't see anyone who looked like Riley, but he knew that he could be disguised. Still nothing looked out of the ordinary.

The wedding began on time, all the cops were in their assigned places and they maintained true vigilance as the wedding went on. The couple joined one another at the front, and held hands as the priest greeted the congregation. After the readings and a short homily, the priest came down to the couple and asked them to stand. They looked at one another lovingly and exchanged their wedding vows. Since Dan knew that this was the moment that the sacrament was truly performed, he was on total guard. He could see every cop in the place looking around, but nothing happened.

After the vows were exchanged, the priest continued with the mass. Everything went off picture perfect. There were no interruptions, no guns blazing, no crashing chandeliers. Dan looked around one last time as the priest introduced the couple to the congregation. They all applauded as the couple walked down the aisle. It was decided ahead of time that if nothing had happened by the time the wedding was over, then they were to go to the back of the church and immediately exit into a waiting limousine. They walked down the aisle arm in arm and immediately entered the waiting car. The limo, followed by three unmarked police cars moved quickly down the street. There was to be no reception until later that night and the couple had explained to their friends and family that they wanted to spend the first hours of their marriage alone at a secret place. What they didn't say was that the secret place was a safe house about five miles away. They would stay there until the reception hall could be checked out.

Dan was disappointed. He thought for sure that this guy was going to make his move today, it would have all fit together so nicely. Dan saw Raferty at the back of the church and approached him. "Kinda disappointing huh Rafts?"

Raferty nodded his head in agreement. "I mean, I 'm happy for the couple, but I was hoping that we could have this guy by now. I thought for sure he would make his move at the church. Think he got wind of our presence?"

"If he did, it wasn't before today, we were so careful about talking to the couple, he couldn't have known what was going on. Anyway, do me a favor and head over to the banquet hall and lead these guys in the sweep of the place. I wanna call Maggie and see if we can grab a late lunch before I head over there. You can handle that, right?"

Raferty smiled. "Hell yeah, no problem at all. You take your time, the couple isn't coming for at least five hours, we'll have everything set up there. You go, enjoy yourself. Maybe this would be a good day to propose to Maggie, with all this wedding mood surrounding you."

Dan smiled back. "You know Rafts, this is the first time I'm not going to tell you to shut up about that. I think I might go home and do just that." Dan patted Raferty on the back and walked back to his car. He flipped open his phone and called his house to tell Maggie that he was coming home for a late lunch or anything else that she had in mind. The phone rang its compulsory five times before the machine picked up. After the greeting Dan shouted into the phone. "Maggie if you're there, pick up." There was no response. "Okay then, well I'll be home in ten minutes, for a little lunch, or whatever. Love you." He closed the phone and drove back to his neighborhood.

Dan pulled his car up in front of the house. If he was only going to be home for a few hours, he always parked in front. He walked up to the front door and put his key in the door, but it was already unlocked. He pushed the door open and yelled through the house. "Hey, I'm home, wanna grab a little lunch?" He looked at the kitchen table and saw Maggie's car keys still sitting there. He looked over at the stove and saw the tea kettle boiling away, the steam shooting out of the top. "Maggie, where are you?"

Dan walked to the back door, he thought that she must be weeding the garden and forgot about the tea, it wouldn't have been the first time. He opened the door and glanced at the garden. The garden hoe was sitting on the ground along with one of her gardening gloves. Maybe she went over to the neighbors for a little gossip, he thought. He walked down the stairs and opened the back gate so that he could go into the neighbors yard. As he closed the gate he heard the peel of tires in the alley. He thought is was the goofy teenager who lived down the block trying to show off again. Dan shook his

head in disgust and looked to his right. He saw a big black car spinning its tires in the alley dust. He had to hold his hand up because
the sun was so bright and he squinted to see who it was making all
the racket. As he looked he could see the car wheels spinning, throwing rocks into the air, as the tires finally made contact the car began
to speed off and Dan could see the distinct outline of Maggie in the
back seat.

Dan's heart raced. Maggie had been kidnaped and he knew it was
the killer who had taken her. He ran through the gangway and back
to the street and jumped in his car. He didn't even have time to put
the mars light on the roof. He drove to the end of the block and
turned left so that he was at the end of the alley where the other car
had just sped away. He stopped for a second and looked down the
alley. He couldn't see the car, but he could see the dust that the car
had raised all down the alley. He turned the wheel and sped down
the alley in pursuit of the vehicle.

Dan turned on his police radio and called for backup. He was in
pursuit of a dark late model Chevrolet going west on the alley behind
School street, between Menard and Austin. The operator assured
him that backup was on the way, she wanted to know if he had a
plate. Dan wasn't close enough to get a plate, but he was doing his
best to catch up to the car. He crossed Austin avenue at amazing
speed. The dust cloud was still in front of him, but he couldn't catch
the car. As he tore down the alley his only thought was to get Maggie
back, he couldn't be concerned about pedestrians or other cars.

Dan followed the car down the alley and he started to gain on it.
He knew that the alley was going to come to a T in about a block in a
half and he radioed again to give his location. The dispatcher assured
him that there were other cars in pursuit and that they should be at
the T in the alley within 30 seconds. Dan put his foot all the way
down on the accelerator, he didn't know which way the car would
turn and he couldn't make out the plate with all the dust that was
being kicked up. As the approached the T, Dan could hear the sirens

of the other police cars wailing. From the sound of it, the noise was coming from the left. Dan prayed that the car would turn to the left, and be stopped by the patrol car. He came to the T in the alley and the big car in front of him veered to the right, side swiping a garage door in the process. Dan turned his wheel hard to the right and slipped in behind the large vehicle. A patrol car, with lights flashing pulled in right behind Dan.

The vehicle in front was on another alley now, heading north. When he came to Addison Avenue he turned right and swerved into traffic. Dan followed closely behind, finally he could get close enough to read the plate. He picked up the radio again to indicate that they were going east on Addison. "The plate is Victor David Zulu One Three One, that's Victor, David, Zulu, One Three, One."

The dispatcher said she would run the plate and that there were more patrol cars pulling onto Addison right now. Dan could see the flashing lights behind him and in front of him about a quarter of a mile down the street. The patrol cars had made a blockade, but the Chevy wasn't slowing down. He was going to crash right into them, light a kamikaze pilot hitting a battleship. Dan radioed that the Chevy wasn't slowing down. The patrol cars heard his warning and drew their guns so that they could stop the car when it got close enough.

"Don't cause an accident, he has someone very special to me in that car!" Dan yelled.

The Chevy sped toward the blockade and the officers fired at the tires. There were three direct hits, blowing out the front two tires and sending the car into a wild skid. The car turned in a complete circle and was now facing west in the east bound lane. The bullets must have also hit the radiator, because steam was streaming up from under the hood. Dan brought his car to an abrupt halt and threw the car in park. He jumped out and raced toward the car with his gun drawn.

"Get the hell out of that car, you scumbag, with your hands up!" Dan was only about six feet from the rear door of the Chevy. "Let's go, get out!" There was no response from the driver. As Dan approached the rear of the car , the uniformed officers approached the front. "Can you see him?" asked Dan.

"Looks like he hit his head or something, looks like he's passed out on the wheel," yelled one of the cops.

Dan crouched down and approached the rear door of the vehicle, he opened the door and grabbed Maggie from the back seat. The other cops ran to the front, guns still pointed on the driver and opened the door to grab him.

"Hey, Detective, you gotta see this," said one of the officers.

Dan untied Maggie's hands and put his sport coat over her shoulders to keep her warm and protect her from potential shock. One of the paramedics who had arrived on the scene took her from Dan and walked her over to the ambulance to make sure she was okay. Dan walked to the front of the car and looked at the driver who was still passed out from hitting the steering wheel.

"Well, Mr. President, you were the last person I expected to see driving this car." Dan reached down and lifted the Bill Clinton mask off the driver. "Holy shit, maybe not the last person!"

CHAPTER 31

*T*he paramedics had determined that Maggie was probably suffering from a concussion so they insisted that she go to the hospital for observation. When Dan arrived at the hospital, Maggie had already been put in a curtained exam room. She was already beginning to form a large bump on her forehead and she was experiencing bouts of nausea.

Dan entered the exam room while the doctor was using a pen light to look into Maggie's eyes. He determined that she did have a slight concussion and should spend the night in the hospital for observation. Dan held her hand as she lay on the gurney holding an ice pack on her newly developed bump.

"What the hell happened?" she asked.

"That's what you need to tell me," Dan said.

She scooted up on her elbows to be more level with Dan. "Let me see, I remember being in the garden, taking care of the weeds. There was a car in the alley beeping its horn, I looked up and didn't give it much thought, but he kept on beeping like he needed something. I thought maybe someone was lost and needed directions. I put down my tools and walked to the car, but I couldn't see the driver, he was leaning over looking in the glove compartment. When I got to the window on the driver's side he popped up, he was wearing a mask of some sort. I remember wanting to run, but I saw he had a gun and I just panicked. I don't think I moved at all. He got out of the car very quickly and pushed me in the back seat, he made me lay down on my stomach and then he tied my hands. The next thing I knew he sat me up and started to drive away, then really pushed the accelerator and tore down the alley. With my hands tied, I couldn't get any balance and I kept falling over, I guess that's how I hit my head. I don't really remember anything else."

"Well, he gave us quite a chase. I called the house after the wedding and you didn't answer so I decided to come home for a little lunch. I went out to the backyard, I figured you were either weeding or had gone over to one of the neighbors to chat, that's when I saw the car tearing down the alley with your head bopping around in the back seat. I chased him through the alleys and eventually onto Addison. We finally stopped him with a road block." Dan leaned in close to her, his own eyes beginning to well up with emotion. "Maggie, I am so sorry that this happened to you, I never want you to have to get involved in my work."

She kissed him, her big eyes giving him the assurance that it wasn't his fault. "You couldn't know what was going to happen Dan, there wasn't anything you could have done about it."

"I should have taken you to the wedding with me, it was a lot safer there."

"Well, what really did happen, I mean who the hell took me? Did anything happen at the wedding?"

"Nothing happened at the wedding, there was no attempt made on the lives of Brad and Laura. Everything happened without a hitch. It made me think that the killer must have known that we were going to be there, so he didn't waste his time with a hit. I thought maybe he would wait until the reception, so I sent Raferty over to the banquet hall to secure the place. He's on his way over here now."

"You were right then, the killer did know that you were going to be at the wedding."

"The killer knew everything we were doing all along. The man who kidnaped you, the man who has been behind all of this was our good friend Bartly."

Maggie look at him incredulously, the ice pack falling from her forehead. "Police Officer Bartly? The man you've known for twenty years, is a killer, Dan are you sure?"

"Well, when I got to the car after it spun out, I reached in and pulled the mask off the driver, you can imagine my shock when I looked down and saw Bartly's face. I didn't know what to think, it didn't make any sense to me, and I'm not sure that it does now. But we did get the gun that he used to kidnap you, and it's the same kind of gun that was used to kill Father Goetz and Anthony Martin. It won't take much time for forensics to run the ballistics test and prove it's the same weapon. We've got him dead to rights on at least two murders, and something tells me that he'll cough about the whole plan. I'm waiting for Raferty and the Captain to get here so that we can question him and find out exactly what was going on. The Captain is pulling in some favors right now, getting warrants to search Bartly's house, access his bank account, his phone records, and all that stuff. We should have a pretty solid case against him within the next four to five hours."

She put the ice pack bag on her forehead. "I knew he was a creep, I remember when you thought he planted evidence against that black man a few years ago. I just hate coming across a bad cop."

"Yeah, we were close at one time too, but his need to be in the spot light started to fog his judgement a long time ago. If I could have proven his corruption I would have tried to have gotten rid of him. It makes me sick to think about what he did to all those people."

The nurse came in and instructed Maggie that she needed to take some medication to help her rest. The doctor had determined that it was safe for her to sleep since she had not lost consciousness. Dan leaned over and gave her a kiss and held tightly onto her hands. "I love you, Maggie," he said.

"I love you too copper," she said.

"It's time for you to go sir," the nurse said. "You can come back tomorrow morning, but she really should just rest for the remainder of the day and through the night. We'll be moving her to a regular room in about an hour, you can call to find out where she'll be."

Dan nodded in agreement and gave a wink to Maggie as he left the exam room. He went back to the waiting area of the emergency room. There were cops everywhere and Dan approached one of the uniforms to talk to him about keeping security on Bartly. The officer told Dan that Bartly was currently handcuffed to his bed and that there was an armed officer waiting outside the exam room. The hospital staff wasn't thrilled with the situation, but there wasn't much they could say at this point.

Dan had already sent an officer to the station with the gun that was found in Bartly's car. One of the policemen had told Dan that the car was a rental from the airport. The car was still being impounded to search for additional evidence. Dan walked out of the emergency room, into the fresh air and lit a cigarette. It was well deserved and he hoped that it would calm his nerves as he waited for the Captain and for Raferty.

Dan saw Raferty walking toward the emergency room doors from the parking lot. He lifted his arm in a wave so that Raferty would see him. Raferty nodded in return and walked toward Dan. He was chewing on a toothpick, he had never picked up the habit of smoking and Dan envied that in him.

"I can't believe all this!" Raferty said.

"I know, it doesn't make any sense. But once the Captain gets here with some evidence it might all come together. The thing I don't understand is the Jerry Riley component. I mean, I thought for sure he was our guy, out to get revenge."

"Maybe we'll find something to connect Bartly with Riley, maybe they were friends or even working together. You still might have half a murder team on the loose."

"I thought about that, we're not going to know much until we get Bartly to fill in the blanks for us. Man, what a day." Dan rubbed the back of his own neck.

"How's Maggie, she doing okay?"

"She should be fine, a slight concussion and a nasty bruise on her head. Those will heal quickly, but the experience won't go away so easily. I feel terrible that she was dragged into this." Dan finished his cigarette and threw the butt on the pavement."

"It's not your fault Dan, there was no way you could have known that he was going to grab her."

"Yeah, I suppose, but he grabbed her because of me, he was pissed that I was getting close. He must have thought that we were onto him, but honestly, I never thought he had a thing to do with this."

"Now that you think about it, it was a little more than coincidental that he took such an interest in the case. He talked to the Captain about it more than you did. And I never liked the idea that he showed up at the scene of that second murder in the abandoned hotel. He was trying hard to convince us that the priest was a drug addict, remember that?"

"Yeah, that's right. He did show up kind of unexpectedly. I just attributed it to his need to be in the spot light, I mean we all knew this was going to be a high profile case," Dan said as he lit another cigarette.

"You're gonna kill yourself with those you know."

"Yeah, I know, I'm gonna quit on Monday, I swear. I don't even enjoy it anymore, it's just habit. And a bad one at that."

"I was thinking Dan, we know that Goetz killed the Archbishop, do you think that Bartly was using other guys to do the other killings?"

Dan took a deep drag on the cigarette. "I don't know, he certainly had access to all the others. It was the Archbishop that was going to be the hardest to get to. I'm sure that he killed Goetz and Martin, I'll bet my life that the ballistics test will prove that by the morning. I'm not sure about Shannon Wallace, she was shot as well as crushed, there's a good chance his gun will match that one too. He certainly was big enough to kill Wysocki in the confessional and to cut the thumb off of Danner. He was also smart enough to leave very little clues except for the gun. I'm sure he thought no one would ever be able to trace that."

It had been two hours since Dan had first called the Captain and he hadn't heard a word back. He hoped that this was a good sign, and that it meant that things were in progress. As Dan and Raferty shot theories back and forth, Dan's cell phone rang. He reached into his pocket and flipped open the phone. "Gill here," he said.

"Dan, it's Captain Kelsh. We were able to get the warrants and the subpoena for his bank account. The bank is working right now to give us his records and we've already searched his desk here at the department. There isn't much, but I'll bring it all with me when I come by to confront him. I don't know what we'll find in his house, but I instructed the team to do a quick sweep, just to look for anything that might relate to this case and to get it to me as soon as possible. I expect to be there in no more than two hours. You want to wait there or meet me here at the station?"

"We'll wait here for you, we can grab something in the cafeteria, although that might be considered cruel and unusual punishment by Amnesty International. I don't want to leave Maggie anyway."

"Yeah, I'm really sorry about that Dan, there is no reason for any of our families to ever have to get involved in our business, it really sucks."

"Thanks, Captain. I appreciate that. She's gonna be fine, I think there's a chance we'll need a little vacation after all this is over."

"Guaranteed!" said the Captain. "I'll meet you in the emergency room no later than five, by that time we'll have enough on him one way or the other to get him to talk. I understand that he already told the uniforms that he wants a lawyer present. Might mean he has no intention of talking at all."

"Yeah, they told me that too. He called for a lawyer, he may already be here as far as I know, but that's fine, give him time to think about what he wants to say. If he wants any hope of mercy from the court, he knows it will go better for him if he cooperates."

Dan hung up the phone and filled Raferty in on the conversation with the Captain. He suggested that they go down to the cafeteria and kill a couple of hours before the boss got there.

"Yeah, well, it'll kill something that's for sure," said Raferty.

Dan smiled at him and walked down the long corridor to the cafeteria. They each got a hamburger and fries and sat in a corner so that they could continue to swap theories about the case. Dan was perplexed, he just couldn't imagine how Bartly could be connected to all these people. He had known him for years, knew that he was never in the seminary. They never really talked about religion, although Bartly would occasionally chide Dan about his mass attendance and religious devotion. There just wasn't anything there to connect him to Riley or any of the other people involved. The time passed slowly as Dan drank cup after cup of black coffee and Raferty downed his Diet Cokes.

They headed back up to the emergency room at 4:30, Dan walked into the exam area and saw that the curtain to Bartly's cubicle was closed, he could hear mumbling as Bartly talked to his lawyer. Dan was glad that he was conscious and couldn't wait to confront him. Dan met Raferty back in the waiting room and anticipated the Captain's arrival.

By 5:00 they could see the Captain's car pull into the lot. He walked toward the door of the emergency room and greeted Dan and Raferty. "We've got him. I had them rush the ballistics test, it's a match on the Goetz and Martin murders, it also happens to match the Wallace bullets that we took from her body. That never even dawned on me, but the computer found it right away."

Dan smiled at Raferty and the Captain. "I knew it would match, I had forgotten about Shannon Wallace myself, but Raferty reminded me of it a little while ago."

"There's something else that is very interesting," said the Captain. "His bank account was huge, he'd been depositing in excess of two thousand dollars a month over and above his pay check for that last ten years. The deposits had varied from time to time, but with a good time line, we can show they correspond to the deaths of the various participants. His cash flow really stopped cold about a month ago. Very little influx of extra income since Wysocki was killed. I don't know how, but he was blackmailing these people. We've got him on one count of kidnaping with intent to kill, the murders of Wallace, Goetz, and Martin. He knows it will go easier on him if he cooperates, if he doesn't he won't like the jail that the judge sends him too, I'll make sure its one that's filled with people he's framed over the years."

"You suspected that he was framing people too?" Dan asked.

"Could never prove it, tried to trip him up a few times, but his arrests were just too lucky, he could find evidence long after the forensic team went through a place, it never seemed to fit together in my mind. I tried to catch him Dan, but he's no dummy."

"Not until today. No one kidnaps my girlfriend and gets away with it."

"It was his Waterloo that's for sure," said the Captain.

The three of them walked through the emergency room doors and back to the exam room cubicle where Bartly was handcuffed to the bed.

"John Bartleanowicz, you are under arrest for the kidnaping and attempted murder of Maggie Cleveland, the murders of Antony Martin, Shannon Wallace, and Reverend Francis Goetz," said the Captain.

"Screw you," shouted Bartly.

"You also have the right to remain silent, anything you say can and will be used against you in a court of law. You have the right to an attorney…."

"Hey, I know my rights, and my attorney is right here."

"Do you understand these rights as they have been read to you?"

"Yeah ,yeah what grounds do you have to hold me, huh? Tell me that."

Dan took a step closer to Bartly, there was rage in his eyes and Bartly could tell that Dan was about to strangle him. "Listen you fat piece of shit, we have enough evidence in just three hours of investigation to send you away for a long time. I suggest that you cooperate and make it easier on yourself."

"There's no reason to be vile Detective," interjected the lawyer.

"I suggest that you confer with your client and urge him to cooperate. It will go much easier on him in the long run," said Dan.

"Go easier on me? Are you kidding, you think you got me on three murders! How could anything I do make it go easier on me?" Bartly asked.

The Captain held up the files he had brought in with him. "You've been a cop for a long time John. You've put a lot of bad guys in jail. Now, I know that in many cases the judge will be a little easier on a crooked cop when it comes time to assigning him to a prison. Maybe one far away, where the cop is unknown, or one that has a protective custody wing for ex-cops. Of course if the cop doesn't want to cooperate, maybe he could be sent to Joliet, where he knows a lot of the inmates by name."

The lawyer pointed his finger at the Captain. "That's coercion! You can't threaten him like that and hope to get a confession. He'll insist on going to trial and getting himself cleared of these trumped up charges!"

"Shut up you asshole," said Bartly. "They've got the gun, they know what their talking about. There's no way I'm going to Joliet, I won't last two days in there. Mind your own business."

"I suggest that you not say anything John, they can use this all against you," said the lawyer.

"You just don't get it do you? I'm guilty and they can prove it. I have to cooperate to save my life."

The Captain reached into his briefcase and pulled out a small tape recorder. He set it on the table next to Bartly's bed and pushed the record button. "This is Captain Kelsh of the Chicago Police Department, you are about to hear the confession of Detective John Bartleanowicz in a series of murders and extortion plots." He turned to look at Bartly who had been visibly shaken when the Captain mentioned extortion. "Please state your name."

"John Bartleanowicz."

"Are you making these statement of your own free will?"

"Yes, and I have been read my rights and I have met with an attorney, it is my desire to cooperate in anyway possible with this case."

Dan shook his head, he knew that Bartly was being complacent and cooperative so that the court would be more lenient on him when it came time to assign him to a prison. Even though he despised Bartly, he knew that if the situation were reversed that he would have to do the same thing. Jail was a terrible place for an ex-cop.

"Do you want me to ask you questions, or do you wish to simply speak?" asked the Captain.

"I'll just speak, but, if there's something unclear, you can ask. I don't think you know how far back this goes, so you wouldn't really even know what to ask at this point. Hey, can you undo this cuff so I can be more comfortable?" Dan reached over and undid the handcuff after the Captain nodded in agreement.

Bartly cleared his throat and began his story. "Eleven years ago, my father died. It was a difficult time in my life. We were very close and I spent a lot of my free time taking care of him. I was all alone now in the world and had nothing to do with my time except go through his things. He had tons of private papers and diaries recording virtually everyday of his adult life. I always admired my dad, he always seemed to me to be a good man, he was an excellent provider and encouraged me to do whatever I wanted to in life. When I told him that I wanted to be a cop, he blessed me and told me he would support me all the way. I knew deep down that he wanted me to be a doctor like he was, but I knew I couldn't handle the years of school and the hours it would take to reach that goal. For years I had seen my father completely absorbed with his patients, often leaving the house at 10:00 at night to be with them. It was hard on my mom and I suppose in some ways on me, but he gave us a nice house and great vacations every year.

"What I didn't know was that my Dad led a double life. He was a caring physician during the day, taking in lots of people who couldn't even afford to pay. But at night he was a completely different person. At night he was an illegal abortionist. He would perform three or four abortions a week, taking the women to a small storefront that he kept on the south side of the city."

Dan interrupted. "That's where he met Mary Riley."

"Yeah, he had performed an abortion on Mary Riley back in 1972. He kept records of all the abortions he had done, but his entry that day in his diary was different. He talked about a whole group of people accompanying this girl to the store. He had never seen a group come in before and it unnerved him a little bit. He recorded the name of the girl and the name of her brother. He mentioned that there were complications with the abortion, the first time that had happened to him, although he knew that it happened to other doctors all the time. He wrote about how he left the whole group there in the store front to care for her and didn't think much about it until he saw her name in the death notices three days later. When he did a little investigating he found out that her death was ruled a drug overdose. In some ways he was relieved, there was no mention of an abortion and apparently no one checked during the autopsy to see if she had bled to death. He figured that the group got scared when she died and somehow had pumped her full of drugs. There was no way she was going to drug overdose on her own the day after that abortion. I think in many ways he knew that he had killed her, but that the group had somehow taken the blame upon themselves and did all they could to mask the death. It didn't make a lot of sense to him but he didn't concern himself with it anymore, there was no way for it to be traced back to him. If anyone from the group had talked, they would be incriminating themselves. At least that's what they would have thought. He wrote that they were all very young at the time.

"Well after I read that, I didn't know what to do. I felt guilt and shame, but I wanted to protect his name at the same time. Then something happened a month later that was pure serendipity. I was still a uniformed officer at the time. I was on a routine traffic stop and asked this guy for his license and registration. He blew a stop sign, it was no big deal, I had every intention of letting him go. It wasn't his car so the registration wasn't in his name, no big deal lots of people borrow cars. When he handed me his license it was Canadian. Pretty unusual, don't get too many of those. But when I saw the name it said Gerald Riley. Now I had just been reading over my dad's diaries and the name was stuck in my head. I looked at the guy, there was no way this could be the same Gerald Riley in my dad's diaries, it just wasn't possible. But I wanted to know, so I introduced myself as Officer Bartleanowicz, just to see the reaction in his face. It was like I hit him with my night stick he was so shocked. I mean this guy was physically shaken. My name's not common, and he had obviously made the connection between me and my father. Not to mention that I look exactly like my Dad, people always thought we were brothers.

"You didn't call in his license to see if he was wanted for anything?" asked the Captain.

"At that point it didn't matter to me. I'm not sure that back then the computers would have picked it up on a Canadian license anyway. But I knew that this guy was scared, which didn't really make

too much sense, I mean in the long run they didn't really do anything wrong, at least nothing that they could be arrested for anymore. But I could just tell that he thought he was in real trouble."

"Well, he probably did think he was in trouble, he had an out-
standing warrant for skipping bail," Dan said.

"Yeah but I didn't know that right away. But he was so nervous
that I figured something was wrong, so I told him to wait while I
wrote up the ticket. While I went back to the car, the guy took off. I
mean he bolted down the street. But his nerves must have got the
best of him 'cause he just stopped two blocks later. When I got out of
the car I had my gun drawn and got him into the back of the patrol
car. I wanted to call it in, you know, but I just had to know what he
knew about my dad. So I found out everything that happened that
night, I found out he was a fugitive and that he would do anything
not to go to jail.

"That's when it hit me that this guy and his little group could turn
into quite a gold mine. I mean if he was afraid of jail, maybe the others were too. So I told him that I would let him go, even see to it that
he could easily get back to Canada in exchange for the name of
everyone who involved that night. I figured that even if half of them
caved to the extortion, then I would clean up every month. Well,
when I found out who was involved it was a sure fire thing. There
was no way that the priests in the group were going to confess to having a hand in an abortion. He told me that if they participated in an
abortion that their priesthood was not valid. I knew I had them
where I wanted them. So the deal was to give me $250 a month for
the rest of their lives to keep my mouth shut. Only Riley knew that
my dad was the doctor who performed the abortion. But that was
okay, because Riley had the most to lose. He was a real fugitive and
these other guys just thought they were guilty of something.

"So it started out very well. Everyone who had participated that
night started to pay me every month. Most of them would drop the
cash off in a garbage can on my beat. It was easy, they never tried to

find out who I was and everything was going along fine. Then Father Carmichael screwed it up. He was a smart man and he figured out who it was that was blackmailing him. He held off for a while, he was afraid because I was a cop and there was no evidence against me, also because he knew that his orders would be invalid if it was shown that he had helped to pay for an abortion while he was a layman. So he made a deal with me to stop paying, he would keep his mouth shut and he wouldn't tell the others, but he wasn't going to pay anymore.

"At first that was okay with me, I could live on the other money that was coming in. But then he got cocky. He said that he couldn't keep quiet and that he was going to tell the others not to pay me either. I couldn't have that. So I made arrangements for his car to crash one night while he was out. It was determined to a drunk driving accident, the guy was loaded with booze, I made sure of that.

"Things went by fine for a couple of years, but then last year, it started to unravel. They must have started to get smart to the idea that there wasn't really anything that they could be arrested for. Anthony Martin wasn't a priest, the Church couldn't do anything to him, so he figured he had nothing to loose. His last payment was accompanied by a note that said it was over. I couldn't take a chance on him telling the others that the game had come to an end so I shot him while he was peddling his supplies in a bad neighborhood. You know your theory about the killer getting guys at work intrigued me, Dan. It was an unexpected set of circumstances that made it look like a serial killer was on the loose. I just kept following your instincts from guy to guy. There was no way it was going to be traced to me."

"But why the others, they didn't stop payment, we know that from their bank statements," said Dan.

"Somehow the priests all got together and decided that enough was enough. Some of them were still playing bridge once a week and the topic was bound to come up eventually, even if they didn't want to talk about it. It started with Wysocki, he played his hand to me like a fool, told me that the game was over, that they had figured out who I was and that he didn't care if he was defrocked. He was going to turn me in. That his last payment was just that, a last payment. Well, I couldn't take a chance on them turning me in. By this time I was a detective, I had too much to loose. I decided that they all had to go. I knew enough about police work to hide my trail and that the cover of a serial killer would be perfect. It sure didn't take you long to see that they were all being killed during sacraments. I thought it was pretty clever myself."

Dan shook his head and looked into Bartly's eyes. "But you couldn't get to the Archbishop could you? He was a difficult target."

"Not only was he a difficult target, but if the public thought he was killed, then the game would have been over. I knew he had to go, but I had to figure a way to do it without it looking like it was connected. I chose to use Goetz, he was the weakest of the group and he assured me that he had no intention of going to the police. He still didn't know who I was, but he took direction well. Those Germans, love to be told what to do. I told him where to get the hemlock and how to buy a book that showed him how to process the seeds to make the poison. He was very effective in playing out his role. I suppose I could have let him go, but I couldn't take the chance.

"It was pretty easy to kill them all, and I never knew about the photo until after the killings started and I found it on your desk one day. I knew then that you were getting close and I had to get it over with soon. I planned to kill Brad Fiore and Laura Walters when they were in Vegas, but I couldn't get there. The Captain had given me a case that needed attention. So I figured I would finish with the serial killer theme at their wedding. But you got in the way of that. It was easy to know what you were doing Dan, the Captain kept me informed all the way.

"I never intended to hurt Maggie, but I needed to throw you off my trail. I rented that car under the name of Jerry Riley and I figured that I would dump Maggie and the car off some place that could be easily found. That would cause you to blame everything on Riley and to spend your time looking for him while I took out Fiore and Walters. But you came home for lunch, I never planned on that."

"You would have probably gotten away with it Bartly, you certainly weren't a suspect. But once we had the gun, we had you dead to rights," Dan said.

The Captain jumped in. "What about Riley, what did you do with him?"

"Nothing, he's still living in Canada, thinks he's a fugitive from the law. My guess is that he could easily return now if he wanted to, statue of limitations has run out on him, but I never told him it was safe to move back. I know that he would occasionally visit Chicago, cross over the border somehow and then return home. The ironic thing is, he was the least threat to me because he felt the guiltiest about what happened."

"Is that the end of your confession?" asked the Captain.

"Yes, that's all I have to say for now."

"It isn't a real confession you realize, this will never hold up in court. You coerced him into it and you know it!" said the lawyer.

"I told you to shut up! There's not going to be a trial, I'm pleading guilty, and serving my time in a secure prison. The governor has seen to it that there won't be any death penalties in Illinois for while."

Dan, Raferty, and the Captain left the cubicle after they had handcuffed Bartly back to the bed. The Captain said that he was heading back to the station to call the State's Attorney and make arrangements for the arraignment. Raferty was going to stop by the Fiore reception and tell them that they could relax, the killer was caught and they should enjoy the rest of their celebration. Dan decided to look in on Maggie one last time, he figured that she would be asleep by now, but he wanted to see her one more time before the night was over.

As he walked int her room he could see her sleeping gently in the hospital bed. The bump on her forehead had already started to go down and the red marks on her wrists from the rope were already gone. He knew that she would be fine, but he was still filled with guilt for having involved her. He walked over to the bed and kissed her gently on the forehead and wiped a few pieces of hair out of her closed eyes.

"I really do love you, Maggie, you're everything to me."

She jostled a little in the bed and let out a sigh, as though she had heard him in her dreams. Dan turned to walk out of the room and head back home where he would try to make sense out of everything that had happened. He decided that his first priority on Monday would be to locate Jerry Riley in Canada and to check for him if he was free to return to the United States. At least something good could come out of all this senseless destruction.

As he got to his car he knew that he had to do something for the woman he loved. He took a deep breath and started the car. He drove out of the lot and headed west just as the sun was beginning to lower itself into the evening sky, he turned on the radio and listened to an oldies station as he drove on to fulfill his mission.

EPILOGUE

*T*wo months had past since Bartly was arrested and Maggie had to spend the night in the hospital. Bartly pleaded guilty to five murders and one count of kidnaping. The District Attorney chose not to charge him with the murder of Father Carmichael or conspiracy to murder in the case of the Archbishop. The Archdiocese had pleaded with him not to push the issue of the poisoning, thinking that the morale of the diocese would plummet. The judge was not lenient on Bartly and sentenced him to five consecutive life terms and one ninety nine year term for the kidnaping. None of the life terms had the possibility of parole. For his cooperation and confession Bartly avoided the death penalty and a trip to Joliet Prison, where he would have been killed by the end of the month. Instead he was sent to a prison in the southern end of the state where no one knew him and that had a separate cell block for ex-cops. It was a humane sentence for a terribly inhumane person.

It was time for Dan and Maggie to put all this behind them. Maggie had spent a restless week after she got home from the hospital, but Dan never left her side. Eventually time heals all wounds and through some good therapy the incident was slowly but surely being put to rest. With Bartly behind bars, life could attempt to proceed as usual. The same could be said for Brad and Laura Fiore. The newly married couple enjoyed a peaceful honeymoon and began to settle into their new life as husband and wife.

Dan had made plans for he and Maggie to go to Paris for a week. It was a wonderful trip, sight seeing all over town, enjoying wonderful food and wine. They visited Notre Dame, the Louvre, and the Opera House. They took long walks along the Seine and realized how wonderful their life really was. They were in love and they now had shared much more than the average married couple. Dan felt so protective of Maggie, he never wanted her to have to go through anything like that again. And Maggie knew in her heart that Dan needed her more than ever. The ghosts of the case haunted him even more than her. Many days she thought that he should have been the one going to the therapist, but she knew that his tough cop image would never allow him to do that.

Their last night in Paris was beautiful. The weather was warm and clear and the city of lights illuminated like a sparkling diamond bracelet above the banks of the river. They made reservations to have a romantic dinner at the Jules Verne Restaurant about two thirds of the way up the Eiffel Tower. It was the hardest place in Paris to get dinner reservations, but Dan had planned this night long before they left for Paris.

The waiter had just taken their order for dinner when the wine steward returned with a fine bottle of Champagne for them to share. He opened the cork and presented it to Dan, who gave it a compulsory sniff as Maggie smiled at him gently. The steward poured a small amount into the glass and smiled at Dan. He picked it up and pretended like he knew what he was doing as he took a small sip and swished the ambrosia around his mouth before swallowing. He nodded to the steward that the bottle was fine. Their glasses were filled and they raised them high in a toast to their trip.

Their dinner was magnificent. Course after course of the finest French food. They talked and laughed and gazed out from six hundred feet in the air at the beautiful city below. They had finished their main course of braised lamb chops with dill and tarragon when Dan reached over and grabbed Maggie's hands. He smiled at her, knowing that words were not going to be enough to capture the sheer joy of this moment. She lifted his hands to her lips and gently kissed them. She was very much in love with this man.

The waiter brought them their desserts. A beautiful chocolate swan sitting in a pool of raspberry sauce. Maggie glanced down at the swan and then at Dan. She couldn't believe her eyes and she began to shake. Draped around the neck of the swan was a beautiful diamond engagement ring. Dan reached over and lifted the ring from the swan's neck and placed it on Maggie's finger.

"I love you with all my soul, you make me the best man that I can be. You make me a whole person and I want to spend the rest of my life with you. Would you do me the honor of becoming my wife?"

Maggie looked at Dan, tears forming in her eyes. She smiled at him and brushed the tears off her cheeks. She looked at the ring on her finger and then took Dan's hands in hers. "Yes, yes, I would love to spend the rest of my life with you. Oh, Dan I love you so much."

The waiter had seen her response and sent a violinist over to the table to play a romantic song for them. Dan stood and then brought Maggie to her feet. They danced next to the table as the violin continued to play. The word had spread through the restaurant that they had just gotten engaged and people began to applaud. Dan looked into Maggie's eyes and then gave her a kiss. It was a perfect ending to a perfect trip.

Sister Chris Rayday hung up the phone and headed back to her bedroom. She was packing the last of her clothes into a moving box. She had told her religious order that she wished to be transferred to another diocese, she was too emotionally exhausted from the events that had happened in Chicago over the past three months. She wasn't sure how the new Archbishop would react to a woman chancellor and she knew that it was time for her to move on. She would be leaving in the morning for her new assignment.

She placed the last pants suit in the box and was looking over the remaining items that needed to be packed. She reached down and picked up a box that had her mother's wedding ring in it. She looked at the ring and smiled. Her mother had given it to her on her death bed, with the hope that one day she might use it herself. It wasn't meant to be. She ran her hands over some of the memories of her life. Diplomas, awards from the diocese, her Phi Beta Kappa key from college, and a pile of old photos.

She reached into the pile and pulled out a photo from days gone by. She looked at the picture, glancing at the faces of the seven handsome young men, and their teacher smiling so proudly in the midst of his little gang. She kissed her finger and placed it on the face of a handsome young man in the middle of the photo. It seemed like only yesterday that they asked he take that photo, to capture the group as they were; young, carefree and innocent .

0-595-22285-4

Printed in the United States
4239